# Walking up a Rainbow

ALSO BY THEODORE TAYLOR

# WALKING UP
# A RAINBOW

*Being the True Version of the*
*Long and Hazardous Journey*
*of*
*Susan D. Carlisle, Mrs. Myrtle Dessery,*
*Drover Bert Pettit, and Cowboy Clay Carmer*
*and Others*

## THEODORE TAYLOR

Delacorte Press / New York

Published by
Delacorte Press
1 Dag Hammarskjold Plaza
New York, N.Y. 10017

Manufactured in the United States of America

First printing

Library of Congress Cataloging-in-Publication Data

Taylor, Theodore, 1922–
    Walking up a rainbow.

    Summary: In 1852, a fourteen-year-old orphan and her elderly
guardian, accompanied by a tough drover and his crew, take several
thousand sheep from Iowa to California, returning by ship through
the Panama Canal, to raise money to save the girl's home from a
villainous debt collector.
    [1. Voyages and travels—Fiction.   2. Overland journeys to the
Pacific—Fiction.   3. Orphans—Fiction.   4. United States—Social
life and customs—1783–1865—Fiction.]   I. Title.
PZ7.T2186Wal   1986      [Fic]
ISBN 0-385-29435-2
Library of Congress Catalog Card Number: 85-16239

With love, friendship and laughter, and other good things, this book is especially for my wife, Flora, who said, on an outstanding summer day, "Write me a tall tale about an adventuresome girl . . ."

# Walking up a Rainbow

# PART I

# By the Big Muddy

"Come one, come all, see the elephant," said Phineas T. Barnum. Then the elephant died and was stuffed.

*Circus Stories,* 1906

# 1

Not long after breakfast that mellow autumn dawn there was a banging on the front door and I dried my hands, shushing big Rufus's deep-throated barking, then went on down the dark hallway from the kitchen, wondering who might be visiting at such an hour.

Pinching his bloodstained right thigh, a gangling, long-armed stranger was what I found lurking on my wide front porch. Eyes pleading, whiskery face shingle long and about as narrow, he looked helpless rather than mean or threatening.

Behind him and the open gate was a new homemade prairie schooner with three yoke of oxen and one of cow hooked on. Heads of a woman and some small children poked out of the white hooped cover, gawking straight at me. Likely Mormon pilgrims on their way to Utah. Overlanders, to be sure, Salt Lake City bound.

"Doctor home?" the man asked. He was positively pasty.

"Nope. Hurt yourself?"

"Sure did, li'l missus."

I was not a "missus," nor was I so little. In my glorious teens at that time, I was single, thank you. My eyes narrowed down to cautious slits.

He went on, "Spent last night 'bout two mile east o' here. Cuttin' firewood at daybreak, an' I got it right in the leg."

"You do need sewing up. I'll do that for you."

Drawing back, alarmed, he said, "Wal', now, I don't rightly know . . ."

I just stood absolutely stock-still in that doorway, tempted to tell him to take his sainted Mormon leg on up the road.

"You're too young to be the doctor's wife," he blurted, frowning widely at me.

"I'm his daughter but I sure know how."

"You sure, are you?"

"Sure, I'm sure. Not much to sewing, is there? Just in and out. I've done it a dozen times." Well, six or eight, anyway.

Unhappily, he clumped after me into the doctor's office. Looking around, his eyes swept over the glittering surgical knives and forceps and saws, the splints and the big jar of hungry black leeches. His Adam's apple jumped when he saw several other jars containing body parts preserved in alcohol.

Well, what did he expect? This was not a candy shop.

The neat blue sign outside read DR. GIDDINGS CARLISLE, M.D. SURGERY AND PHYSIC IN ALL BRANCHES. SETS BONES. DRAWS TEETH. BLEEDS. ADVICE GRATIS.

"I sure hope you know how," the skinny man mumbled.

Truth was, that Mormon didn't have much choice. My father, lone physician in Kanesville, Iowa, was far, far from these parts.

I ordered, "Now, take off your boots and pants, and crawl up on that surgical table."

I'd seen privates before, having assisted the doctor a number of times. My mother was always too squeamish, prone to fainting.

"Slip them right off," I demanded.

"Wal', I . . . I . . ."

Then he turned his back to me, and to ease his manly feelings I said, "I've got to go wash my hands, anyway." The doctor was always so careful before he did surgery.

When I returned, my patient was in his long johns, flat on the table, still pinching the right leg, fear etched all over his pastiness. "Just keep pinching it," I instructed.

My first chore was to cut the crimson underwear leg off up near the crotch, but no sooner had I reached for the scissors when he asked, "Why do you need those?" I told him why.

The main job of that suspicious Mormon was to hold himself stock-still and not butt in. Finally, when I was over at the surgical tray, picking up the curved needle and spool of gut, he asked plaintively, "You gonna give me something?"

Lordy, this was the frontier! Not that fancy hospital down in St. Louis. I said, "Nope, mister. Just lock your teeth and hang on."

Mollycoddles needn't ever visit my table. There was chloroform and opium in the doctor's drug cabinet, but I did not know enough to fool around with them casually. I'd seen occasions when strong men had to hold a patient down while the doctor worked with quick, bold strokes of the saw even though whiskey and opium had been administered. This occasion was minor, in the splinter-removal category.

While in preparation, dipping cotton balls into alcohol, I asked, "You westering?"

"Yep. Gonna cross the river an' stay in Misery Bottoms till spring, then go on to Salt Lake in a wagon train." His voice was high-pitched and jittery.

"That's a good idea. Trail in the spring," I said, with a

quick scan at the gleaming stitcher. I took a moment to
hone it while he anxiously watched.

That done, I advanced on him and he looked as if he
might jump off and run for the Big Muddy. His eyes were
the size of walnuts, whites pulsating.

Standing beside him, I said, "Mister, I'm going to swab
some alcohol on you, then do the stitching. This needle
ought to go in and out real easy. Now, I'm going to count
to three and you take your hand away and hold on to the
table. Don't grab my arm or I might puncture you where
you don't want to be. Understand?"

Already gritting his teeth, more pasty every second, he
just nodded.

"One-two-three," I said, and he let go of the wound,
which was about the length of a standard ax blade. I
daubed alcohol to it and I bet you could have heard that
Mormon yell all the way to Keokuk.

"Hold still," I ordered, swabbing his wound just as gently
as I could.

Then I pinched down on the upper edge with my left
fingers to get a nice tuft and began stitching. In went the
needle and out came a long moan.

To help calm him down, I said, "Hope it'll be a mild
winter for you over there." The weather was always slightly
different on the Nebraska bank of the Missouri.

Another dreadful moan was his only answer as I tied off
at the top and started working down.

"So far it has been warm this fall."

"Owwwwww," he answered, pitifully.

"Looks like you have a nice wagon."

"Ummmmmmh." His teeth were locked shut.

"Where are you from?" I asked, making a slick-as-a-whis-
tle puncture, from which a little red squirted.

"Illi—Illi—oh, owwwwww."

"Illinois. Well, no wonder your wagon looks so good." Four more stitches to take and I thought my patient was doing very well. Dribbling a bit out of the corners of his mouth; breathing a little shallow. Otherwise, he was fine.

"You sure got a late start," I remarked. Most overlanders departed in late spring. Winter on the trail to Utah, Oregon, or California was never recommended. Just ask any Donners still alive.

He said, "My wi—my wifffff—aw, owwwwww."

"Just two more," I said. "What did your wife do?"

"Had a babeeeeee . . ."

"A baby. Oh, that's what made the delay. Congratulations. Now, I've got to pull this tight and then we're finished."

There was one more terrible mollycoddle scream left in him and the whole western plain must have heard it.

"All done," I said, looking down.

I was very pleased. The flesh was pulled together in a straight line and would heal nicely. Not much of a scar would result, which had always made the doctor happy.

I said, "Now, I'll bandage this and you can be on your way."

Still breathing hard, he just nodded, eyes closed.

While securing the bandage, I asked, "How many children do you have?"

Eyes still closed, as if he was afraid to look at his leg, he replied, "Three."

I'd always wished I'd had a big brother or sister. Now it was far too late for that. Far too late.

"There, you're all bandaged. If the doctor was here, he'd tell you to keep it clean."

The stranger finally opened his eyes and sat up.

I said, "Now, that wasn't so bad, was it?"

He looked at me intently. "Yes, it was," he said, suddenly sweatier and pastier than ever.

My, he was certainly not displaying much gratitude and I turned my back again while he eased into his pants and boots. Meanwhile, he asked, "What's your name?"

"Susan," I said.

"My name is Hopper. How much do I owe you, Susan?"

"Twenty-five cents," I replied, without hesitation.

Digging into his pocket, he came up with a quarter dollar. Handing it over, Hopper asked, "How old are you?"

"Almost fourteen," I answered.

To my great surprise, that tall, tough-looking, rawboned Mormon pilgrim fainted dead away on the spot, crumpling like a dried-up beetle shell.

With the help of smelling salts, I had Mr. Hopper on his feet a few minutes later and escorted him, wobbling a mite, out to his wife and children, wishing them all good luck on the overland trail next spring.

Then I returned to the kitchen, finished washing my dishes, dressed myself appropriately, saddled up Gabriel, and promptly rode to Mrs. Myrtle Dessery's farm.

I had a midday court appearance before the Honorable Cause Tuttle.

# 2

"Do you, Susan Darden Carlisle, solemnly swear . . . ?"

After the tubby clerk, Mr. Evan Green, had finished rattling it off, I said strongly, "I do," then lowered my right hand, which had hovered over the Holy Bible. Alongside me, Mrs. Dessery took the same oath in that stuffy log courthouse on Madison Street, near famed Cottonwood Jail.

We then sat down on the smooth oak bench, likely in the same spot where murderers had rested guilty haunches, and waited for His Honor, Cause Tuttle, to finish reading seven sheets of paper my lawyer, old Tinley, had prepared.

Judge Tuttle plain dawdled, now and then sucking yellowed teeth, wrinkling his large nose and muttering. He then looked up, asking matter-of-factly, "How'd your folks get killed?"

"Buggy accident," said I.

Early August, they were crossing Mead's Meadow where Linch Creek runs through it, and the big earthen dam on Farmer Kinchlow's place gave way. That high wall of water swept my parents a hundred yards. The mare died, too.

The judge nodded and lowered his head once more. The Honorable Cause Tuttle presided over cases that ranged from premeditated murder, which occurred now and then in Kanesville, to probate of wills such as my dear father had left behind.

Anxious and restless, I fidgeted openly and Auntie "Indian" Myrt Dessery, who wasn't my aunt at all, whispered, "Be patient, Susan." She was always a calming influence.

A beefy, red-faced white-haired man, Judge Tuttle was known as a "no-nonsense" jurist. Beneath a rumpled black suit, shiny from wear, a checkered vest was visible, crossed by a heavy gold watch chain. A double-over black bow tie was under his ample chin. Midway of the third page, he looked up again over his gold-rimmed spectacles to ask, sourly, "Where you livin' now?"

"In my own house, Your Honor."

"Not alone?"

"Yessir."

That wasn't quite true, either. The dog also lived with me in that two-story house, recently completed. Rufe slept in the same lovely room with me, near my four-poster, following me around as if attached on an invisible rope. About the only place he didn't go with me was into the outhouse.

The judge shook his head disapprovingly. "Alone in that big house and you're only thirteen?"

Finest house on the frontier, without question. Nothing downriver, in St. Joe, or upriver, in growing Sioux City, to match it. The front veranda had four graceful Grecian-like columns and there were fluted balustrades beneath the veranda railing. Summer past, I'd sat on the porch swing many late afternoons, smelling the prairie clovers, thinking about all the places I wanted to see. St. Louis, New York City, Paris, Rome.

I answered, "I do have a ferocious dog. He's outside. Shall I bring him in?"

Rufe was faithfully with old red Samuel, Mrs. Dessery's horse, out by the buggy.

"Absolutely not," said the judge.

Then he shifted his cold gaze to the woman on my right. A fetching bonnet was on her head. Her hair, parted in the middle, was a striking deep auburn, flecked with gray; brown eyes bright and sharp behind Ben Franklin specs. She was always a "pithy" lady, as they say.

"And you're her aunt, and you petition to be guardian?"

"No, sir, I'm but a close friend of the family, and yessir, I do petition to be Susan's guardian."

"My best friend," I added, in a loud voice, hoping to make a strong point.

Though she wasn't vain, Indian Myrt Dessery kept her

years a secret. But it was generally believed she pushed seventy. Aside from a few wrinkles, she was otherwise a free spirit and quite sassy though remaining ladylike. She lived about two miles from me, up winding Stutsman Road. Though not everyone knew it, Mrs. Dessery was a LeClerc, from Dubuque, father blue-blooded French-Canadian and mother Pottawattamie Indian. She could speak excellent French as well as Pottawattamie and Sioux. Though she mostly thought like a Gentile, her Pottawattamie part resented the white man paying only fourteen cents an acre for Indian land hereabouts. It was a hushed-up scandal.

Judge Tuttle mused on and then shook his curly head. "Alone in that house, with all the gold rush thieves in town, whores, gamblers, riffraff criminals of all ilk . . ."

I thought to myself, Oh, Lordy, I do wish you'd get off that scare talk. I was merely protecting my own property, that's all. Yes, paddle wheelers coming upriver were always littered with adventurers. Arriving also were Santa Fe Trail traders in striped blankets and somber Quakers in black homespuns; various Indians. And there was nothing worse than the profane U.S. Cavalry. Yet not a one had ever accosted me.

"Who gave you permission to do that? Live alone? You're thirteen years old, female, and have no more rights than a starving squirrel."

I answered, unafraid, "Your Honor, I made that decision myself."

Judge Tuttle frowned, as if he couldn't quite believe it. "You did, yourself?"

Lawyer Tinley had carefully coached me to respond "Your Honor," and I was mightily trying to do so. Be feminine, respectful, even humble. But where in "howlin' hell," as Dr. Giddings Carlisle used to frequently shout, was old

Tinley now? He'd promised to be back by this fateful hour. Maybe the *David H. Pyle* had hit a snag in the river? Those puffing steamboats were never reliable when you needed them most. Tinley was due back from St. Joe the past night.

"Yes, I did. Your Honor. *Sir.*"

Tuttle's big warty nose did a little rabbit hop. He stared at me, clearly disturbed, and I got to thinking about it later. It really wasn't over me living in that elegant house alone. What the judge was seeing was certainly not a "starving squirrel" but an unmeek girl who'd look him straight in his bloodshot eyes; a girl with long honey-colored hair, up-turned nose, and a few discreet freckles, probably a lot spicier and prettier than his own daughter, if he had one.

Sensing the judge's resentment, Mrs. Dessery spoke up in my behalf. "Susan is a very self-reliant girl. Always was, Your Honor."

He grumped and muttered unintelligibly again.

I added, "I'm quite safe, too. I sleep with a Model 1841 point 54 Mississippi loaded rifle that belonged to my Daddy on one side and a Presentation Pocket Colt point 31 five-shot, four-inch barrel, on the other side. That gun belonged to my mother. Rufe is at the foot of the bed."

"Rufe?"

"The dog."

"Oh, yes. And you know how to shoot those guns?"

"The doctor taught me before I could ever hold them up two-handed."

He sniffed and bunny-hopped his nose once more. "Your mother should have taught you something else. Young ladies shouldn't be handling guns. Looms are for them." His Honor resumed reading.

Just after the tragedy, Indian Myrt said to me, "You

have three choices. Put yourself up for adoption to a family wealthier than you, blue bloods of mental substance who want a ready-made daughter. Second choice is college. Third choice, find yourself a respectable man and get married a year from now when you are pushing fifteen. That's when I married Mr. Dessery. If not one of these suit you, then I volunteer to be your guardian for a while."

Having always wanted a daughter, never able to have children of her own, Indian Myrt, I think, was very much hoping for the last choice.

"I'll have to think about it," I said, even though I loved her very much.

Think I did for several days.

Though the whole nation was rapidly changing, it just wasn't appropriate for a quickly blossoming girl in her early teens to go around Iowa begging for a new family. Besides, after Judge Tuttle's verdict, it was likely I'd have my own ample resources. So I needn't be "kept" by any man. Having already finished what school there was in Kanesville, plus home tutoring, I had decided, for the time being, not to go to a college for women, though one had been founded in Davenport and another in Dubuque.

My genteel mother was always distressed that I wasn't domestically or socially or intellectually inclined. To me, hunting grouse or wild turkey with the doctor was much preferable to fiddling with a sampler or reading Chaucer. Shooting a gun was always better than tatting. Marriage? From all I knew, such a union would only lead to my belly getting big in a hurry. Marriage was not for me. Ever.

"I like your fourth choice best," I finally told Indian Myrt.

And so it was all settled, providing the court agreed, which brought us around to today.

# 3

The judge lifted his mass of sugary curls to eye me directly. "The court knows your mother and father came from Virginia? Do you not have kin back there?"

"Your Honor, I've never seen any of them. I was born in this state before it was a state."

"Your mother and father talk about kin in Virginia?"

"Yessir. Mostly about her only brother who lives in California, in Sacramento City, name of Roblett Chauncey Darden. He is a partner with Clarence J. Hudnut in the finest general store in that city."

"And it is your desire to stay in Kanesville?"

"Yessir, it is." But not forever. I certainly wanted to see the rest of the world.

"And you wish to be placed under the guardianship of Mrs. Myrtle Dessery?"

I replied, "That I do, Your Honor," with a glance and smile at my future protectress.

He nodded. "All right, now, tell me about the sheep. For some odd reason, they aren't part of the will. You own them outright. Your Daddy assigned them to you when he bought them."

Until that moment, I had no idea I already owned those dumb woollies.

"Go on," said the judge.

I pulled in a long breath. "Just this June, the doctor bought nineteen hundred head of ewes and wethers from a Mormon lady for fifty cents a head. She was with a bunch of Mormons passing through Cass County when her husband had a heart seizure. Though the doctor tried to save him, he upped and died and the lady had no desire to go to Zion without him. So that's why I have all those sheep."

"Where are they now?"

"At Mrs. Dessery's farm, or wherever there is good grass or corn stubble. Most of the ewes are pregnant."

"Who's taking care of them?"

"A farmer named Blackwell, from Ohio. He is Mrs. Dessery's hired help. Also his son, Roy, who is dim-witted somewhat but likes sheep."

The judge sighed. "What do you plan to do with 'em? Sell 'em? You don't look like you're up to handling that many sheep."

He was dead right. "We plan to sell 'em, I guess."

"You guess?" The judge was suddenly exasperated.

I nodded.

Judge Tuttle said, "Perhaps we should continue this until next spring . . ."

Mrs. Dessery rose up swiftly. "Your Honor, nothing will be accomplished by that. Susan shouldn't have to suffer simply because her fool lawyer isn't here."

"Tomorrow is my last day sitting this session and I want to shoot me some game for winter," the judge informed, feeling a little sorry for himself.

"I appreciate that, Your Honor."

The judge then addressed her head-on and none too kindly. "You could be Lucretia Borger for all I know. I have no idea you'd be a fit guardian and adviser for this young lady, who seems uppity, headstrong, and spoilt already."

My mouth was agape.

Under her breath, Indian Myrt said, *"Tête de mule."* I'd heard her say it before—French for "pigheaded." Thank goodness the judge didn't hear her. Aloud, she said, "It shouldn't take you long to find out."

Judge Tuttle's eyes narrowed. "No, it shouldn't."

He dug into that soiled checkered vest for his watch, glanced at it, and then pounded the gavel on the desk, making the inkwell jump. "Court dismissed until ten tomorrow."

Lawyer Tinley never did show up.

In the street, my possible guardian dabbed snuff into her nostrils and then sneezed explosively, clearing her head. "I been wanting to do that for two hour," she said, and then asked, in afterthought, "Who is Lucretia Borger?"

I said I didn't know but would look her up in the doctor's office.

We climbed into the Dessery buggy and moved up Madison Street, Rufus preceding us like a four-legged chocolate knight. The street was busy but nothing like late spring and early summer when it was jammed with adventurers. In truth, Kanesville was just a price-gouging, lickety-split jumping-off place. It had been on the natural trail west for centuries and buffalo and elk used it long before Indians ever did.

"Town is quieting down for winter," Indian Myrt observed as we briskly turned the corner at Broadway and First.

"Yep," I said unhappily, thinking about the dull, dark snowy days ahead. The town would almost hibernate from December to March.

During May and June, when the pilgrims, pioneers, greenhorn gold seekers, and such passed through, streets were shoulder to shoulder, muddy boot heel to toe. Gambling and drinking houses such as the Ocean Wave, Humboldt's, and Bloomer's did boom business. So did houses of ill repute like Sweet Frenchy Moll's. Gaming even flowed out over the puddles between the tents, log houses, and stores. Upturned packing cases were used for tables, stacked high with twenty-dollar gold eagles for three-card monte, chuck-a-luck, and thimble rigging. As of this fall of 1851, Kanesville was the sinningest place west of Philadelphia, full of "ladies of the night."

# 4

Before I relate this next part, I want to make it very clear that Dr. Giddings Carlisle was probably about the finest Daddy that ever lived, breathed, and died before his time. Yet he had a weakness common to us all. Money, and the want of it! The doctor wanted to be the richest man in southwest Iowa.

At precisely ten o'clock, Judge Tuttle, appearing weary and hung over, gaveled the court to session and picked up several pages of writing that were on his desk.

Meanwhile, I had looked up "Lucretia Borger" in the books in the doctor's office and had told Indian Myrt about that woman. The name was really "Lucretia Borgia," a thoroughly wicked Italian poisoner living about four hundred years ago. Seldom one to show outward anger, Indian Myrt said quietly, "I'll bide my time with the judge today."

I looked around. There weren't many people in attendance. It took a killing or some other scandal to bring them out. Yet, I did see Lawyer Brookins sitting there, and that was odd. A scrawny little man with shifty eyes, he usually represented the scummy side of Kanesville.

As the first order of business, the judge settled an authority. "The court hereby appoints Mrs. Myrtle Dessery, of Stutsman Road, Kanesville, Iowa, as the sole and legal guardian of Susan Darden Carlisle."

Indian Myrt and I exchanged smiles, and I reached over to grasp her small hand and squeeze it.

Judge Tuttle continued, "The court hereby awards all property of the late Giddings Carlisle and his wife, Alice, to their legitimate heiress and daughter, Susan Darden Carlisle, this to include . . ."

In other words, everything. The court, with the help of Tinley, had set the value of the estate at $10,000, of which $2,000 was in hard cash, a fortune at that time. I was a rich girl, no doubt.

The judge finished up with a few more clauses and then stared straight at me. Without previous hint, he said, "Now that I've said all that, I don't know that it'll do you a bit of good. A lien has been placed against your entire estate."

I looked over at Indian Myrt for help. I wasn't sure what a "lien" was. She'd turned the color of an overripe pear.

"A lien means that your estate owes a debt," said the judge.

"Why didn't you tell us this before?" snapped Mrs. Dessery, recovering some color in her papery cheeks.

"Lawyer Brookins didn't file it until yesterday."

There was no better example of a mud-crawling serpent than measly Hazel Brookins.

"It means your father borrowed fifteen thousand dollars at three percent interest from G. B. Minzter and now Mr. Minzter wants his money before the estate can be settled."

Minzter! He owned the Ocean Wave Hotel & Saloon, one of the worst places in the nation. In addition to selling whiskey and providing gambling, it harbored ladies of the night. The Ocean Wave was well known for hot sin as far off as wicked Sydney Town, in San Francisco. I pretended to be shocked.

"The doctor was never in that Ocean Wave in his life. I know he would never have anything to do with G. B. Minzter," I protested emphatically. To tell the truth, however, I was well aware that Daddy had visited the Ocean Wave many times. He was not past carousing now and then.

Lawyer Brookins spoke up. "Why, he used to play poker with G. B. all the time, and drank—"

"Hazel," barked the judge. "Just tell her what occurred and nothing else."

Lawyer Brookins then said to me, "Your father borrowed fifteen thousand to buy one-quarter share in the *Missouri Rainbow.*"

If that was true, he needed say no more. The *Rainbow* had been destined to be the most luxurious steamboat on the entire lower Missouri, with a schedule to St. Louis, Independence-Westport, St. Joseph, Kanesville, and Sioux City. The doctor had talked a lot about her. She had cut-glass chandeliers, carpets from Brussels, and Windsor armchairs. The ladies' cabins had pink and white carpets; ten bridal chambers had every flummery known to man.

April past, on her trial run, the brand-new *Rainbow* had lodged on a sandbar near Leavenworth, Kansas, burning down to the waterline. But the doctor had never mentioned that he owned an inch of her, much less a debt to G. B. Minzter.

"Does Lawyer Brookins have papers to prove what he's talking about?" asked Mrs. Dessery.

"Indeed he does," said the judge.

One minute I had a fortune; the next, nothing.

"What do we do?" I inquired of my new guardian.

Though appearing fully perplexed, she said, "We need time to think," and asked the judge for just that.

He recessed for twenty minutes, and we went out into the street. I was numb. "I don't want to lose my house," I said.

"Especially not to G. B. Minzter," agreed Indian Myrt. "I think I know why he wants it. People around here might think better of him if he lives in a nice house and not above his saloon with his floozies."

There wasn't an eviler man in the whole nation. Not too much was known about G. B. (Gustav Bollmeier) Minzter, who'd come out from Philadelphia, but it was said that he'd had a bad reputation there, too. He was a short, fat man with a round Dutch head, mostly balded. Henchmen fought his fights and kept order in his raucous saloon.

But it was evident that Minzter wanted the finer things in life, such as my house. For instance, the mirror behind his bar had been the talk of the lower Missouri. Imported from England, it was thirty feet long, and seven high. Minzter had it polished every day and bragged that it was the largest saloon mirror in the world.

Auntie Myrt broke my train of thought, reminding me, "You still have the sheep, Susan. They belong to you, not the estate."

I was in such a funk that I barely heard her. The dumb sheep.

"But even if you sold them at a dollar a head, you'd still be thirteen thousand dollars shy."

I couldn't think. I'd started off this day with such a grand, good feeling. My life was to begin anew. Now . . .

She went on. "I could lend you some money but not near enough to pay off Minzter, even if we do sell the sheep."

There are times in life when you just want to sit down in the rotten dirt and cry.

Brightening, she said, "One thing is certain. We can't solve it standing here. Let's go back in and ask for an extension to pay back Minzter." Then she laughed a little, which helped. "Maybe by that time someone will shoot him."

Wiping some water from my cheekbones, I laughed too. What a horrible man he was! "Maybe I'll do it," I said.

French and Indian blood suddenly boiling up, she sang out, "That's the way," and on that uplifting note we returned inside. Soon, Mrs. Dessery said, "Your Honor, we respectfully request that the court grant us an extension in repayment of the debt to Mr. G. B. Minzter. One year and one month."

Hazel Brookins was on his feet immediately. "Your Honor, on behalf of my client, I object—"

"Sit down, Hazel," admonished the judge.

Lawyer Brookins was livid.

"What's the extra month for?" asked His Honor.

"Emergency," said Mrs. Dessery.

"What makes you think you can pay back fifteen thousand dollars next November second?"

"That will give us time to contact Susan's kin. They may want to help. She has that uncle out in the California gold-fields."

I added, "My Uncle Roblett is a very wealthy man." I had no knowledge of his wealth, but it seemed a good thing to say.

Judge Tuttle pondered a moment, looking at Brookins and then back at me.

Then my new guardian offered the classic decider. Indian Myrt said, quietly, "Fate has pitted this innocent thirteen-year-old girl against G. B. Minzter, and the least the court can do is to give her an opportunity to save her home and life."

No actress could have done it better and not a pin dropped in that hall. Short as it was, it was as eloquent a plea as had ever been heard in Iowa and a female commoner, not a lawyer, had done it.

While Cause Tuttle did not exhibit moist eyes, he did say, "Granted! Be back in this court one year and one month from today with fifteen thousand dollars plus three percent interest."

Hazel Brookins looked bloody daggers at us as we departed.

Thank the Lord, I thought, but before I thanked Him too much, I asked Indian Myrt, "Where am I going to get fifteen thousand by next November?"

"That's something we'll have to think about," said she.

Yes, we would.

There was a throng at the end of the street. Auction Day always brought out a lot of buyers. Most of the household things were from people going west who got chicken-hearted when they reached the Big Muddy and decided to turn back. Too much false gossip on the streets about trouble on the trails, about white renegade and Indian attacks, dying of thirst on the desert, drowning in the rivers, or expiring of cholera or spotted fever.

Well, no one ever, ever, said it was a cakewalk once you crossed the river.

# 5

Going home, Gabriel tied off and trotting behind the buggy, Rufe bouncing along in front, I said to Indian Myrt, "You know, it's funny, I just remembered something the doctor said in June, just after he bought those sheep."

She looked over and waited.

"Well, he'd just inspected them. He said, in his own unique way, 'Susan, my love, they're healthy and strong and they're going to save us.'"

"Wonder what he meant by that?"

*"Save us,"* I emphasized. "Save us from G. B. Minzter! That's what he meant!"

"If so, you still better multiply them by thirteen thousand."

I fell silent, drooped in spirit again.

"Have you ever written your uncle Roblett?"

"Nope."

"Does he even know your folks are dead?"

"Nope." I should have written him long ago.

Mr. Blackwell had the sheep grazing about a quarter mile from the house, and we went out into the field to see him and his son.

"How'd it go?" he asked, always interested, a caring man.

Mrs. Dessery answered for both of us. "I am now Susan's legal guardian. After all these years, I have a daughter in a manner of speaking."

"I'm glad to hear that," said Mr. Blackwell. "And what about the sheep? Do we have to sell them?"

"That's up to Susan and me," she replied. "The court just gave her everything and laid down not too many rules. We're completely satisfied."

He waved his head toward the merinos, of which about two hundred were old and barren; fourteen hundred–odd had bellies full of unborn lambs; the rest were wethers. The rams had done a good job back in Indiana, just before the ewes departed. "You'll sell 'em in the spring, eh?"

Though he was a tall man, he had a hump in his back

and walked in a queer way, kind of throwing his feet out in front of him. He and Roy had lived in a little house on the south edge of Mrs. Dessery's property since Henri, her husband, had died back in '49.

I said, "I don't really know, Mr. Blackwell. We'll get your advice."

He nodded, pleased. "These are fine sheep, good Spanish merinos, but they are an awful lot for this farm. Spring, summer, and fall don't worry me. Winter does. But let 'em season through is my advice. We'll start lambing in not too long a time an' have a bigger, healthier flock by spring. Shear off all the wool from those wrinkly sheep, sell off the buck lambs, and most of the ewe lambs, as well as the ewes. Just keep a few younguns here. The doctor would have made a good profit on his deal, almost doubling his money. Now you will, Susan."

I said, "That's good advice, Mr. Blackwell." I hadn't thought about wool. "How much can we get for that fleece?" I asked, already counting my unliened assets.

"Oh, close to two thousand, I guess. Down in St. Joseph, Connaught-Venable buys for a New York company."

I exchanged crafty looks with Indian Myrt. That would help pay G. B. Minzter. She nodded.

Openmouthed, dim-witted red-haired Roy was standing there, listening. I said, "Hello, Roy," often feeling sorry for him.

"Hi, yah," he said. Almost six feet tall, he had hands the size of plates but was only fourteen. Poor Roy was likely to stand out in winter hail in bare feet unless someone told him to come inside.

"Well, the sheep'll take care of you if you take care of them," said Mr. Blackwell.

Roy laughed, as if it was funny.

Wasn't that odd, the sheep taking care of us? It fit right into what the doctor had said and what I'd been thinking about.

The first I ever had anything to do with sheep was in September when Mr. Blackwell was lancing a ewe's leg and Roy was off getting salt, which sheep like a lot. So I, not Roy, was holding the animal when Mr. Blackwell drew down with his sharp knife. She kicked and a glob of pus hit me square over the left eye.

Mr. Blackwell had laughed heartily and said, "They do it on purpose."

Not on my naked forehead! Still, I was thankful I had all those sheep free and clear, and was glad to be reminded about the wool.

Samuel was clucked around and we moved off toward the farmhouse without further conversation.

After Indian Myrt changed into her house clothes and slippers, I helped her make piccalilli until late in the afternoon, and even then we only talked about silly and inconsequential things, fending off the evil cloud of G. B. Minzter.

Just as I was leaving she said, in a new "guardian" voice, "Susan, I do hope you'll quit treating patients. I've heard you were doing it again. Mrs. Bayliss told me."

That talky crow! I said, "Same as a month ago. The wagon train people keep coming up and knocking on the door. I swear I've treated only one man recently." I'd never attempt to do anything like setting bones. Buckshot? Yes. I'd seen the doctor flip those out with the point of a knife.

Indian Myrt, in her new role, said sharply, "Susan, you shouldn't be sewing anyone up."

I agreed wholeheartedly, except in emergencies. *Meeting the emergencies is what life is truly all about,* as Mrs. Myrtle

Dessery herself had said repeatedly. I had no reason not to believe her.

We hugged each other. I kissed her cheek; she kissed mine. She said "Daughter," as if saying it experimentally.

We laughed about it.

Once home, I fed the chickens, Gabriel, and Rufe, then had a light cold supper of leftover pig ribs and Shawnee johnnycake with apple butter, wanting to get down to business in the office. I had the strangest feeling that something was secreted in there. Perhaps the doctor, on high in Beulahland, would guide me to it. About seven, lighting a lamp, I proceeded down the hall.

Starting first with the pigeonholes in the big rolltop desk, I discovered an assortment of correspondence but nothing about the Minzter loan or the *Missouri Rainbow*. I went through all the drawers. I looked everywhere, even under the pad cover on his surgical table; studied his pharmaceutical bottles. After them, I'd have to tackle, page by page, all of his medical books and I despaired of that.

But beneath the bottle of *Acidum tannicum*, on the shelf with such as *Galbanus*, *Oleum recini*, and *Oleum rosae*, was a folded notesheet, and an unmailed letter. Just as I was beginning to read the notesheet, which had to do with a man from Taos, New Mexico, there was a sharp rap on the door. Rufe roared loud enough to shake the windows. For a moment, I debated about running upstairs to get the point 31 five-shot. Rufe ferociously by my side, hair prickled up, leathers laid back, I called out a tentative "Yes?"

A female voice answered, so I decided I probably wouldn't need the Pocket Colt after all. Opening the door, I peered out. A young woman was standing there, orange lamp glow lighting a face that was well painted. My immediate guess was—*lady of the night.*

Glancing around behind her nervously, out into the chill blackness, she said, "I'm Aimee, may I come in?"

"If you want treatment, I'm not supposed to do that. I'm not the doctor's wife." However, she didn't look sick. But her rouge would have covered any paleness and there was enough cheap perfume floating around her to stifle gangrene. I invited her into the parlor, always the proper room for guests.

She said, "I'll only stay a minute. You're Susan, the doctor's daughter."

"That's me," I admitted.

"I work at the Ocean Wave. . . ."

I knew all about these women and what they did. I was never, ever, as innocent as I looked and talked. Some you'd guess as thirty-odd when they were only twenty. Rouge and whiskey and sleeping around did it. Indian Myrt called them "demonidestes" or "bar keepouses." Aimee was one.

"It's all over town what happened at court today," she said. "But G. B. wants your house and wants it bad. He'll do anything to get it, no matter about you. I just came here to tell you."

"I have a whole year," I said, suddenly alarmed.

"You hope you do," she advised. "Just be careful, Susan. You shouldn't be here alone."

"I have this killer dog," I said.

Her laugh was high-pitched and lacking breath. "The men who work for G. B. just as soon shoot you both down."

That really stunned me. Until that day, I didn't know I had an enemy in the world.

"Just be careful," she repeated. *"Minzter wants this house."*

Wondering why she'd come out this time of night to warn me, I asked her point-blank.

"I have a child," she said. "Last spring he was mighty sick. Doc Carlisle got him well. You be careful." She was just being motherly and neighborly and kind.

"I am soon to go to San Francisco, just to escape G. B. Minzter," she said.

With that, she left in a hurry, and I bolted the door behind her, thoroughly rattled. I was so scared, I forgot all about the notesheet in the doctor's office. Rufe at my knees, I went upstairs and locked the door tight. Fully clothed, I went uneasily to sleep with one hand on the Mississippi point 54, the other on the point 31 five-shot.

# 6

Awakeness usually comes upon me slowly, like the approach of midsummer dawn, eyelids lazily opening a slit, closing again, opening again, outside sounds coming from far away, then closer. This time, it was like popping open a jar of bees. I was on my feet and down the steps, having had a flash of memory about the notesheet of the night before.

It was right where I'd left it. And I sat down and began to read the difficult scrawl. One of the very few faults the doctor had was an unsightly hand.

Struggling with the loops and scratches, I made out that sheep were selling for the fantastic price of up to twelve dollars a head in the vicinity of Sacramento City, Coloma, Hangtown, Poker Flat, and so forth, just to feed the ravenous gold panners. I also made out that there was a man in Taos, New Mexico, named Bert Pettit, who was driving sheep for a living. *Trustworthy,* the doctor had underlined in notes to himself.

*Am worried, however, the Drover will not do business with me. Last year he took nine thousand head from Taos to Sacramento City. Alas, I don't have that many sheep. I'll try to buy some more . . .*

Poor Daddy! Now I understood what he meant about the "Sheep saving us." I quickly figured it up. Two thousand-odd times twelve. Why, he could have paid off the *Missouri Rainbow* debt to G. B. Minzter and have some left over.

Slicing open the unsent letter addressed to Drover Pettit, I saw that it was dated August 3, only two days before the tragedy in Mead's Meadow. In it the doctor proposed a deal whereby Drover would take our sheep to California and they'd split all expenses, Drover taking half the profit. But then the doctor sadly admitted he had only a couple thousand head.

Suddenly I yelled so loud that Rufe raced around the room barking his fool head off at nothing at all. I yelled again and again and again. Surely, from above, I'd been led to the *Acidum tannicum* bottle and that correspondence to Drover Pettit, of Taos, New Mexico.

Ever since a few weeks after the funeral, when the loss was felt in every lonely corner of the house, when my innermost fears had to be dealt with and conquered, I'd been tamping down a terrible itch and urge to go to California and see my uncle Roblett Chauncey Darden.

Even before Farmer Kinchlow's dam had sent that fatal wall of water down the creek, I'd had this tiny itch and urge to go westering. That was natural, my Daddy said. Almost everyone who lived along the Mormon Trail did. He'd had the very same prickling, I knew. In '49, he'd thought about going out as a doctor for a wagon train company, then setting up practice in the gold fields.

My Daddy, all excited, had bought Ira Willis's *Best Guide to the Goldfields* and Clayton's *North Overland Trail Guide.*

Well, my dear mother wouldn't even look at them and they began to gather dust. She said she'd already pioneered enough and that was that for us westering as a family.

Why *was* it such a big thing? The Mormons were doing it all the time, taking their sheep and cattle, even gobbling turkeys, with them. Gold miners were walking across the country with no more than a canteen and pistol on their hips, bedroll on their shoulders.

I'd seen the Mormon girls, wearing their straw bonnets, making nosegays as they went along; watched the smiling Latter-day boys as they walked behind the creaking, clanking covered rigs, now and then goosing the oxen with their long sticks. They looked happy, as if marching off to heaven.

Yet when *I* talked about going to California, Indian Myrt was alarmed. "It's across a whole continent. . . ."

I certainly knew where that coastal state was. "Blood kin is powerful to me, and important. The last we heard of Uncle Roblett he was living near the American River, where they discovered the gold. Mother always said he was a 'first class gentleman and family man.'"

"For all you know," warned Auntie Myrt, "he may be halfway around the world."

That could be true. We hadn't heard from Uncle Roblett in almost a year, but it was an occasion when we did. He seemed so romantic and devilish, a spicy man. My mental picture of him was tall and handsome, with a crisp, black mustache, a real Virginia cavalier who could dance a quadrille.

I said, "I could always take a ship to Panama and go up that way. . . ."

Ships left New York and New Orleans every few days for Panama; then you crossed the isthmus by canoe or mule, and steamed on up to San Francisco.

"Suppose you got out there and he's gone away. What then, Susan? A child alone in Sodom and Gomorrah?"

I was no child, and that's exactly how perfectly good dreams are squashed.

Triumphantly, I yelled once again there in the doctor's cluttered office, then ran down the hallway and out the back door, heading for the barn.

*It was all settled! I was going westering with my sheep.*

I'd rent the house and the medical equipment to a doctor from Des Moines. He'd already made inquiry.

*Awestering I'd go.*

# 7

Saddling up Gabriel, I was on my way with Rufe in a few minutes that rosy fall morning. As I was riding by Mrs. Carol Foote Thompson's place, she came out in her highboard Moline wagon and matched black mules. The Thompsons lived in a warm sod house, mostly underground.

"Mind if I ride with you?" I called out.

The pipe-smoking lady in the floppy red hat answered, "C'mon over, Susan."

She made a living buying secondhand things from overlanders and reselling them in a hut located near where the

Ogden Hotel is now. THIRD HAND GOODS was the sign on it. By the time overlanders reached Kanesville, some were ready to part with unnecessaries; lighten their loads.

I eased over to the high wagon-seat and let Gabriel pace alongside. "You ever thought about going to California, Mrs. Thompson?"

Nodding, the junk lady lifted the pipe from her lips, spat over the side, and said, "Many times. If I was still thirty-five, I'd be off tomorry."

"You'd leave your husband and sons?"

"I'd give 'em a choice. Go with me or stay behind."

"Would you be worried about the dangers?"

"Nope. It's just grit an' grime an' sweat an' say your prayers you don't get cholera. . . ."

I nodded a thanks, then slid back on Gabriel, waved at the junk lady, and headed in the opposite direction at a full gallop.

Mr. Blackwell had the sheep back where they'd been the previous afternoon. I rode Gabriel up to him, and some of the ewes scattered, bells ringing.

"Think these sheep could get to California?" I asked.

He laughed behind his bushy beard. "Sheep can go any-where. Or almost anywhere, up hill and down. They can swim. They take their overcoats with them. They can eat off the land. They are a meat and wool factory. Sheep are a lot tougher'n mules or cattle or oxen. They can go without water longer. They may get the scours, that's plain diar-rhea, once they drink from alkali pools, but most survive, I hear. Why do you ask?"

"Oh, I was just wondering," I said, innocently and care-lessly.

Mr. Blackwell smiled thinly at me, estimating exactly what I was thinking about. He knew! The westering bug bit almost everyone. Young or old or in between. Some could go. Some couldn't. Some tried, as he had, and failed.

I rode off, mind doubly set.

Now, I hadn't been all that unhappy with life in Kanesville, on high river bluffs, and truly, Iowa in the spring and fall is as pretty a place as you could imagine. In early fall, the prairie grass is still hub-high, with gentian, goldenrod, and white and purple asters peeking through. In the early green glory of spring, baby false dandelions and bird-foot violets always winked at me from the knolls. Then came summer with wild plums and wild grapes and crepe-petaled primroses. There was no lack of beauty here.

Nor, up to that time, was I lacking in attention at picnics or husking bees or sleigh rides. I'm not bragging when I say there were a half-dozen boys who got all fumbly when I smiled at them. One, Hans Jochem, turned the color of a rooster's brick-red breast if I so much as glanced at him. Another, Billy Bundy, who stuck his hand up my dress when I was eleven, was still chasing me despite the fact that I knocked him flat one morning.

Galloping into the Dessery side yard, I was yelling, "Auntie Myrt, Auntie Myrt," before I left the saddle.

The contents of the information about Drover, of Taos, New Mexico, was then divulged, along with my plan, or part of it, to defeat G. B. Minzter. I was not about to tell all of it, just yet.

The widow beamed with excitement.

# 8

Chill, gentle rain was falling the next morning, providing time to do things inside the house. These damp autumn days, with the leaves turning red and gold, smoke twisting up into the gray sky, were always good. The cottonwoods had yellowed and the wild Pottawattamie plums were safely in jam crocks.

Mrs. Dessery was there, having spent the night. Her new Navy Colt six-shooter, a point 36, bought down at Lazenby's, came along with her, and had Minzter and his men decided to test us, a hot, whistling reception would have followed. I told her all about the kindly visit of "Aimee," the helpful "demonideste."

Over breakfast, we discussed the two letters I was to write that day. Auntie Myrt advised my throwing myself upon the mercy of the drover, explaining my lien problem in detail, then offering him all profits over fifteen thousand plus three percent. She had to return home to start her own daily chores, so I helped hitch Samuel to the buggy and off she went in the drizzle, feeling a sense of accomplishment. We now had a plan.

Giddings Carlisle, M.D. had bought embossed stationery from Dumas & Company, in St. Louis, and there was no better time to use it than now. Sitting down at the heavy square table in the kitchen, its top whitened from doses of lye, I began:

September 15, 1851

Mr. Roblett Chauncey Darden
Hudnut & Darden's General Store
J Street
Sacramento, California

Dear Uncle Roblett:

I've never met you but I hope you've heard of me, Susan Darden Carlisle—your niece from Iowa.

First, I have some very sad news. Your sister, Alice, my mother, was killed in a buggy accident in August. My father was killed at the same time. I grieve them very much. However, I must now plan my own life and that plan includes me coming to California.

One reason is that I'm in trouble here. My parents willed me a fine house and property but a terrible man named Minzter wants to take it all away.

I will be coming with several thousand sheep, my mission being to sell them in Sacramento to feed the hungry miners and raise money to pay off Minzter.

I would appreciate your advice on sheep prices, etc., around Sacramento.

Please give my regards to your wife and children, assuming you have same, and I await your reply.

Your loving niece,<br>Susan Darden Carlisle

At this point, my new guardian had absolutely no idea that I planned to accompany those animals to California. *Where go the sheep, go I* was my new motto. She'd learn of that part soon enough.

I then began to concentrate on the second letter. I laboriously practiced the bird-track scrawl of the doctor. The exact scrawl was not necessary, only that it look masculine. There was never any mistaking Dr. Carlisle's heavy hand as feminine.

Finally, I dipped the quill into ink, copying from the letter the doctor had written in August but had never mailed.

September 15, 1851

Mr. Bert Pettit
Post Office
Taos, New Mexico Territory

My dear Mr. Pettit:

I understand that you are a professional sheep drover and for hire cross-country.

In that regard, I have 10,000 healthy merino sheep that I would like to have driven to the Sacramento Valley of California next spring. I am prepared to offer you half ownership in these fine animals for your labors and leadership in delivering them safely to market.

I will advance expense money which will be shared equally upon sale of the sheep in California, as will herder salaries, etc. Wagons and supplies can be purchased here.

Having heard much of the difficulties of the Overland Trail, I will not hold you responsible for losses resulting from natural causes or theft.

I look forward to your early reply.

Sincerely,
Giddings Carlisle, M.D.

The only changes I'd made from the original were the number of sheep and the date. If I admitted I had less than three thousand woollies, Drover was apt not to write back. On the other hand, if I could lure him to Iowa, there was always a way to explain anything.

The next to final touch was to heat the doctor's personal seal over the stove and push it down through red wax, making a flowery GC on the back flap of the envelope. Without doubt, Drover Pettit would think: Ah-hah, a letter from the well-fixed Kanesville doctor, Giddings Carlisle! Minutes later I got my cape out and went down to the barn to employ Gabriel, and we rode away to town. Rufe never liked the rain but came along anyhow.

Court Clerk Evan Green was also postmaster and I asked him how long it would take for a California letter. "Coupla months, I'd say. It'll go downriver to New Orleans and then to Panama, cross the jungle there, and then go up the coast by Pacific Mail Steamship to San Francisco. Long trip."

"How about New Mexico Territory?"

"Where?"

"Place called T-a-o-s." I spelled it out.

"That's pronounced 'Touse.' It'll go the Santa Fe Trail, then on up to the mountains. Month to six weeks, I'd say. That's eight hundred miles away. What you doin' writing to all these foreign places?"

"Oh, friends of my daddy," I said airily. Evan Green was an awful gossip.

After I posted the letters, I couldn't resist going to so-called Tent City, five minutes distant, where most of the emigrants camped until crossing the river. At one time, it covered two square miles. Tents, wagons, mules, oxen, horses, milk cows; people milling around. Now it was down to a few dozen people as the wintering Mormons made their last big push west. Gold seekers were still coming through, however, as well as plain Gentile settlers westering for one reason or another.

I liked to look at the names gaily painted on the wagon sides: GOLD OR A GRAVE or DAVY CROCKETT THROUGH BY DAYLIGHT or BOBTAIL COMPANY EAST BEAT or BURY ME NOT BY SODA SPRINGS. Each late spring dawn, some would roll down the bluffs, brakes screeching, to line up and wait for the ferry.

A lot were headed for towns named Jackass Hill and Shinbone Peak and Angels Camp and Gospel Swamp. Never had the nation thumped and bumped so much.

Is it any wonder that I, Susan D. Carlisle, suddenly pushed into change of circumstances by tragic mishap, had my own special dreams and visions? What should I paint on my own wagon in red and gold letters?

The next late afternoon I took time out to go into town and see Sweet Frenchy Moll, having some urgent questions to ask that wise woman. Frenchy's real name was Josette Moll, and she was only half French at that, like Indian Myrt, but unlike my guardian she couldn't really speak the language very well. She'd come up out of New Orleans, by steamboat. Quietly, she opened a high-class house of ill repute, recruiting her girls from St. Louis. None from Iowa. She was that smart.

I got to know her when Sweet Frenchy came into the doctor's office for an operation. She had a hard-core cyst in a private place and Dr. Carlisle expertly chunked it out. I assisted in that operation and we became friendly. A woman of the world, to be sure, she was very interesting to talk to.

Smallish, dark-haired, with an hourglass figure and baby-bottom skin, she sometimes spoke with a put-on French accent, which is how she got her name. Aside from her

girls, I think I was the only female in town that would talk
to her. If she'd fallen into a mud puddle on Broadway,
every man in town would have jumped to help her out;
every woman, including Mrs. Dessery, would have stepped
on her back.

In Sweet Frenchy's fancy parlor, we usually had tea and
small Chinese almond cakes. I always filled her in on any
gossip, and she discussed world affairs, never what went on
in the bedrooms. I avoided the house when customers were
there. But in the fall and winter, things were quiet and the
girls took their holidays in St. Louis or New Orleans. No
horses or buggies were tied up outside Frenchy's this wintry
day and I went on in.

"Suzanne," she said, wrapping her arms around me,
smiling widely. She was always perfumed; best-smelling
woman in town. "Today I am lonesome and you make the
sun come out."

My eyes always went to the big painting entitled "In the
Pond." It was a daring picture of a nude lady in a pond, up
to her knees. Her back was to you, and it left a lot for
imagination. I'd never seen such a daring picture. It was in
the red velvet parlor.

Now, there are a lot of things you can say to the Sweet
Frenchy Molls of the world that you can't say to the more
or less sheltered Indian Myrts. The Frenchy Molls have a
different view on life.

"You heard about Minzter's lien on my house?" I said.

"I did," she replied. "He is a terrible man. I steer clear of
him."

Then I told her what I'd done, summoning the drover
from New Mexico on false pretenses. "I had to tell somebody."

"I'm flattered," Frenchy said.

"Did I do right, considering the circumstances?"

She sighed. "No."

"But I had to do something to save my house and property."

She nodded emphatically. *"Oui! Oui!"* Yes. Yes. Sometimes she lapsed into French without trying to put it on. But I was now confused and she saw that, adding, "What you did was wrong but at least you did something. Now you must see how it all works out."

"Should I tell Mrs. Dessery?"

"By all means."

"But she'll make me write another letter to him and tell him the truth. Then he'll never come here."

Sweet Frenchy said, frowning widely, "I see the problem." Tell the truth, lose the house; tell a lie, perhaps save it. The world turns on such dilemmas.

She spooned her tea around delicately for a few thoughtful minutes, then said, "I have the solution. Tell the truth but wait a while before telling it."

"To who?"

"To both. To *Tante* Myrt, and to the sheepman."

"How long should I wait?"

She considered that question for a long time, then said, solemnly, "You should wait until you know that whatever you say will make no difference. That is how politicians do it."

I was relieved. We talked about other things and then I took a last look at that daring "In the Pond" and went on home.

# 9

Lambing took place for the next three weeks, with the weather growing steadily colder, winter approaching our prairie lands in low scudding clouds and hints of snow. Frost-bearded brown was now the color of the wire and buffalo grass. There was thin early-morning ice in the rush-grown sloughs. We separated the "readys" from the "soons" and brought the readys up near the Dessery barn, largest in the country, and they began to drop lambs on schedule within a few days. Fifty or sixty a day.

Having to forgo hunting, barely celebrating my fourteenth birthday, I had never worked so hard in all my life, sometimes around the clock, catching naps in the barn hay. However, I was constantly adding to my flock, thinking often of Drover, wishing I had five thousand pregnant ewes.

As each lamb was born, mother licking it and soon feeding it, I made a mark in my notebook. Some ewes had twins and two wonderful ewes had triplets. The overflow of mothers and lambs went into my own barn. At the end of three weeks, I had nine hundred and seventy-six additions to my band.

Harsh winter began to descend upon Iowa the first week in November and I was glad the sheep had thick coats. They huddled close together, almost disappearing in the new snow, except for rising steam. You'd have thought there were thousands of kettles out there. They walked to the barns for feed each day, and we pitched it out.

I was so occupied with the sheep and weather that I almost forgot that letters were due from California and

New Mexico. Then one arrived, in the chubby fingers of Postmaster Green, who said, "This is addressed to your late pa." He was curious, of course. I kept my strict silence. G. B. Minzter would know soon enough of my plans via other town tattletales.

Outside, I ripped it open.

The first thing that impressed me was the educated handwriting, firm and masculine but cultured. Here was a real gentleman, I thought. The *l*'s flowed up nicely, the *g*'s had a rhythm to them, and the grammar was correct, insofar as I knew. I take great stock in first impressions and Mr. Pettit's quill painted a picture of a businessman of substance, even though he was a sheep drover.

> November 13, 1851
> Fernando de Taos,
> New Mexico Territory

Dear Dr. Carlisle:

I gladly accept your generous offer.

I will bring several experienced herders with me and hire several more in Kanesville. Those I will train on the trail. With that many sheep to bed down each night, we'll need extra protection against theft. I suggest we hire four guards in Kanesville—riflemen! I'm bringing my own trusted dogs, goats, and Spanish mules.

I estimate total expenses, up until we sell the sheep, at about $3,000. I will need $500 in advance for travel expenses to Iowa.

Unless you hear from me, I'll arrive in Kanesville about April 1st of next year (1852) and leave for California as quickly as possible to take advantage of summer weather for the crossing.

I look forward to meeting you.

Your obedient servant,
Bert Pettit
Drover

I had thought a favorable reply from Drover would send me spiraling in joy. Well, it did not. *Three thousand dollars? Dogs, mules, goats, herders, guards!* All I wanted was to take a few sheep across the country and save my house. Nothing more. It now appeared to me that I had started a pebble down a long, treacherous hill and it might well turn into an avalanche and bury me.

At home, I lighted a fire in the parlor and sitting in front of the roaring flames, using Rufe's warm back for a pillow, I must have read the letter fifty times, with a tiny but growing gollop in my throat each time. Outside couldn't have been more than six degrees and the parlor was still cold, but I suddenly found myself sweaty damp from throat to toes. Though I'd seen wagons and tools and food rations piled up over in Tent City many times, it hadn't really occurred to me that I'd be buying the same things.

For instance, why did he need to bring goats all the way from Taos? I could find several good milk cows for five dollars each. Four riflemen? Did we need the U.S. Cavalry just to walk the sheep and watch over them? Not daring to show the letter to Indian Myrt just yet, I hid it beneath the bottle of *Acidum tannicum* in the doctor's office. Before I went to bed, I looked in my late mother's big French mirror and asked myself, "Oh, Susan, what have you done?"

I really didn't want an answer, and throughout the twisty, turny night I debated about writing back to Bert

Pettit immediately, not waiting, and confessing that I was the late doctor's daughter, not the doctor himself; that I had been known to be impulsive.

But came the jonquil-colored dawn, with early golden sun spanking off the snow blanket, birds flitting about happily, my courage and resolution returned.

If life was not a gamble, what was it?

I went straightaway over to Indian Myrt's, kissed her, hugged her, and said, "I have good news for you."

"The Ocean Wave burnt down?"

"No. Drover Pettit sent his reply. He'll be here April first."

"You heard from him?" she exclaimed, astonished.

"He's bringing goats and dogs and herders. And he needs five hundred in advance for expenses." She would have to lend it to me, since my own funds were tied by Minzter's lien.

Happy for me, Indian Myrt smiled widely. "That's just fine, Susan," she said. "We'll have breakfast and then go get the money." The banking house of Haines and Kimball was open.

I was glad she didn't ask to see the letter, but she did make a prophetic comment that Drover would be arriving on All Fools' Day.

# 10

The grandfather clock in the hall ticked on through February and into March, nervousness and sleepless nights of late December beginning to return. Triumph's hour or the sword of doom was approaching. By this time the drover and his men had likely started to walk out of the New Mexico mountains.

I sat down and wrote a confession to Drover Pettit, knowing it would never reach him in time. I'd done, partially, as Sweet Frenchy Moll had suggested.

Then gusty March began to slide to unstable April on the plains. Flowered paintbrush would soon pop out of the moist earth, along with blankets of groundvetch and pasque flowers. About the third week of March, feeling the need for wisdom and advice, I finally mustered up enough courage to show Indian Myrt the December letter from Bert Pettit. She was horrified. "You actually told him you have ten thousand sheep?"

I nodded.

"I can't believe it, Susan. Ten thousand?"

"I did."

My guardian gasped. "It's too late to stop him now. He probably left Taos a month ago."

I agreed, and told her about the too-late letter.

"Susan," she said sharply, "you are a heathen liar."

I was indeed.

"You've tinkered with his life and his business. He's expecting profit from all those sheep. Ten thousand. Not three thousand or whatever you have."

I stayed silent. I was guilty of everything.

"How could you do it? Forgeries, lies . . ."

She went on for another five minutes. I'd never had such a dressing-down, even from my own mother. When she ran out of words, I asked, "What do I tell him?"

"Tell him the exact truth the minute he gets here and ask for his forgiveness. He may skin you alive and I wouldn't blame him at all."

We talked on about the situation for almost an hour and

plainly there was little to do but await his arrival and let the Lord's bountiful mercy take its course.

When I'd exhausted that possibility, I asked, "How do you think he's traveling?"

"Santa Fe Trail, most likely, over to the Missouri, and then upriver by steamboat. He's probably already across Kansas and down at Independence."

"I hope he's had good weather," I said, not knowing what else to say.

She just sighed deeply and shook her head.

A few days later, discussing final strategy, we decided I'd be innocently alone in the house when my new business partner arrived. Mrs. Dessery would be utilized only when it became necessary to save the day.

I'm sure impulse is often a practice of the living devil. On the sleepless night before Drover was scheduled to arrive, "impulse" once again got the better of common sense. Up to the earlobe, I snipped my long, beautiful honey-hued hair, the silky adornment of which I'd always been so proud drifting ignobly to the floor. Why? For a few fleeting, dangerous moments I'd had in mind impersonating my late Daddy, God rest him.

However, on looking at myself in the long mirror, turning sideways and backways, thinking about mummy bindings on my chest, wearing a pair of the doctor's trousers, I decided the whole idea was ridiculous. No matter what, I'd still look like and talk like Susan Darden Carlisle.

Come dawn of the next day, the day of All Fools', with my partner due to arrive by sundown, I washed the shortened hair in rainwater until it sparkled, put on my prettiest taffeta dress and the black shoes the doctor had bought me in St. Louis, then dabbed some of my mother's expensive Paris perfume behind my ears.

Jittery while preparing myself, I finally told Rufus, "If things go wrong and that man attacks me, bite his privates." Brown eyes solemn, that big dog just sat there, gazing at me curiously. I was never, ever, really sure when I was communicating with him.

In case of full, life-threatening emergency, I took the fully loaded point 31 five-shot from upstairs, placing it behind the fern in the parlor. Firing it would be a last resort, a quick shot into the ceiling to tell Bert Pettit "Hands off!"

Then began the daylong ordeal of waiting. Sitting down in my late Daddy's carved oakwood rocking chair in the parlor, I creaked away, having many thoughts, rehearsing exactly what I planned to say to the visitor, especially about the difference in the sheep count; about the obvious absence of the doctor. Both from thinking and rocking, I was weary by the time the sun began to dim across the river, and gave up on Drover's arrival.

Up to that point, my intentions were to follow my guardian's good advice and throw myself on his mercy. But then, during the evening, I had a brilliant idea about writing one last note from the doctor. . . .

## 11

On the sunny, coolish morning of April 2, 1852, I heard and smelled Drover Pettit before I ever saw him. Hobnail boots pounding on the porch, the odor of strong cigar smoke went ahead of him like a foul breeze. Rufus began to rumble and the hair along the ridge of his back arose, as if old Lucifer himself had set foot on the premises. I shushed him down and slowly got out of the rocking chair, smoothing my dress, patting my hair, readying myself, knees suddenly watery.

Drover's first words were, "Tell your pa the drover is here."

Oddly enough, he had the smooth, soft, quiet voice of a thorough gentleman, though certainly not the diction. I first looked beyond his chunky body, thinking that dogs, goats, and herders from New Mexico would be out in the road. But there was only a single big, dusty brown mule tied to our front gate, slashing away at the chokeberry buds. Rinaldo was his name, I later learned. Spanish riding mule.

Then I did look at Drover. Though they'd gone out of style, a tall trail-worn beaver-coated hat was on his keg of head. Beneath the floppy brim of it, under red-brown furry eyebrows, were a pair of the clearest blue eyes I'd ever seen. He had a windburnt weathered bulb for a nose and over his jaw was a month's beard. His knee-length animal-skin coat might have been black at one time, but the trail had turned it brown. Beneath the coat were wide shoulders and on down were bargeman's legs. I estimated him to be forty-odd.

No collar was attached to what had been a white shirt, open at the neck, exposing prickly reddish-brown hair. Around his wide chest and over his back was an equally dirty sheepskin vest. But what finally drew my attention was the point 36 Navy Colt, a hogleg exactly like Indian Myrt's, strapped on his right hip. On the opposite hip, I saw the handle of a long knife. It appeared to be an authentic Bowie.

Rufe was still rumbling, teeth showing. Drover said to him, "Pppp ht," as if flicking a fly. Rufe immediately shut up, and tucked his tail between his legs, which made me doubly uneasy. No one had ever before intimidated that ferocious dog.

Drover fixed those penetrating eyes on me and said insultingly, "You sure don't look like you're deaf, girl. Go get your pa!"

I stammered, "He, he . . . the doctor isn't here now," which was certainly no lie.

"Where'n blazes is he, then?"

Heart slamming, I answered, "He's away."

The drover snorted and looked around our fenced-in yard. "Show me the sheep."

Oh, Lordy! "Out grazing." Then I said, just as quickly, "Won't you come in?"

In the parlor, I asked, "May I bring you some nice cold water?"

"Nothin' stronger, Hoss?" he inquired.

I shook my head. Hoss? What a thing to call me.

When I returned to the parlor with the bucket and dipper, Drover was sitting in the rocking chair, creaking it back and forth as he pleased, beaver hat still rudely on his head, dusty hobnails on the round rug from Brussels, my mother's favorite. He'd also dropped ashes on our splendid cherrywood floor.

As he downed the dipper in one long gulp, I asked, "How was the journey, sir?"

He gazed at me thoughtfully. "Lot of rain and sleet in Kansas." Then silence gripped us, except the rocker creaking.

I broke the quiet. "Who else came with you?"

"Five old men. One youngun. Twelve mules. Three goats. Four dogs."

Nothing to do but press on. "Where are they now, sir?"

"Waiting for me."

"Near here?"

He eyed me suspiciously. "On the bluff."

"Why do you need so many mules?"

"Don't drink as much water. Mule team can make thirty miles a day; oxen only fifteen."

"Sir, I'm also very curious about those goats that you brought along."

He looked at me as if I were a total ignoramus. "Goats lead the sheep. Dogs keep order. I'd rather have goats and dogs than herders."

Creak, creak.

I was now finding it hard to breathe. "Did you walk all the way?"

"Walked, rode, got carried on a steamboat," he said wearily.

My brain whirled. "You know, I've never been outside Iowa except to cross over to Nebraska Territory and go down to St. Joe. You know that Iowa is an Indian name? A-y-a-u-w-a-y. It means—"

Drover suddenly stood up and locked those drilling eyes on me. "Damnitall, girl, where's your pa? Where's your ma?"

I said to him sharply, "No profanity in this house! I will not allow it!"

Steam began to form under his nostrils, something I had never seen before. Blue eyes turned icy, he said to me in a voice short of thunder, "Damnitall, where's your pa?"

The emergency had begun! "He left a note for you. I'll get it."

I went across to the doctor's office, lifting my begging face toward the perfect gold streets of Paradise. Plucking the note out from under the *Extractum anthemidis* jar, I returned to the parlor and handed it to Drover. A master-piece, I'd thought at the time of writing:

March 28, 1852

My dear Mr. Pettit:

Welcome to Kanesville.

This will introduce you to my daughter, Susan Darden Carlisle. Called away at the last minute, I will not return for quite a while but have left all my instructions with Susan, who is a very bright girl. She will accompany you to Sacramento City and take my share of the sheep sales.

She is reliable, trustworthy, a hard worker, and a very good cook. So she will add tremendously to trailing the sheep.

She may look and act a little young but she is actually nineteen.

Good luck on the trail.

Sincerely,

Giddings Carlisle, M.D.

Drover handed it right back saying, "I got temporary sun blindness."

His eyes didn't look sunburnt to me. Nonetheless, I proceeded to read to him, using a very positive tone of voice when I talked about myself. But he finally exploded when I reached the part ". . . she will accompany you to Sacramento City—"

"No, sir, Doc Carlisle," he shouted. "No siree! No female on my drive. Never! Not a one!"

Calmly, I waited until the rampage was over, and then continued steadily until the end, gaining confidence with each second. When I finished, I added firmly, "Those were his wishes, Mr. Pettit."

Drover had calmed down somewhat, but his quiet words were every bit as threatening as his loud ones, perhaps more so. "Your pa must be crazy," he said to me, in icy outrage. "Even thinkin' 'bout sendin' his daughter on that trail. There's the heat o' hell out there, Hoss. If we get slowed down, there may be blizzards in the peaks. There's Injuns, not to mention murderin', stealin', rapin' white renegades. We got two ranges to climb. Fifteen rivers an' two hundred creeks to ford. There's wolves an' coyotes an' mountain lions. There's buffler stampedes . . ."

I did not even blink.

"Has your pa ever heard of the Humboldt Sink? Forty Mile Desert? Worst places on earth. Burnin' sun, alkali dust, no water. Forty miles o' killer sand. A hot spring that'll scald your tongue. People droppin' dead, oxen dyin', mules fallin' over . . ."

"The doctor knew all that," I said calmly, without being sure at all.

"That's where you see the elephant!"

What elephant? I didn't ask.

He went on, "I'll bury at least one herder 'fore we get to Forty Mile. I don't need to bury no girls in addition."

"I'll take care of myself," I said. *Elephants on the overland?*

Almost murderously, Drover said, "You ain't going!"

I looked straight back at him, pulling myself up to my full five feet three, shoulders back. "Either I go, or the sheep don't go" was my ultimatum, tough as horseshoes.

His nose got to within an inch of mine, cigar breath almost gagging me, and he said, emphatically, "That first letter from Doc Carlisle don't mention no girls."

"This does," I replied, waving the forged missive at him.

Just then, Mrs. Bayliss, who lived over on Father De-Smet Street, stuck her head in from the hallway to say, "I'm sorry to interrupt your conversation, Susan, but I'd appreciate some of the doctor's good wild cherry cough medicine. For Fred. He's got the bads today."

Breathing relief, I said, "I'll get some for you, Mrs. Bayliss."

When I returned, that crow Klara Bayliss was saying to the stranger, "You know, we all miss Dr. and Mrs. Carlisle so much. Why, when they got killed last year part of Kanesville went up to heaven with them. . . ."

Drover turned slowly to look at me, so slowly that he seemed to be mechanical; on cogs.

I froze, in total breath and body.

Blinking, Drover said, "Uh?" It was a childlike, hurt sound.

Faintly, I heard Mrs. Bayliss thanking me for the cherry cough syrup. Then she departed.

I thought about the Pocket Colt nestled behind the potted fern. I'd certainly shoot him if I had to.

However, Drover Bert Pettit just stood there numbly, looking at me in amazement. I don't think he could quite believe that he'd come all the way from the Sangre de Cristo range in New Mexico at the beckoning of a four-teen-year-old. I tried to think of something appropriate to say and messed it up instead, sounding trivial. "You see, I had this itch and urge to go to California and sell the sheep—"

He said, "Uh?" clearly stunned.

I said, "Well, you see—"

Suddenly, a stream of molten curses poured out of him, many of which I'd never heard before. I quickly discarded the idea of the Pocket Colt, thinking that this New Mexican could dismember me before I could even aim right. Running out of the house as fast as I could, I dashed past the barn and over the fence at back and crashed on down into the thicket, ruining my taffeta dress and busting one St. Louis shoe. Rufe was at my heels, terrified as I was. I went so deep into that tangle that even rabbits couldn't have found me. Much to my surprise, the drover made no attempt to follow.

About a half-hour later, I ventured back up to the house and crept around to the front. I was glad to see that Drover and his brown mule, Rinaldo, were gone. I went straightaway to the Dessery farm, telling Indian Myrt of my encounter with Bert Pettit, and how Mrs. Bayliss wrecked the whole thing.

"You deserved it," she said, showing little sympathy. "You caused him to walk seven hundred miles or more, maybe for nothing."

"They rode some of the way on mules and steamboats," I said defensively.

"Susan," said she, with sharpness, "You are guilty of fraud, forgery, and I don't know what else."

"But you will come with me tomorrow when I see him? Tell him I meant well?"

My guardian shook her head in frustration. "You'll have to tell him yourself, but I'll come along."

I hugged her, but Mrs. Dessery remained coldly withdrawn. The half Indian, showing her ways, didn't return the hug.

## 12

Next morning I went to the Dessery farm before sunrise, just when cook fires in Tent City were being stirred anew. Five hundred westering travelers must have been around Kanesville that morning. The annual trek would soon begin.

As I bumped along in the pale, early light, smelling damp sedge and wild flowers, hearing the birds chirp, I couldn't help but think it would all be so different if Drover was the kind and understanding man I'd first estimated him to be.

No sooner had I reached the farm when my guardian said, "I suffered a sleepless night. It isn't likely that Mr. Pettit will want to walk home with his herders without wages. He may threaten to take us to court. Make you sell the sheep here, then all is lost."

"Take us to court?"

"You misrepresented yourself and caused damage to him. Then again, you are still a legal child."

"I didn't cause him much damage."

"I think Mr. Pettit can prove you did."

Any man was a "mister" to Indian Myrt. She never called her late husband, Henri, anything but "Mr. Dessery," to my knowledge. One evening when I stayed over there, I heard her say to him, "Good night, Mr. Dessery," even though they were under the same quilt.

We had breakfast and were soon on our way. Rufe ran along, now and then detouring when he saw a cottontail or woodchuck. They were plentiful. Dogwood and redbud were beginning to bloom, also shadbush, with its feathery whiteness.

Wood peewees were flicking around and the prairie horned lark, a good singer, added his music to the harness jingle. Floating on the nearby ponds were white and yellow crowfoot, and the little stream that flanked the back road was visited with yellow star grass and moccasin flowers.

"What a lovely day," said Indian Myrt, ridding her mind of what was to come, and trying to ease mine.

She was wearing a prim blue cotton dress and her head was covered with a blue polka-dot sunbonnet. A silver brooch was at her throat. She looked to be a woman of substance. Every day except Sunday she wore boots made in Boston.

The Missouri takes a bend around Kanesville and at the south end of the bend, up on the bluffs, the drover had set up his camp of three dingy, well-worn tents. Everybody was up and about, sitting around the cook fire, when we arrived. The big mules were tethered nearby, deleafing new growth. I guess the goats were off on a morning feed of early yellow lousewort, which thrived where Bert Pettit happened to camp. His sheep dogs began to bark.

Indian Myrt drove within thirty feet of the little group by the fire. I could smell strong chicory coffee. It appeared that they had just finished their meal, and were relaxing, having lit their pipes and cigars, a good time to parley.

She reined to a stop, saying, very pleasantly, "Good morning to you from us. I am Mrs. Myrtle Dessery, of Kanesville, Iowa," as if Drover didn't know which state he was in, "and this is Susan Darden Carlisle, my legal ward."

Drover replied evenly to her, "I know who you are, Hoss. I already been told."

I wondered who'd told him about Mrs. Myrtle Dessery

and eased discreetly to the ground, my eye catching that young herder that Drover had mentioned. I took a longer look at him and was totally stunned. He was six feet or over, with a strong jaw and greenish eyes, and it looked to me like he had everything I wanted. He was dressed strangely and I later discovered it was Mexican attire. A black flat-topped, wide-brimmed hat was on his head, a red kerchief was about his neck, and a serape was over his shoulders, a woven wool thing of green and red. This man was surely striking, and I couldn't have been more stunned if I'd been hit by a ball of thunder. I also noticed that his fingers were long, something I've always admired in a man. I finally tore my eyes away from him, little realizing that I was looking at *the first authentic American cowboy.*

The dogs had been sniffing each other out, Rufe doing his usual rumbling. Just then all four attacked and Rufe ran up the road, yelping in fear. I was so embarrassed.

The old white-haired man by the fire, whose name was Clem Epps, I later learned, a Missouri mule skinner, cackled, and then yelled, "Those dogs are all bitches."

I was shocked. Ferocious Rufe running from four little females?

At that moment came a second shock of a different kind. A man whose skin was muddy black began to unfold from the fireside and I thought he would never stop rising. With a woven turban on his head, he was dressed in a long, collarless robe, sandals on his big feet. On both cheeks were scars arranged like crescent moons. Strapped to his side was a long curved dagger. I had never seen such a man. He was nothing less than a black giant, fearsome at first sight. I looked away from his piercing brown eyes, though I noted Auntie Myrt nodded to him cordially.

Meanwhile, Drover ignored me to look at the mite of

woman in the buggy seat. Including her clothes and boots, Mrs. Dessery weighed no more than a hundred pounds.

Without removing his dirt-infested hat, Drover said to her, "I want damages for travelin' all the way from Touse under false summons. You're both liable."

He still wasn't aware I didn't have ten thousand sheep. I looked toward the lady in the buggy. She replied pleasantly to Drover, "I'm sure we can negotiate any damages. Susan meant well. There's a long story if you'd care to listen. . . ."

"Oh, ho, a story, eh?" said the drover. "Well, I engaged legal counsel yestiddy afternoon an' can get a hearin' within a few days, I'm told."

"Who is your counsel, Mr. Pettit?" asked my guardian.

"Hazel Brookins," said Drover.

We both sucked rancid air.

Nonetheless, Indian Myrt smiled warmly at Drover, saying, "Such a pity for you to go to all that trouble, hiring Mr. Minzter's lawyer. Such a loss of money and time, which is so precious to all of us."

When she said "money" I could see Drover's keggy head cocking over a little, a glint of greed appearing in those clear blue eyes. So that was his flabby weakness, like the doctor's.

"Oh, haven't you heard?" Indian Myrt went on smoothly. "No, of course not. You've been traveling all those hard and dusty miles. Why, Mr. Pettit, sheep are now selling for fifteen dollars a head in California, and here you are, wasting valuable time. . . ."

I detected gold eagle pieces beginning to faintly spin behind all his sharp squinting. "Fifteen dollars a head? Who told you that? I sold 'em for twelve there last year."

A preacher couldn't have been more sincere when she answered, "Heard it only yesterday from the stage driver."

I turned to look at my guardian in astonishment. What she'd just said was an absolute impossibility. The Concord of the Western Stage Coach Company wasn't due in for another three days, if then.

"Is that so?" asked Drover, his interest clearly piqued. He turned to the small audience by the fire, talking rapidly in a language strange to me. Spanish, I later learned from Indian Myrt. She spoke a smattering.

A stocky swarthy man grinned and answered, "Bwayno, bwayno," or something like that.

"Well, now, Hoss," said Drover, seeming to become pliable at last. "Yep, we should get those sheep movin'. You sheared yet?" He was looking direct at me.

I also felt my guardian's eyes on me. "You might as well tell him right now," she said.

I knew exactly what she was talking about.

"Tell him," she insisted.

I took a deep breath. "Mr. Pettit, I don't have ten thousand sheep."

"Some die?"

"A few," I hedged.

"How many?"

"Tell him," my guardian repeated.

"How many sheep do you have? Nine thousand five?" he asked hopefully. His income was involved.

It wasn't that I wouldn't tell him. For a moment, I couldn't. Everyone has had that experience. A lot of short swallows within a dry throat, and then an "eek."

Drover tried to be helpful. "It's hard to count them all. You may have more than you think."

"Susan!" said Indian Myrt, like a whip-crack.

"Less than four thousand."

Drover suddenly looked ill and weak.

Oddly enough, in all this exchange not once was it mentioned that I intended to go to California with my sheep. I suppose he simply forgot that ultimatum, and I had no desire to bring it up at this time.

Never have I been much of a weeper, but I managed to produce some glistening water in the corners of my eyes while relating all that had happened to me. After describing the awful mishap in Mead's Meadow, then the shocking discovery of the lien, said I, bravely, "All I can call my own is those sheep and what I have on my back." An innocent female purely down on her luck was what I hoped he clearly understood.

Drover sat with his arms folded, puffing on that smelly cigar.

I went on, "Humbly, I ask your forgiveness and—"

Mrs. Dessery broke in wisely. "—and she's willing to give you *all* profit above fifteen thousand, plus three percent interest."

Hopefully, I added, "Expenses can come out of the wool money."

Mrs. Dessery continued, "Now. Mr. Pettit, if you reach Sacramento City with most of the sheep, that will give you a profit of over twenty thousand dollars, and you will have done a good deed."

The "good deed" would not amount to very much to him, I suspected.

Drover began thinking hard, some of it aloud. "With those few sheep, I won't need to hire any guards. . . ."

That sounded very promising and I quickly grasped the opportunity to speak out. "You don't need to hire anyone.

You're forgetting something, Mr. Pettit, I'm going along. . . ."

"You're doing what?" coughed my guardian, flabbergasted.

"I must go along," I said. "By the time the sheep reach Sacramento City, it'll be late August. The money is due in November."

I already planned to return via the Isthmus of Panama, and via ship to New Orleans, reversing the mail route. Evan Green had told me a railroad was being built across the isthmus. Maybe I'd take the train across. Maybe not. Maybe I'd walk or canoe. Or ride a mule.

Now it was Indian Myrt's time to be speechless.

I went on logically, "Someone has to bring the money back on schedule." Selling the sheep and having money in pocket would be of no avail unless it was brought back to Judge Tuttle.

"I got no time for wiggle-tails on the sheepwalk," flatly said Drover, echoing his sentiments of the previous day.

"I'm not asking for time, I'll work equal," said I, with some anger.

Indian Myrt said, "I won't hear of it."

What this was really all about, as usual, was that these people, Myrtle Dessery included, did not give me brawn enough to make such a trip. That was the core of it, nothing else.

Drover eyed me. "S'pose you git kilt? Drownded? Scalped? Maybe the fevers? All kinds o' ways on the trail. The elephant will stomp you."

I replied, matter-of-factly, "You just say some Bible words over this 'wiggle-tail,' bury me, and go on."

Old Clem Epps cackled and spat into the fire.

"I won't hear of it," Indian Myrt repeated. "The idea of

you going alone with these . . ." She stopped short of saying "dirty ruffians."

". . . these strangers."

Drover slapped his knees. "That settles that, Hoss. You stay home," said the drover to me, quite happily.

I eyed them both and remained silent, but Where go the sheep go I was still my motto.

"All right," said Drover, rising up, all business again. "We shear tomorrow. Get us some burlap an' make wool bags today. Start clippin' 'em tomorrow, if it don't rain. It's way early to shear, an' if we get a cold snap, we may lose 'em all, but that's the chance we got to take."

Well and good, I thought. Drover would wester, after all. I'd won that much.

Just before we departed, the young herder in the serape came over, surprising me. He smiled and asked, in the Queen's pure English, "What do you call your dog?" He had a lot of shining teeth and they were set in perfect.

I felt like I'd been hit over the head. We'd be able to converse all the way to the gold mines. "His name is Rufus and I'm ashamed of him." The drover's dogs had returned, but Rufe was nowhere in sight. The coward had probably sneaked on home.

"Rufus! That's as good a name as any, I'd guess." I heard a foreign drawl in his voice.

With a marked ticking in my throat, I asked, "How do you call yourself?"

"Clay B. Carmer."

I ran that around my tongue, certain there was curly hair under that flat-topped Mexican hat. The red and green serape was handsome, close up. "I'm Susan Darden Carlisle." I sounded too high, I knew. A squeezed sound.

He kept smiling and nodded his hello.

My feet elevated off the ground. He was nineteen or twenty, I guessed, and like nothing at all in Kanesville. Nothing like blushing Hans Jochem or Billy Bundy, with his loose hands. *Clay B. Carmer!* Lordy.

I didn't know what else to say to him and what I did say sounded foolish. "Are you a profaner?"

He blinked. "A what?"

"A cusser?"

He frowned. "I have been known to do that but never in front of ladies."

"That is to your credit," I said.

He frowned some more, shook his head, gave me a strange look, and sidled off.

On the way home, I said, "Auntie Myrt, I must go with them." No matter what!

"I won't even talk about it. A fourteen-year-old girl on the trail with seven men . . ."

"Going on fifteen," I corrected. Six old fatherly types, I thought. One young one, curly-haired and maybe not so harmless.

"Put it out of your mind, Susan," she added, chin poking up stubbornly.

I thought I knew what it really was. She was suddenly lacking in true pioneer spirit. Prairie years had taken a toll, I guessed. Like my late mother, she had no more zest for grand adventure and that was too bad.

I reminded her, "Thousands of women and little children have been over that same trail, and you know it. Here I am, healthy and strong and almost grown . . ."

She kept her eyes grimly on Samuel's bouncing mane.

I said, "You pioneered. You even got married when you were fifteen. . . ."

She closed her lips terrapin tight and I decided to break

off for the time being, wishing I'd never asked the dumb court to be guarded by anybody, much less her. We clopped on in silence.

No sooner had we reached the farm when I sought out Mr. Blackwell and Roy at their little house. "We'll be shearing tomorrow," I announced, in a businesslike tone.

Mr. Blackwell was dumbfounded. So was Roy.

"I'm now in partnership with a drover from New Mexico. The sheep are going to California. I'm going, too." I felt defiant. Those were my sheep, down to the last hoof.

The Blackwells just stood there gape-mouthed, as if I had told them the woollies and I were going to Jupiter and Mars. Then Mr. Blackwell broke his spell of surprise. "Take us along," he pleaded, eyes glistening with hope.

He'd been headed west himself once upon a time, leaving Ohio in '49, secretly hungering for gold but claiming he wanted to farm in Oregon. The Blackwells had made it as far as Kanesville, but then Mrs. Blackwell upped and died of lobar pneumonia, the worst kind. Grieving, Mr. Blackwell stopped his westering here by the Missouri but had never lost the urge to "git an' go."

"I can't make that decision for you and Roy," I said. "You talk to the drover. He's bossing the trail. He'll be along in the afternoon."

I tipped my hat to Mr. Blackwell and went on.

# 13

In not long a time, Drover brought his menagerie of goats, dogs, and mules over Stutsman Road to the Dessery farm, causing some raised eyebrows as they passed through Kanesville like a circus. From Bert Pettit, with his outdated beaver hat, to that towering black man with his crescent moon scars, they all had a foreign look to them. Our visitors selected a site near the barn and erected dirty tents. I wouldn't have slept in them for a poke of gold pieces.

Soon, introductions were being made by Clem Epps, not by Drover Pettit, who seemed to be occupied talking to and kissing his oldest goat.

Clem said, "This here is Salvador Maria Baca, an' this here is Clay Carmer," someone I already well knew. I said my hellos. Baca was about fifty, a chunky, round-faced man with swarthy skin and a walrus mustache. In addition to being chief herder, he was a smithy. He spoke Spanish. Not a word of English.

"This here is Abber Doof, the African giant, an inch under seven feet. Tallest man I ever seen. He prays three times a day to 'Aller' on his own rug an' has his own teakettle for washin'. Speaks almost nothin' but French. He looks fierce enough to eat anvils, but he is gentle 'less you rile him up."

With those marks on his cheeks he did look fierce enough to eat anvils. I swallowed and said, "Hello."

He smiled back and said, " 'Allo."

Auntie Myrt would be interested in his French speaking.

"This here is Will Pless, the sheep doctor." He was a sallow, skinny man and just nodded, which I did in return.

"This here is Charlie Quarry, the cook." He even looked like a cook, round and dumpy, capable of a lot of sweat. I said hello. Then I noticed his skin was as smooth and hairless as mine. I'd only seen one other man like that. Not even straggly beard would grow. He had dimples, as well.

Epps went on with his introductions. "That best-looking mule is Rinaldo, the drover's mule. It eats anythin' an' turns it right into gas. Never git into a closed space with it."

I said I wouldn't.

The mules, I soon learned, were all Mexican; much stronger and tougher than U.S.A. mules.

"The dogs are Rosita, Juanita, Blanca, and Maria," said Clem. They were already gone, much to Rufe's relief. They had spotted the sheep over two knolls distant, and went for them.

"There is nothing a sheep dog likes to do more than work sheep," Clem explained.

Next, Clem pointed to the short-eared goats. "That old one is Graciela. She has arthritis. That other nanny is Cholula, just call her 'Cho,' and that castrated nervous buck is Hector."

Bert Pettit was still talking to Graciela and hugging her.

Clem commented, "He sure loves that old lady. Cross between a French Alpine and a Toggenburg. Smartest goat I ever met."

With coarse hair the color of tarnished silver, Graciela was most notable in the eyes. They were vivid yellow. She also had whiskers about eight inches long, a most unusual-looking animal.

I didn't know what more to say about goats, so I asked, "You been with the drover long?"

Clem cackled and shook his head. "Nope, I'm a freighter out of Independence, Missouri, but more lately out of Touse. I'm driving sheep instead of a freight wagon because I owe Bert Pettit some money. He don't let you forget that."

Odd how your life changes when you owe money.

Casual-like, as if I really didn't care, I asked, "Has Clay Carmer always been a herder?"

Clem laughed. "He's no herder at all. Doesn't even like sheep. Texas boy, he's a cow handler."

"Well, what's he doing here?"

"Like me. He owes Bert Pettit money. Gamblin' debt. That boy is workin' off a poker pot. Along with some *vaqueros*, he brought four hundred half-wild longhorn steers up from Messico, sold 'em in Santa Fe to the government, then went over to Touse lookin' for fun an' lost all his profit to the drover. He owes more 'n me."

"What's a *vaquero?*"

"Messican cow handler. Best there is."

"Drover take their money, too?"

"Nope, just mine an' Clay's. Same game."

I had more in common with handsome Clay Carmer than he knew. What was I doing but heroically "working off" my Daddy's steamboat gamble to G. B. Minzter?

I said hello all around again and went on my way back to the house, thinking they were not really "dirty ruffians" as Mrs. Dessery had called them.

There soon came another sharp turn in the day's events. While his men and the Blackwells were sewing big burlap bags for the wool, Drover came to me and said, outside the kitchen door, "Had a visitor after you left the bluffs this morning." He was kind of smirking.

"Who?"

"Your Mr. Minzter."

"Well, he isn't mine," I said emphatically. "What did he want?"

"Oh, jus' wanted to know what my plans were regarding your sheep."

"And you told him?"

He nodded. "Why not, Hoss?"

"The less he knows the better off we are."

"Hah an' hoot," said Drover. "He offered to entertain us down at his saloon tonight. Drinks on the house. Said he didn't often have visitors from New Messico. . . ."

"He's trying to entice you," I warned. "It will come to no good. Ask anyone who lives in this town. Old Lucifer is a lamb compared to that Dutchman."

"You wouldn't know ol' Lucifer if you put your mooney down in his lap."

"How dare you speak to me that way?"

Drover just roared with coarse laughter and walked off, giving me cause to further worry. He could be traitorous as well as foulmouthed.

A little later, Auntie Myrt went down to the barn herself to meet Abber Doof, being curious about that seven-foot French-speaking man from Africa. Beaming, she came back to say "His name is not Abber Doof. It is Abdou Diouf and he is a Muslim from Sene-gaul, which is on the west coast of Africa. Can you imagine that, in Kanesville?"

I could not.

"Mr. Diouf is a member of the famous Wolof tribe and his tribal name is Doudou Dombele, pronounced 'Dombee-lie.' He is from the province of Kayor and his grandfather was a crown warrior slave, a Tyeddo, which is pronounced 'tie-edo,' who was so fierce that he became an aristocrat general."

"Well, what is Mr. Diouf doing here?"

"Mr. Pettit hired him after the last sheepwalk to help get the mules and goats back to Touse. There were a bunch of Indians on the way back to New Mexico who always gave Mr. Pettit trouble. One look at Mr. Diouf and they all rode off."

"Well, how did he get to the States in the first place?"

"A wealthy New Orleans doctor found him in Paris

three years ago and hired him as a bodyguard. The doctor died in a Sacramento City saloon and that set Mr. Diouf adrift."

Now I understood. "He is not a slave?"

"Not at all."

My auntie Myrt said excitedly, "I can't wait to talk to him about Africa and the Wolofs."

That night, the drover and his men went off to town, excepting Mr. Diouf, who did not drink whiskey, being a good Muslim. The reason I know is that I checked them after sundown and they were all gone except Abdou Diouf, whose black feet stuck far out of his tent.

The rest stayed until very late, because I fell asleep and then was awakened past midnight to the sound of off-key singing and laughter. Looking out Auntie Myrt's eating-room window with disgust, I saw the six of them stumbling along in the moonlight. They were bobolink drunk.

# 14

Morning dawned sunny and warm, which was fortunate. Wool comes off more easily in warm weather, luckily so this time, since my shearers were all grossly hung over. Men were drinkers in the days of the Romans, and before, I'm told, and not much has changed. On the other hand, I felt uplifted and wholesome and said a cheery good-morning to them as they sat by their cook fire. But they only mumbled back, gazing at me bleary-eyed, obvious and predictable result of their night at the Ocean Wave. Even Clay Carmer looked wounded from old John Barleycorn. Abdou Diouf was chipper, of course.

They'd erected temporary pens late the previous afternoon and had a cotton cloth enclosure where the sheep would be stripped of their thick coats. The dogs had rounded up the woollies about five hundred yards away.

Twice, during rest periods, I had a chance to talk to Clay Carmer. I certainly made the chance. Each time, I tingled, as before. My heart was taken. Impulse made me roll *Mrs. Clay Carmer* secretly around my tongue. Openly, I asked him how old he was.

"Twenty-three."

I'd guessed almost right. Eight years difference between us wasn't that big a river.

"How old are you?" he asked.

"I'm a lot older than you think," I replied, putting a serene gaze on him. What difference did it make how old I was?

He laughed, which I didn't appreciate, though I must say he laughed easily; even his green eyes laughed.

"Mr. Epps tells me you're from Texas."

"Born there," said he. "Place you've never heard of— Sleeta."

"How do you spell that?"

"Y-s-l-e-t-a. On the Mexican border, at the Rio Grande."

"How long did you stay in Touse?"

"Just long enough to lose some money."

I concentrated on his eyes before asking the next question, registering them for truth. "Do you have many girls?"

"Where?"

"Anyplace?"

"As many as I want."

I did not know how to respond to that statement, which sounded very boastful and untrue to me. Yet his eyes stayed true. Then he laughed and they twinkled. That Texas man was going to be very difficult.

I said, "I'd like to ask you a personal question. Do you have curly hair under that hat?"

He said, "Yes, I do," and took off the Mexican hat. The hair was indeed curly and the color of light pitch. Green eyes, black hair, and a strong jaw all on the same head has to be a wonder of the world.

Just then Drover shouted for us to get back to work. He spoke as much Spanish as he did English, I was discovering. "Tra-ba-ho, tra-ba-ho," he yelled.

Clem said, "Work, work."

The second time that I talked with Clay Carmer was late in the afternoon. That time ended up with him patting me on the head, a very dangerous thing for any man to do.

After supper, I caught Clem Epps away from the others. He was having a pipe and rubbing lanolin into his boot tops. "Makes 'em soft as baby belly," said he. Mr. Epps was a rather small man, wiry and leather-skinned, every bit as old as Indian Myrt.

After we'd talked a little while, I said, "I can't get over you and Clay Carmer walking all the way to California without getting paid. . . ."

"Bert ain't very charitable with his gamblin' debts. Matter o' honor, he sez."

"Well, he's a strange man," I said. "Hugging and kissing that old goat yesterday."

Clem cackled. "He ought to hug an' kiss her. She led him six thousand sheep to Californy two years ago. Led him nine thousand last year. Commands those sheep like an army, take 'em right across rivers, up mountains, over deserts. Bert couldn't pay for what ol' Graciela does. That's why he hugs and kisses her. . . ."

"Is he trustworthy?" I asked, point-blank. If he was a scoundrel, I wanted to know about it now.

Clem stopped rubbing the boot top. "Real mountain man, an' they ain't many left. Till he started doin' this two years ago, he'd trapped beaver, hired out as a mountain guide for the U.S. Cavalry; fought Injuns now and then. Fought in the Messican war four years ago. Bert's taken more scalps than any Injun alive. First met him in St. Louis at the Rocky Mountain House when he wasn't much older than Clay Carmer, sittin' on a buffalo rug in greasy buckskins, gamblin'. He was wearing a fur cap, with a horsetail braid on it, and had on beaded moccasins made by some Injun woman. In those days, he was more Injun than white man. He carried a tomahawk, a short-barreled rifle an' powder horn an' bullet mold. Now an' then he'd get up an' start jumpin' round with those French coquettes. You couldn't call it dancin'. Jus' stompin'. Then his fur money'd run out, an' he'd head back to Colorado an' those mile-high lonesomes. . . ."

"He never got married?"

"Yes, he did. Two winters ago in Touse. I was there an' remember the exact ceremony, in a saloon right off the plaza. Sheriff married 'em, all legal:

"Underneath this roof in stormy weathah
    This buck an' squaw come togethah
    Let none but Him who rules the thundah
    Set this buck an' squaw asundah. . . ."

"Married an Indian?"

"Prettiest one you ever saw," said Clem. "Mestizo. That's Spanish Indian. She had a dusky baby a while back. So ol' Bert's gettin' ol', gettin' married an' settlin' down. When he's home, he's startin' to sit on the sunny side of the house. Sure sign of age. But don't never sell him short.

He'll take you down with a knife sooner'n you wink an eye. . . ."

I shook my head. "I just can't understand him writing such a beautiful letter to me."

Clem Epps laughed and laughed. "Bert Pettit? He can't read nor write a lick. What you got, little lady, was a letter from the educated hand of the priest of Fernando de Touse, an' no one else. . . ."

Old Clem cackled and cackled over that.

Sunburnt eyes. Hah!

About noon of the next day, two hard-looking men rode right up to where we were shearing the sheep and looked at what we were doing. Well, New Mexicans clipping sheep in Pottawattamie County was very unusual and I could readily understand their curiosity. Yet these men appeared as if they couldn't care two loud buffalo grunts for what was going on. Both of them had Whitneyville Walker point 44's on their hips and those pistols, with a fifteen-inch barrel, weighing over four pounds, are as big and mean as howitzers.

One of them went over to where Bert Pettit was lolling and asked him something. I saw Drover answer and then those two men rode away toward town, an evil pair if I ever saw two.

The first opportunity I had, I asked Mr. Blackwell who they were. He answered, "Couple of Minzter's boys."

No wonder.

# 15

Mrs. Myrtle Dessery had a bad case of spring sniffles, so it was decided that I'd go with Drover on the *Prairie Queen* of the Missouri Mail & Cargo Line to officially represent the interests of myself when we sold the wool to Connaught-Venable & Co., of St. Joseph, Mo.

Five wagonloads had been required to move all the bags of wool down to the Kanesville landing, where it weighed out at 11,406 pounds. Oh, if only the doctor could have seen those big brown bags of wool stacked up on the deck of the *Queen*—solid proof of his good business sense despite the burnt-out *Missouri Rainbow*.

As Clem Epps took the New Mexicans back to Indian Myrt's, having loaded the fleece, I boarded the steamer, saying to Drover, "The captain's a close friend of mine, so I can sleep in his cabin if I choose."

Drover said firmly back to me, "Hoss, you can sleep on top the wool, an' that's no choice. Somebody's got to guard it."

I said, "Nobody would steal those big bags."

"That's what you think," he replied.

"Where will you sleep?"

"On the wool, when I got time," he replied, but I did not understand his full meaning until later.

Soon, Captain Tom Killoran rang the bell and blew the departure whistle, Irish roustabouts pulled the gangplank in, and the *Prairie Queen* shivered as the mighty wheels bit the muddy water, and we circled grandly out into the channel to head south. The big river was running moderately high, though the real spring thaw in the Dakotas and Montana hadn't begun as yet. Still, the trip to St. Joe would be fast.

With twin smokestacks, topped with fancy crowns, the *Prairie Queen* was a fine side-wheeler. The main deck was only three feet above the water, crowded with the engines, fireboxes and boilers, stacks of cordwood up front. Lower-class passengers stayed down there.

The next deck up was the "boiler" deck, on which sat the dining saloon, with passenger cabins all around the outside. Astern were the single ladies' cabins, designed for the likes of me. The third deck was the "hurricane" deck, containing a few cabins beneath the pilothouse. This was called the "texas," occupied by steamer officers, honeymooners, and politicians. Above the texas was the glass-enclosed pilothouse.

The *Queen*, like a lot of other riverboats, carried her cargo in the "guards." That was the space that went around the entire boat like a belt, width of the side-wheel paddles. Our wool, loaded last at Kanesville, was in the guard on the right-hand side, just behind that paddle wheel, and next to the cargo door.

Bidding Drover "adieu" for a while, I went on up to visit distinguished Cap'n Killoran in the pilothouse. Stepping away from the giant steering wheel for a moment, he hugged me and said, "Susan, I'm glad to see you. Heard about your ma and pa, and am sure sorry. You bound to St. Louis with that wool?"

"Nope. Connaught-Venable in St. Joe."

"Who's that with you? Rough-looking character."

"He is that, Cap'n Tom. Roughest man I've ever known, and he may even be rougher than I think," I said. "He's a sheep driver from Touse, New Mexico, name of Pettit."

"Well, if you need help with him, just call on me,"

Cap'n Tom said, giving his steering wheel a slight turn. We flowed with the sparkling river, past prairie lands and patches of beautiful cottonwood and white elm.

"If I need help, you'll be the first to know," I promised, standing beside him, watching from high over the hurricane deck. The wide, rushing yellow water was cold flat and roiling on this golden day when not a leaf was moving ashore.

There wasn't a regular town below Kanesville for miles, the river so lonely that it was owned only by birds and other wild game. Now and then there'd be an Indian village. Iowas or Shawnees or Otoes or Omahas. We'd exchange waves.

Fretting about my guard duties for the night, I then asked, "You think there's a chance somebody would steal my wool?"

He chuckled. "Anything littler than this boat can be stolen."

That wasn't encouraging news. I'd thought my burlap bags were too big to steal. After telling Cap'n Tom all about G. B. Minzter trying to take my home and property, I loitered up in the pilothouse until almost five o'clock and then went down to Drover. He was in the "social hall," or dining saloon, at a table with four other hatted men, his left hand holding playing cards.

Money, and quite a lot of it, was by his elbow.

Standing beside him, I said, "I see this is how you spend your time and why you can't help me guard the wool."

He glanced at me with a frown and took a puff on his odorous cigar but didn't answer.

"This your daughter?" asked one of the players.

I was quick to plainly say, "No, I am certainly not his daughter. I'm his business partner."

Raucous laughter followed me to the dining area nearby, but I did not want anyone to think that gambler Bert Pettit was my father.

Mealtime on the *Prairie Queen* was always a treat where the quality and quantity of food was concerned; not so much a treat where the eaters were concerned. I have never seen such bad table manners anywhere. Pigs slop with more care than these men.

Served up, family style, were three kinds of fish, three kinds of soup; then platters ranging from fricasseed kidneys to spiced pig head; roast beef, roast pork, and wild turkey; white potatoes, sweet potatoes, rice, and corn.

Most of the diners were men and they ate with their hands instead of forks, stuffing themselves as if they were starved savages. I'm surprised Cap'n Tom put linens on his tables. His eaters didn't deserve such treatment. Soon, the fat man directly across from me, his greasy cheeks bulging, asked, "You attached?"

"Yes," I said, "that is my husband," pointing to the keg-headed man in the ancient beaver hat.

That diner said no more to me after taking a puzzled long look at Drover, having no desire to test the New Mexican.

I arose to take some air out on deck and watched the *Elsie Close* go by us, northbound. Cap'n Tom and her captain exchanged steam whistle greetings.

The only civilized-looking man at the table then came out for an evening pipe and I struck up conversation with him. His name was Cradock and he worked for the American Fur Company, founded by John Jacob Astor, the New York scoundrel.

I was still worried about my wool being stolen and asked for his advice.

"Petty thieves do not fare well on Cap'n Tom's boat. I am on this river all the time and I can tell you. Last trip, he caught a watch thief, a perfumed Frenchman. So he lined up all the passengers and handed them barrel staves, the most splintery ones that he could find. Then he made the thief run that gauntlet. I took my whack at that Frenchy."

I felt better and went back to the social hall to tell Drover I was going to retire for the night. I saw that his money pile had somewhat decreased. He looked glum.

I announced, "I'm going down and go to sleep. I have to guard the wool, you know." That latter was a sly dig.

A few minutes later, I crawled up on the bags of wool with my valise, took my boots off, and prepared for the long night. There was a hot, wet smell of steam engines on that main deck and a lot of noise. Through cracks in the guard walls I could see the roaring flames of the fireboxes. A few feet away, the big paddles were slapping water, driving us forward. That was a pleasant sound. Soon, the paddle wheels slowed and then stopped. I could feel the gentle bump as Cap'n Tom put the *Queen* up against the Iowa bank for the night and tied her off. The roar of the fireboxes and the drum of the engines died away. Voice babble of the main deck passengers arose. In not too long a time, I drifted off into needed and peaceful sleep.

However, I did not awaken very peacefully. About midnight, I felt movement under me. The wool bags seemed to be moving. I inched up to the edge, and peered down. Two men were in the shadows and in the square of pale moonlight I could see that they'd opened the cargo door. One bag of my wool was already near that wide door. My heart pounded.

Thieves were operating!

I inched back and slipped the Pocket Colt out of my

valise and went again to the edge, cocking the revolver quietly and aiming it toward the shadowy figure outlined in the door opening. I could barely breathe because of fear, I do admit. Suddenly, I realized that my gun hand was shaking, something that had never happened when the doctor was training me. Just as suddenly, the little Colt slipped, fell to the deck, went off with a loud boom and blast of red-blue flame, and I saw the shadowy figure near the cargo door go overboard and heard his splash.

The other man disappeared into the dark guards and I quickly scrambled down to retrieve my pistol, then climbed back to my position atop the wool bags in case he returned to attack me.

Within seconds, there were footsteps and shouting and yelling: "Who's there? What's happening? Who shot?"

But no one appeared in the dark space, so I finally yelled, "I'm in here. Someone tried to steal my wool." My heart was still hammering.

Then I heard a very distinctive New Mexico voice. "What'n tarnation did you do?" The gambler, Drover, of course! Late to the scene!

Calming down, I answered, "I was protecting my wool. *Where were you?*"

"You shoot somebody, Hoss?" Drover asked.

I had to think. That my gun shot that man was doubtful. He did go promptly over the side, but he just jumped over in fright and surprise, I reckoned. Nonetheless, I said evenly, "Yes, I shot a dirty thief. There were two of them. I'm sorry I didn't shoot the other one."

Just then, Cap'n Tom came into the guards and raised a lantern to illuminate me up on the bags. Gone was his gold-brimmed captain's hat, but the rest of him was dressed in a long white nightgown. His feet were bare. His white, silky hair was mussed. I'd never seen him looking so undignified.

Drover's face was illuminated. On it was a definite look of respect, if not pure awe. He said to the captain, "Hoss, she just shot a thief, by golly."

Behind them, I could see two-dozen faces. They were all wide-eyed, curious, and panting for news.

"What are you doing with a gun, Susan?" Cap'n Tom asked.

"Protecting my own property," I replied.

He said, "Well, come on down off there and come up to my cabin and let's all get some sleep." He looked at the spectators and ordered gruffly, "Go to bed."

Cap'n Tom didn't even ask how I'd shot that man, which disappointed me. Thankfully, for my purpose, he didn't launch a skiff to go and look for the body. Thieves were just not accommodated.

Finally, Cap'n Tom looked at the drover and asked, in disgust, "You put this girl up to guarding those bags?"

"Well, I . . ." started Drover, sputtering around foolishly, obviously guilty.

"Guard 'em yourself, Hoss," said Cap'n Killoran, and off we went to the hurricane deck.

Departing, I smiled sweetly at Bert Pettit, of Taos, New Mexico, and said, "Good night." He deserved to be thoroughly humiliated for his drinking and gambling and generally obnoxious ways.

# 16

The *Prairie Queen* was well down the river when I awakened in the texas. I could feel her quiver and the *patsplat* of the paddle wheels. We were making great time toward St. Joe, I knew. The Big Muddy was flying south with her yellow syrup, and we were already off Missouri, with Kansas on the other side.

I quickly went about facing the bright day with handfuls of cool water on my face and a mouth rinse. I did not use the community toothbrush.

Then I went up to see Cap'n Tom and the first thing he said was, "In light of what you told me yesterday, I don't think those men were trying to steal your wool."

"What were they trying to do?"

"To steal it, they'd need wagons on shore and a lot more help. I looked around on shore early this morning. No wagon tracks. No foot tracks. I think they were just going to ease it all overboard and let the river carry it away."

"Why?"

"You told me yesterday about G. B. Minzter's interest."

"Yes," I said. Now it made sense.

Suddenly, I was wishing I *had* shot that man. To think of them pushing all my wool into the river. With it, of course, would have floated away the expense money for California and my home.

Drover was already having his breakfast when I arrived in the dining saloon. A huge stack of flour cakes, Iowa beans, and sausages were on his plate. Looking up, he said to me, "You kilt that man last night!" He was obviously impressed.

"Yes, I did," said I, trying to be casual. I sat down with no signs of remorse. Drover seemed to respect violence.

"Did he make a noise before he fell?"

"What do you mean?"

"Did he grunt, did he cuss, did he cough, did he say somethin'?"

"Nothing. All I heard was the plop when he hit the water."

Drover shook his head in awe. I don't think he knew too many women shooters.

"What kind of pistol you carryin'?" he asked.

"Colt Pocket, point 31, five-shot, four-inch barrel."

"Just be careful where you aim that thing. I'd be happy to keep it for you."

"No, thanks," said I.

"Well, just be careful with it," he advised.

With Cap'n Tom's estimate fresh on my mind, I said, "And perhaps you should be careful to whom you talk."

He gazed at me curiously.

"The captain thinks those men weren't trying to steal the wool. They just wanted to dump it overboard and ruin my plan. He thinks they might have been G. B. Minzter's men."

Drover's curious gaze turned to a mystified frown.

So I continued. "While we were shearing wool, I noticed you talk to two men who came to Mrs. Dessery's. They were from the Ocean Wave. What did you tell them, Mr. Pettit?" I thought I had him on the fast run, at last.

Ashamedly, he admitted that they wanted to know when we planned to ship the wool and on what boat. He saw no reason not to tell them.

"Need I say more?" said I, grandly, and ordered some eggs.

# 17

When the *Prairie Queen* went around the final bend north of St. Joe, Cap'n Tom pulled on his whistle rope to blow wetly for arrival: one long, two shorts; one long, two shorts. My spine tingled, as always. Whether on boats or on shore, those two-toned melodious whistles have a sound like none other, filled with promise, *Steamboat 'round the bend.* They are true trumpets of heaven. *Hallelujah!*

"When's the last time you were here, Susan?" asked Cap'n Tom.

"About three years ago, with my Daddy."

"It's grown a lot. Bigger'n Independence or Westport now. It's got three hotels, twelve mercantile firms, blacksmiths, wagonmakers, four taverns, two livery stables . . ."

St. Joseph, Missouri, on the banks of Blacksnake Creek, had long ago been founded by a Frenchman named Joe Roubidoux, who also ran the ferry.

"Town is thriving. But '50 was the big year. They sent thirty-two thousand travelers west that year. Now they're getting a reputation for fleecing everybody. Never buy horses or mules in St. Joe. They're all has-beens."

Thinking about Drover, I asked, "Is there a lot of gambling here?"

"Worse than Kanesville," said Cap'n Tom.

That spelled big trouble, I thought. Gambling was the curse of the nation.

I soon thanked Cap'n Tom for all his information and hospitality and went down to the guards, where Drover was supervising the roustabouts in unloading the wool.

Soon, the *Prairie Queen* departed, heading for Leavenworth, Independence-Westport, and on to St. Louis. Cap'n Tom gave me a little good-bye tattoo on his whistle as the *Queen* began to stride south, trailing her twin plumes.

St. Joe was even noisier than Kanesville. Steamboats hissing and clanking, cows bellowing, mules braying. Drunken men were spilling out of taverns and fiddles were already hard at it. I agree with Cap'n Tom that St. Joe was the worst place on the river, next to Kanesville.

Connaught-Venable & Co. was within eyesight of the landing, up on Market Square, so up there we went and began to bargain with Venable. He was a typical mercantile man, I learned, dressed fashionable and all for himself, starting off at fifteen cents a pound. He wore an oozy smile and we took him back to the landing to show him all that good merino fleece. He wanted to know who I was, seeming offended whenever I opened my mouth.

"I own that wool," said I, straightening him out.

Venable blinked.

I must say that Drover, despite the fact that he couldn't read nor write, got along pretty well. He kept nudging Venable up until the price was twenty-five cents a pound.

At that point, Drover said to me, "We should sell."

I was of no help in those deliberations. So I nodded.

Venable said, "I can pay you in Dix or in English sovereigns, the latter at a cent more than actual value. Spanish gold coin?"

I said to him, "What about good old U.S. currency?"

"Dix is better," said Drover.

I asked him to please come outside with me and he did. "What is Dix?" I asked. I didn't want to show my ignorance in front of Venable.

"Dix is ten-dollar notes issued by the Banque des

Citoyens in New Orleans. Best currency in the land. I been dealin' with 'em since my fur-trappin' days," said Drover.

So Venable paid us $2,851.50 in Dix and for those who don't know their history that's how "Dixieland" was named, courtesy of the Banque des Citoyens, of New Orleans, Louisiana.

I'd made a fine profit on those woollies, and was gaining more respect for them each day. It had cost us thirty-five cents a hundredweight to ship the fleece south on the *Queen*, plus two passenger fares of twelve dollars.

Outside, there was a brief discussion as to who would have possession of the ten-dollar Dixes in the cloth bag. Drover was holding it for the moment.

Our steamboat north, the *David H. Pyle*, wouldn't depart until three-thirty and my inner fear was that Drover would go to one of those taverns and become involved in drinking and gambling. Then, farewell to the expense money for the overland trail.

Drover argued, "S'pose that other hoss on the boat last night is here an' sees you walkin' 'round town with all this money. You kilt his partner, so he'd jus' as soon drop you down, anyway. That Pocket Colt won't help you against a real shootin' man."

Without going into who "kilt" who, or my abilities with the point 31, I argued that the safe thing to do was to stick together and go get something to eat at one of the hotels, particularly if he thought I might get shot down on the streets of St. Joe.

Drover snorted and grumbled, but finally agreed to it. I'm sure he'd originally planned to go to a tavern and I suppose being seen with a real lady made him feel uncomfortable. Instead, he should have been proud. Even at his old age, he had a lot to learn.

In the hotel dining room, I suggested he take his hat off. The doctor always did. Drover leaned low across the table and said back to me in a deadly voice, "Mind your own chickens, or you'll not see me till that steamboat blows."

I decided to mind my chickens.

To pass time, while waiting for pork chops and rice, I said, "Please tell me about the Humboldt Sink, the Forty Mile Desert. Clem Epps tells me that the 'elephant' to which you referred is death."

Drover gazed at me and then said, "That it is, Hoss. I can best describe the Forty Mile Desert by sayin' that it is a blast furnace with sand on the floor. But you'll see the elephant long before we get to Nevaddy Territory. . . ."

# 18

On the morning we arrived back in Kanesville, we were both standing up on the hurricane deck of the *David H. Pyle*, watching the shore go by, before the big bend, and I said idly to him, "Does your wife have a name?"

That surely caught him by surprise.

"Jarramilla," he said, squinting at me. "How'd you know I was married?"

"Clem Epps told me. He said you had a baby, too."

"She did, not me. Name is Ramon Noah. . . ."

"You live in a house?"

"You 'spect me to live in a cave?"

I shrugged. I didn't know how people lived in New Mexico.

"Adobe house, made of sun-baked bricks. Inside is whiter'n snow. Plaster walls made o' caliche, that's hard lime. An' I whitewashed 'em with gypsum burnt in ovens

an' ground into powder. Cut the pine beams myself an'
Jarramilla painted 'em red an' green. Dirt floors is hardened
with oxblood. Nothin' like your house but jus' as
pretty. . . ."

I could tell he was proud of his house. "You miss New
Mexico?"

He stared out across the river. "I first saw Touse in '25,
comin' down from trappin'. There's three of 'em up on a
desert shelf a mile an' a half high. Indian pueblo of San
Geronimo de Touse, Spanish village of Ranchos de Touse,
an' where I live, Fernando de Touse. They sit like nuggets
in the palm o' your hand. You look aroun', up to Wheeler
Ridge, or to Pueblo Mountain to the north; look at Touse
Valley an' the Rio Grande, smell the piñon smoke comin'
out o' the fireplace; go inside an' lay a little piece o' cedar
on the cookstove an' let it smolder. No sweeter smell anywhere. . . ." Then he lapsed into silence for a moment
before saying, "I guess I miss it."

I said, "Please tell me about San Francisco." I dreamed
of that place, too.

" 'Frisco? Place is gone mad. Ships comin' in from all
over the world, besides the overlanders. Growed from three
or four hundred people three years ago to twenty, thirty
thousand now. Mebbe more, gold-crazy."

Thinking about a time ahead, I asked, "Is it dangerous
there?"

"I should say it is. Scum o' the earth has come to visit
'Frisco, especially them Aussies. They jus' emptied the jails
over there an' put 'em in a ship for the U.S.A. Sydney
Ducks, that's what they call 'em."

My temples throbbed.

"Don't they have any nice places?"

Drover gazed at me. "El Dorado! Parker House! Two of the finest gamblin' places you'll ever see."

"I don't mean that kind. Nice restaurants, theaters."

"Well, there's fancy places like Tortoni's an' Delmonico's an' the Alhambra. Chinese places like Whang-Tong's, on Sacramento Street . . . Tong-Ling's on Jackson Street . . ."

I just couldn't wait.

"As to entertainment, I saw the damnedest fight there I ever saw anywhere. A grizzily bear an' bull."

Just then, the *David H. Pyle* blew one long, two shorts; one long, two shorts, ending the first civilized conversation I'd ever had with Drover Pettit. I had no idea he knew as much as he knew.

*Steamboat 'round the bend!*

Kanesville next stop.

# 19

"Someone has to face up to G. B. Minzter and I plan to do it myself, even if no one else does. Avenge those poor, innocent Blackwells!" said Indian Myrt darkly. There was rage on her thin face.

What was this all about? We hadn't been in my guardian's house for thirty seconds and I was all primed to tell her triumphantly about the sale of the wool for a top price at St. Joe; show her the bag of Dixes. Now this . . .

"What happened?" I asked.

"Tell us, Hoss," enjoined the drover.

"Two days ago, three of Minzter's men rode up to where the Blackwells were grazing the sheep on some of Archibald Morgan's land. All of a sudden, they started scattering the sheep, riding into them. When Mr. Blackwell protested, they rode him down, breaking his leg. Then they turned on poor helpless Roy and chased him until he hid in a ditch. They killed several of the sheep and one of the goats, just by running them to death. . . ."

In utter disbelief, Drover broke in, "One o' my goats?"

"Ran her until she just keeled over and died. The oldest one, Mr. Pettit."

That would be old Graciela, the drover's favorite, the one he always kissed and hugged.

"What did my boys do?" asked Drover, in a shocked whisper, tears suddenly welling in his sky-blue eyes. I never thought I'd see the day that happened.

"Your boys didn't know until it was all over. They said they'd wait for you to get back from St. Joe but they are feeling mean."

Drover nodded, fighting emotion.

Aside from poor Graciela, Drover had taken a liking to Mr. Blackwell and felt sorry for Roy's slow-minded condition, I knew. On top of that, we'd lost two sheep worth twenty-four dollars in California. Ancient Graciela, of course, was worth a lot more than that to Bert Pettit. He hadn't taken the trouble to walk that lead goat all the way from Taos to have her chased to death in Iowa.

To console him, Auntie Myrt said, "We buried her Christian-like. I said the Twenty-third Psalm over her."

Drover nodded appreciatively and stepped over to the window, looking out over the prairie land to seek solace.

I said, "Now I have something to tell you, Auntie Myrt."

I told her about the attempted wool washing in the river, sticking to the truth except for the "unsolved" part about whether or not I really shot that shadowy man who splashed into the water.

"You didn't, Susan," she said, in a hushed tone. "Shooting somebody? At your tender age?"

"I was defending my wool, and that is fully legal," said I.

A few minutes later we all three marched over to the Blackwells' to pay a visit and check on their condition.

Mr. Blackwell's lower left leg was now in oakwood splints and he was sitting up in his bed, looking very glum. There were bruises on his face and his hands were skinned in places. Roy had a whopper black eye, a cut lip, and a sprained wrist. I could picture him, scared out of what wits he had while dodging those big Minzter horses, feeling like Graciela.

"Any of 'em say anythin'?" asked the drover.

"Not a word that made sense," replied Mr. Blackwell. "All liquored up, they just rode in there and started yahooing and chasing sheep. I yelled at 'em to quit and then they went after me and Roy. When they did us in, they ran two sheep out of their hearts and then picked on that old nanny, running her until she was dead. They were laughin' and laughin'. Mean men, Mr. Pettit."

"I'd say they were," agreed Drover. "Well, I want to talk to those men." Then he looked over at Roy. "Son, could you pick 'em out for me?"

Roy nodded and licked his battered lip. I could tell he was scared to his very toenails at the thoughts of entering the Ocean Wave. Drover saw Roy beginning to quiver. "No one is gonna hurt you, Roy, believe me." Big as Roy was, people often forgot he was only fourteen.

Indian Myrt's anger surged up again. "They won't be back, Roy."

Then Mr. Blackwell looked over at her in sorrow. "You know, this means we can't go to California, Roy and me."

"I guess not, Mr. Blackwell," she replied. He couldn't

very well hobble all the way to Sacramento City. "There'll be another time."

"I hope," he said. Drover gave a little hand salute to Mr. Blackwell and said, "I'm goin' to town."

"Wish I could go with you," said Mr. Blackwell.

"Well, I'm going," asserted Mrs. Dessery.

"Me, too," said I.

Drover shook his head. "Don't need no women along for what has to be done."

"Need me or not, I wouldn't miss it," said Indian Myrt, firm as granite chunks.

"You two jus' stay out o' the way an' mind your chickens." With that advice, which we would not heed, he departed. I went down to the barn to hitch Samuel to the buggy and while doing so saw Clem Epps and Abdou Diouf load two rifles in the Dessery wagon. The very worst mistake Minzter's men could have made was sending Graciela to a painful death. Bert Pettit was as close to total sorrow as he'd ever be.

Back in the house, I wrapped the point 31 in some toweling and then went out to the buggy, placing it beneath the seat, returning inside just in time to see Indian Myrt amble into the kitchen gussied up like she was going to court again. She wore a new spring bonnet and her Sunday shoes; a fine French shawl was around her shoulders. The bonnet, with little cloth flowers around the brim, sat back on her head and tied in a wide ribbon beneath her chin. She looked elegant and I detected a light cologne in the air. She was togged out for a wedding or funeral.

I said, "You're all dressed up."

She replied, "You know I always dress up when I have something important to do."

We went out to the buggy and climbed in, waiting for

the New Mexicans and Roy. Soon, they rattled out from
the barn area, Drover with the reins, frightened Roy on the
seat beside him. Sitting in the back was old Clem Epps,
Salvador Baca, Abdou Diouf, Clay Carmer, and Will Pless.
They acknowledged us as the mules drew them smartly by,
and then Indian Myrt popped Samuel away, and we followed them at a discreet distance. Off to war against G. B.
Minzter we went.

On the outskirts of Kanesville, Drover abruptly stopped
the wagon and Indian Myrt reined in Samuel. Drover
walked back to look me dead in the eye. "You got that
peashooter with you?"

I hesitated a moment.

He said bluntly, "Give it to me, Hoss. I don't want my
head blowed off from no quick trigger."

"Hand it to him," ordered my guardian.

Thus intimidated, I reluctantly reached under the seat
and passed over my Pocket Colt still wrapped in toweling.

Drover said, "I should throw this in the river. The world
don't need no women shooters."

We rolled into Kanesville like ordinary, peaceable citi-
zens on a provision run, but our destination was the hitching rail in front of the Ocean Wave Hotel & Saloon. From
the number of buggies, wagons, and horses tied up outside,
it was busy inside. Whiskey and cigar stench billowed out
of Minzter's two-story building. Hotel rooms upstairs and
bar below. There was a boardwalk all around it; veranda in
front.

Drover and his party climbed down from the wagon,
hitching quickly, Clem Epps and Abdou Diouf and Will
Pless picking up the rifles. Indian Myrt and I debarked
from the buggy and followed the seven of them up to the
veranda and then to the side door into the saloon.

I'd never been inside.

The first thing I noticed was that big mirror in a wide gold-leaf frame, the most famous mirror in the west, maybe in the world. It took up most of the wall dead ahead, behind the bar. I also saw that much drinking and gambling and merriment was going on in there. Some of the "demonidestes" were around, in tight satin dresses, all rouged up. The Ocean Wave was crowded and noisy, as usual, but nowhere to be seen was the round, half-bald Dutch head of G. B. Minzter.

Indian Myrt and I stood a little back of the New Mexicans and Roy, who were all crowded in the doorway. Then I heard Drover say softly to Roy, "Point them out to me." He was talking about the goat and sheep chasers, of course. Roy did so.

Two were sitting at a poker table, backs to the door. The other man was asleep, head cradled in his arms, at another table. Drover nodded and said to Roy, "You go take a walk down by the river." Roy seemed glad to do that and departed us without looking back.

Then Drover, Salvador Baca, and Clay Carmer pulled their pistols and each headed for one of the goat killers. Meanwhile, still standing in the doorway, Epps, Abdou Diouf, and Pless raised their rifles to keep general peace and order.

Drover, Carmer, and Salvador Baca arrived at their destinations simultaneously. Cold barrel holes were pressed at the backs of three heads, just below that skull bump. They were very surprised criminals and froze in their seats, afraid to even blink.

Quiet descended rapidly on the rowdy Ocean Wave and Drover said, in as loud a voice as you'd ever hear from him, "Everybody jus' keep on havin' good times." But the whole place was frozen-herring stiff now, so quiet you could almost hear cigar ashes fall.

"Where's that G. B. Minzter?" Drover asked the bartender.

"In St. Louis."

"Well, that's too bad for us," said Drover.

No sooner had that disappointment escaped his lips when Indian Myrt whipped out her Navy Colt from beneath the French shawl and put a bullet into the largest bar mirror in the world, Minzter's shiny monument to himself, all the way from England.

*Boom, crash—then tinkle, tinkle, tinkle!*

As it shattered into a million pieces everyone in the Ocean Wave jumped a foot. Usually, a bullet just makes a small hole in glass, but that mirror was so big and heavy that it just totally collapsed.

"Damnation," yelled Drover, still holding his pistol to the target's skull. "Who did that?"

"I did," proudly said Indian Myrt, the smoking Navy Colt looking awesome in her small hand. A wide grin was spread over the papery cheeks.

"Hah an' hoot," said the drover.

I shall never forget that moment of pride and glory. Glass seemed to tinkle forever and the bartender must have had it up to his knees. Then it stopped and total quiet settled over the Ocean Wave.

Breaking the silence, Drover chuckled. "You almost caused me to float this man's head to Nebraska."

Everyone was still stunned and stared at the empty space behind the bar. The big gilded frame now looked ridiculous. When G. B. Minzter returned from St. Louis and saw what had happened, he'd surely weep.

In a moment, Drover and his men were marching the

three culprits outside, barrels still contacting the backs of their necks, a surefire New Mexico method of "gettin' attention," Clem said. It worked! Those men walked like they were treading on knife blades.

A crowd began to gather, sensing a lynching. There hadn't been one since the last spring when a Louisiana horse thief was stretched. I thought that was exactly what Drover had in mind, because once they were clear of the saloon, Clem Epps went to the wagon for big rolls of rope.

In the middle of the street, Drover said to the Minzter men, "All right, boys, jus' ease down real slow, hunker right down in the dirt, legs out, hands up in the air."

They did as directed, and had yet to say a word. Finally, one did work up his courage. "Wait until G.B. hears about this!"

Replied Drover amiably, "Hoss, you tell him for me that I'll put a bullet through his eye an' burn this place to the earth if he ever gets tricky again. Now, which one of you jay-poppers killed my goat?"

None confessed, but soon one man broke down and babbled, "Don't lynch us!" His name was Dave, we later learned.

Clem Epps was already making knots around Dave's legs, and then drew the rope back around his waist and looped it up over both shoulders. It did not look like the usual necktie arrangement.

Epps expertly trussed the other two men in the same fashion, using his long experience of lashing freight on Murphy wagons. The men were in the dirt on their behinds, looking scared. The crowd was now enjoying it. The saloon had emptied.

In a moment, Clay Carmer came up leading three huge stallions, then Clem Epps took a length of rope and looped it around a saddle horn, bringing it back to weave a knot in the "sitting up" harness he'd made.

Three bewhiskered, tough-looking big grown men were tied off to horses, about thirty feet behind flicking tails, trussed so that they'd bump across the prairie on their behinds.

Drover said, "Hosses, I'm gonna dedicate the next minutes o' your lives to a goat who was a great lady."

Then he went to the back of the first horse, slapping the big stallion on its rump. The crowd roared as the Minzter henchman went bumping up the street, yelling in agony as his tailbone hit the ruts and bounced. He was quickly joined by his companions. Soon, three trails of dust headed east and echoes of pain came from that direction, too. The Ocean Wave bartender jumped on his horse to follow and cut them loose.

Drover eyed the dust clouds and said, "Them jay-poppers'll be half dead by the time he gets 'em. They'll never ride a hoss again."

# 20

Drover said, "I want to start provisioning early in the mornin'. I'm leavin' in four days."

In all the excitement over the Ocean Wave, I'd almost forgotten the sheep drive to California, the most important thing of all. It was already April 18. Time was galloping by. We'd be face-to-face with Judge Cause Tuttle before we knew it.

"We'll go to Isaac Lazenby's," said Auntie Myrt. He was the best provisioner in town.

"Me an' Clem will work on a list. I want to travel light.

None of them big wagons with seven-foot wheels. You pull your bladder out jus' heavin' 'em over a rock."

Drover and his New Mexicans went on down to their camp by the barn while Indian Myrt and I went to her house to unbend. As soon as she'd changed into everyday clothes, I asked something that had been strongly on my mind. "Have you lost the spirit to adventure?" I'd seen the doctor get separated from his itch and urge.

She regarded me for a moment and then said, "You know I was beside my ma and pa, my sisters and brother, taming wilderness before I was your age. I worked beside Henri when France still had this land. They stole it from us Indians."

I was already beginning to be sorry I'd brought it up.

"Most of the time I don't feel too old but I'm getting that way, Susan."

"I understand."

"Do you?"

I nodded again, then said, "You know, we've never decided about me. . . ."

"About you?"

"About me going to California with the sheep."

She'd turned to fixing linden tea. "Until the Blackwells got hurt, I thought of little else. I felt better about you going. Now . . ." She paused a long time.

There always seemed to be a "now" in life, along with an "if" and a "well."

"And . . . ?" I said.

She looked over and smiled one of those secretive smiles I knew so well. "Now, I'll be going along myself."

"But you just said you were getting old."

She smiled. "I am that, but I have some time left."

I could hardly believe it. I jumped over and hugged her.

I couldn't believe it! Mrs. Myrtle Dessery on the sheep trail to California!

We laughed together, and marched down to Drover's camp to tell him. He was sitting with his back up against the barn in the late afternoon sun, telling Clem Epps what we'd need to go westering. The latter sat with a stub of pencil and a sheet of paper.

Indian Myrt didn't waste any time in interrupting to say, "Mr. Pettit, I have decided that Susan and I will go along with the sheep to California."

He just eyed us and tapped cigar ashes off his cheroot. "How else you gonna get the money back to Minzter?"

Just the same, Drover gave us a little lecture. "You'll pull your weight or I'll leave you to the wilds. You travel light on my sheepwalk an' I'll tell you what to take. I don't want no weepin' an' moanin' when the goin' gets tough."

Drover more or less dismissed us then. People never quite do what you expect them to do.

Charlie Quarry, who was from Reunion, outside of Dallas, almost buried a pencil stub in his fat fingers when he wrote down the victual list at the table in the Dessery kitchen. Charlie's face was a sunburnt moon, jowls flabby beneath a receding chin.

"You get caught in the gambling trap, too, like Clay Carmer?"

"Nope," said Quarry, "just wanted to go out to the gold fields. I regret that now. Bert Pettit is the worst pay in the nation."

"How so?"

"I'm getting sixteen dollars a month plus my keep. In Dallas, I was cooking for thirty dollars a month at the Palo Duro. I shoulda stayed there."

Sleep was hard to come by that night as I thought about

so many things, from how many pairs of stockings to take along to what I should name our wagon. It was the same for Indian Myrt, so age was of no matter in the mounting excitement.

In early morning, we headed to town to spend most of the day at Isaac Lazenby's. There were other trail supply houses in Kanesville, but Lazenby's was the biggest and best, offering everything needed. Anvils and spinning wheels; plough molds and churns; wagons and carts; saddles and guns; candle molds and chamber pots; green goggles and palm-leaf sun hats for the desert. Barrels of victuals.

Only Will Pless, the lanky Kansas "animal doctor," stayed behind. His chore was to do a last-minute check on the sheep to see if any were lame, or had worms, or "bluetongue," with high fevers. Pless wasn't really an animal doctor but had some talents in that direction. He'd worked for a vet in Fort Leavenworth. Neither was he a regular herder. He just wanted to go west and Drover picked him up in Taos, for sixteen dollars a month.

"We'll buy the wagons first," said Drover. He'd trailed some of his mules to pull the wagons home.

We went out into the lot behind the store. Thirty or forty wagons sat in the sun out there. "I don't want no Murphys," said Drover. They were about sixteen feet long, with rear wheels seven feet high and two hands wide. "You need ten ox to pull them rock-busters," said Drover.

Then I saw a Caster prairie schooner and ran for it. For those who didn't go westering in the 1850s, the prairie schooner was a smaller, lighter version of the old Conestoga freight wagon, with its high bows and poke bonnet canvas top. Crossing the flatlands, on a shimmery summer day, the Conestogas looked like graceful ships. But they were far too big and heavy for the overland trail.

I called out to Drover, "How about this one?"

It was a green-colored Caster twelve-footer, made of hickory and oak. The white cover gleamed in the bright light. When I touched the wagon bed, it seemed to say, "Take me along. Give me your mules and I'll see you through." It was about five feet wide.

Drover walked around it slowly. He knelt down to look at the axles and then grabbed a rear wheel, shaking it roughly. Then he climbed up into the bed, under the canvas hood, and jumped up and down. The wagon would have to carry about twenty-five hundred pounds of supplies. Clem Epps also inspected it.

Drover took a finger and poked at the hood, two thicknesses of canvas, varnished. The ends could be drawn together for a snug home on wheels, though I'd heard they all leaked during heavy rainstorms. Drover finally hopped down and looked at me. "All right, Hoss."

Clem Epps, to be in charge of that wagon, agreed, and Mrs. Dessery nodded her approval. So we bought it.

Soon, we bought another, slightly smaller Caster, a red one, for Indian Myrt and myself, perfect for four mules. We didn't need big wagons, since we weren't going to haul furniture and household goods. We'd need to travel light and fast, which was to Drover's liking and ours.

I will not attempt to list herein all that we bought that first day at Lazenby's, but included were india rubber raincoats and woolsack coats and wool pantaloons and buffalo robes; a sheet-iron stove and two huge Dutch ovens; six hundred pounds of flour and fifty pounds of pilot bread; a hundred and fifty pounds of bacon and fifty pounds of ham; dried fish and lard and coffee and rice and raisins and oats and axes and skillets and shovels and rope and mule buckets and wagon parts and bake pans and two dozen bottles of medicine for sheep screwworms; eight hundred pounds of licking salt for the sheep. Two quarts of lime juice were purchased to help beat scurvy.

We didn't need beef. We'd have mutton on the hoof traveling with us. Clem Epps went through three quarters of his list by late afternoon, as did Charlie Quarry. We still needed such things as ammunition, four good tents and so forth. Another half day of shopping and we'd be ready. Meanwhile, the New Mexicans could start packing.

Minutes later, we were bound for Stutsman Road and home. I sat up beside the Drover as we tested the heavily laden schooner. Four of his mules pulled it along as easily as if it were laden with thistle. Clay Carmer had the reins on the other wagon, following us, pulled by two mules. Bringing up the rear was Auntie Myrt, in her buggy.

What to take still vexed me. What does a fourteen-year-old female pack for a three and half months walk across the continent? I was quite mindful I'd be under the daily gaze of Clay Carmer and had no intention of looking like a scarecrow.

The decision, at last, was to fill my mother's best Boston-made leather stagecoach trunk, which was bound with brass straps, with three of my best dresses plus accessories, all from fashionable St. Louis. When necessary, on the trail, I could put on proper perfumed airs. I also put trail clothes, linsey-woolsey shifts and the like, into the trunk.

Between such terrible decisions—putting things in and taking things out—I found time frequently to walk down by the barn and look at my gleaming red wagon, on which was now painted WALKING UP A RAINBOW.

I also took the responsibility for packing the medicine chests, which we'd store in the red wagon. I robbed the doctor's office of jalap, for sweating and purging; of ipecac, a very fine laxative; and of the most precious of all medicines, quinine, of which he had a small amount. I took what he had, plus the all-around calomel, which had a lot of mercury in it. Too many doses and your teeth fall out. I copied down my daddy's cures for cholera—tablespoon with sixty drops laudanum in it, in half a glass of cold water —his cholera pills in case you vomited up the laudanum mixture; his cholera clysters to be put in warm gruel; his recipe for mustard poultices to be applied to the belly and soles of your feet. Cholera was the killer to face.

I had one final mission before leaving Iowa for California. I needed to talk to, and thank, and say good-bye to, Sweet Frenchy Moll. Weeks had passed since I'd last seen her, and her busy season had begun again, with all the overlanders now carousing around in town.

Two of them were in her parlor, seated beneath "In the Pond," talking to one of the painted "demonidestes," and I ignored them while following Frenchy on into the kitchen, where we could converse freely. Quickly, I told her about Drover's arrival and thanked her for the good advice, which had certainly worked. Despite my deception, he was taking the sheep on to California, I said.

"Frenchy, I need some more advice," I said, earnestly. "I have decided to marry a man named Clay Carmer, from Touse, New Mexico. He's one of Drover's helpers and I need to know how to trap him. He's treating me like a child."

She laughed. "Why marry him? I've been married three times and still don't have a husband. In your lifetime, I think you should have fifty men and not marry a single one."

I said, "Well, I can't do that. I'm a Christian, and have my principles."

"I understand. Is this Clay Carmer an old man? Never marry an old man."

"He's twenty-three, a cow handler."

She smiled and clucked her tongue like Indian Myrt might have done. "Suzanne, why don't you wait? You're so young."

"I will certainly wait until the sheepwalk is over. For a long time I thought I'd never get married but after meeting Clay, I think I will. There's never been anything like him around Kanesville and I don't want to miss my chance. So now I need to know how to land him."

"What does he think of all this?"

"He doesn't know," I admitted.

Frenchy's laughter filled the kitchen. "Well, if you really want to do it, and not wait a few years—"

Determined not to be put off, I interrupted, "Someone else will get him. He's already told me he has many girls back in Texas."

"Well, all right, you must be nice to him, of course. Then you must impress him that you are intelligent and can talk to him about things he is interested in. Also flatter him, and it doesn't hurt to let him know you can cook and sew. . . ."

"I can cook but I can't sew. . . ."

She shrugged. "Not important."

"What else?" I asked.

"You must be romantic. To stir his imagination, show him some flesh but not too much. A fleeting glimpse, but be very feminine."

I reddened. I felt as if my veins were on fire. But why not? "Like 'In the Pond'?"

She nodded. "Umh-huh."

"I'll try," I said.

"When is all this going to happen?"

"Starting tomorrow. We're leaving in the morning."

"I'm going to miss you, Suzanne," she said.

"I'll be back in autumn, for sure, with the money to save my house, and a husband," I promised. Then I thanked her for all she'd done.

She saw me out to Gabriel, and called after me, "Good luck with your Clay Carmer."

Yes, I'd need that.

# 21

Stars still out, long before first light, April 22, Year of Our Lord 1852, we were up and having breakfast and saying good-bye to the watery-eyed Blackwells, wishing them a good summer. Entrusted to them were house and barn, old Samuel and Gabriel, and my chickens. Rufus, of course, would go with us. Left behind, he'd die of a broken heart.

I strapped on my new holster, shoved the Pocket Colt firmly down in it, put on my new wide-brimmed black hat, and prepared to go westering. Checking myself in the mirror, I jutted my jaw. Of course, I did not look nearly as tough as my partner, Drover, but certainly tough enough.

Already in the back of my mind was how I'd look when we got to Sacramento City, and I grandly introduced myself to tall, handsome Uncle Roblett Chauncey Darden, there in his general store. Though he hadn't written back in all these months, I was certain he was still alive and well in California. He'd say, "My, oh, my, Susan, you look exactly like I thought you would. Pretty and spicy." He'd introduce me around, mindful that I'd led thousands of sheep across the country to feed the starving miners. Toast of the gold rush, no less.

Meanwhile, the goats, dogs, and New Mexicans were arousing my woollies, an easy job, since they will awaken and begin eating at the slightest provocation. Normally, they have only three things to do in life. Eat, poop, and sleep. Now these particular merinos had another task. Walk and swim across most of the nation. Little did they know.

When the first thin grays of dawn began to illuminate Tennessee, Kentucky, Illinois, and Missouri, finally reaching us in Iowa, the drover looked over our little contingent that would soon wester.

A few minutes later, he said, "Sun's comin' up." If we had expected a speech about the glory of overlanding and God looking out for us, we didn't receive it. Smoking a cigar, sitting sidesaddle on Rinaldo, he yelled to Hector and Cholula, *"Adelante!"* Nothing more. That meant, "Get going," I later learned. Drover led off, like Napoleon.

The goats stepped along and the sheep followed, about ten abreast, striding out through the gate, nose to tail, baaing and pooping, bells ringing, onto Stutsman Road. The dogs went out on the flanks, two lagging behind to bring up the rear, letting the goats do the leading.

Clay Carmer, Abdou Diouf, Will Pless, and Charlie Quarry took up positions to right and left of the column, without so much as saying a word to each other. The wagons were still in the barnyard, Indian Myrt poised in the seat of the red one; old Clem Epps with the reins of the laden prairie schooner, six mules up. The spare mules packed big bags of oats.

I truly had expectations of something a little grander than this, some feeling that a great historic pilgrimage was under way. But Drover was acting as if we were going to take a walk to town. Even Salvador Maria Baca looked a little bored and sleepy as he waited with Rufe and me to trudge at the rear of the band.

Let me try to fix this firmly. It is unfortunate that cowboys always get nationwide credit for cattle drives but not one thing is ever said about us continental sheepwalkers. You hear about the great Chisholm Trail, but woollies were driven west by the thousands well before bleating cows ever came near Chisholm. It wasn't until after the Civil War that all the cattle drive commotion began, yet all people talk about is trailing steers and "tall in the saddle" flamboyant cowboys. Well, just because you sit tall in the saddle doesn't make you a national hero, even if you are a Clay Carmer with woolen pants sometimes fortified with buckskin and woolly chaps and steam-bent stirrups.

Soon, the sheep cleared the property, and I fell in behind with Mr. Baca, unable to communicate my feelings of severe letdown. I reminded myself to try and find a walking partner who spoke English. Clay Carmer, for instance.

At the same time, Clem Epps shouted to Indian Myrt, "Let's roll," and she popped the reins on her quartet of mules as the schooner dropped in behind her.

My six best hens, riding in a wooden pen strapped to the rear of that red wagon, were due for a lot of bumps over the next three months. How they were going to lay eggs without cracking them was something they'd have to solve.

The Blackwells were out in front of their place as we went past in the spring dawn, which had now turned pinkish. I had a sudden lump in my throat, saying good-bye again. It really got to me when Mr. Blackwell, hunched on his crutches, shouted, "God bless you and good luck." Roy was grinning and waving.

I looked back at Mrs. Myrtle Dessery. She was bundled

in a heavy coat, since it was still icy this early in the day, and had on her favorite polka-dot "traveling" bonnet. Her head was high. Never in her lifetime did she think she'd wester beyond the Big Muddy.

Soon, we were on that part of the road where there's a gentle knoll, just behind Archibald Morgan's land. By now, it was full light and I could see my white woollies stretched out down that slope for a quarter mile; hear their softly tinkling bells. I began to feel better about the grandeur of it.

Indian Myrt had caught the magic of the moment, too, and was smiling widely.

*Glory all!*

Suddenly, it was a sight to be seen going along Stutsman that April dawn, a pageant no less.

A little later, Clem Epps, handling his six big mules as if they were ponies, took out his harmonica and began playing "Old Dan Tucker." The reedy, bouncy tune floated out on the crisp air:

> *Old Dan Tucker was a mighty man*
> *Washed his face in a frying pan*
> *Combed his head with a wagon wheel*
> *Died with a toothache in his heel.*

Well, it couldn't have been better if the U.S. Army band was playing us away with "Hail, Columbia" and "The Star Spangled Banner" combined. Besides, "Dan Tucker" was more appropriate to what we were doing.

But that's the way we went to the Big Muddy bluffs and onto the ferry landing.

One boat had already made its first trip across this morning with a bunch of gold rush foot travelers. It was on the far side of the river, six men pulling the long oars. Two other flatboats were being launched. Soon, my sheep would begin to float over the wide Missouri, bound for California.

# PART II

# Seeing the Elephant

*Oh, don't you remember sweet Betsey from Pike*
*Who crossed the big mountains with her lover Ike*
*With two yoke of cattle, a large yellow dog*
*A tall shanghai rooster and one spotted hog.*

From "Sweet Betsey from Pike,"
song by J. A. Stone, 1850s.

# 1

My name is Clay Carmer and the true story I have to tell is not about fiery-eyed Texas longhorns.

It is about a h--lish sheepwalk I once took as a young buck; also about the female who connived it. Mangy sheep being what they are, I am scarcely proud of my part in it, and am only telling that part for the sake of state history.

So, on the second day, nodding back toward the river, Clem Epps said to me, "Clay, look over there. . . ."

I did.

Three boys from Minzter's had indeed crossed over and were now loping toward us. Either on this side, or over there, in Iowa, across the river, they had picked up four more riders. Coming slow and steady, they were spread about six feet apart, and I probably swallowed a few times. From a couple of unforgettable earlier moments in my life with bandits along the Rio, I knew what approaching trouble on horseflesh looked like.

Drover, Salvador, Will Pless, the fat cook, and the girl who got us into this whole mess were still over on the Iowa side, busy ferrying the last of the sheep, and that left Clem, Abber Doof, the Dessery woman they called Indian Myrt, and me, along with about two thousand-odd peaceable grazing woollies on Nebraska soil.

Nearing four o'clock, in fine weather, we were camped

outside Florence, which became Omaha later on, about a mile from the Indian agent's slab shack.

Without further words, old-timer Clem reached down for his rifle and Doof, the giant, went to the back of the big wagon to get his. Having been appointed by Drover to take temporary command on this side of the Missouri, I said to Doof, in sign language, You go on over with that lady.

He said, "We," which means "Yes" in French, I understand.

Doof liked that old lady a lot, and I would not have tampered with her when he was around.

I said to Clem, "They are going to try and stampede us or worse."

He declared, "They ain't gonna try, Clay. They gonna do it. They got us seven to three." He was not counting that Mrs. Dessery, always a mistake.

I did not know how well the African giant could shoot, but I had an idea that old Clem was peg-eyed with a rifle. Most good mule skinners can shoot, cook, doctor, blacksmith. Do almost anything. I, myself, did not have a good eye. I am a cow handler, not a shooter.

I yelled to Doof, who was standing by the red wagon like a black beanpole, "Get up in there with her."

He did so.

Then I yelled to her, "You get down flat, lady."

I remember pulling my hat brim a shade lower so I'd look older, then I went around to the side of Clem's wagon so I could roll under it in a h-lluva hurry, saying to him, "If they start something, I will take care of that man in the center. You get the one to the right."

They came on slow and easy, saying nothing at all, just staring at us hardlike, stopping about ten feet away, horses still wet; riders wet up to their shirt pockets. A mean group, you could tell. None looked to be much more than ignorant, shiftless hired hands, the kind that would ride for anyone for a few measly dollars. Steal, rape, gunfight, too. The paunchy one in the middle, on a great sleek roan, a whiskery, slack-jawed man of about fifty, with dark eyes tucked so deep in his skull that I could barely see them, said, "You know you boys messed up G.B.'s very favorite nephew, Dave."

Truthfully, I said, "I did not know he had a nephew. I am not from these parts. I am from Sleeta, Texas."

The paunchy man went on. "Rope got all tangled an' that horse you trussed him to stomped his front hoofs down like it was mashin' a rattlesnake till Dave's chest weren't no wider than a bread pan. Broke all his ribs. He has trouble breathin' at the age of twenty-three."

My own exact age! Yes, that was a crying shame and I waggled my head in sympathy. "Sorry to hear that about Dave. One of those unfortunate things, I tell you."

Slack-jaw went on, "Mr. Minzter got back from St. Louis yesterday and has sent us to take you back for trial in Kanesville. Attempted murder."

I did not hesitate to say, "Well, I do not think we will go."

My idea was to get to California to pay off my debt and back to Ysleta as fast as I could. A trial in Kanesville was not wanted. Leaning against the big wagon, right arm hanging limber, Colt .44 at the end of it for all humanity to see, I expected I sounded and looked cocky. I was not.

"You some kind of law?" Clem asked the man on the roan. Rifle aimed, Clem was ready to fire.

Glancing over toward the red wagon, I could not see the lady anywhere, but Doof's rifle was beaded on the man to the left of Slack-jaw. Then I looked closer and saw a gun

barrel peeping through slightly raised canvas. Be d--ned if
that Mrs. Dessery was not drawing herself a careful bead.

"You might say we're the law," was Slack-jaw's evading
answer.

I said, "I didn't get your name, sir."

"Shacklett," he said.

I said, "Well, Mr. Shacklett, we are out of the States
now, law or not. We are in Indian nation, as you see, and
none of us is crossing that river again at this time."

Mr. Shacklett was having a problem making up his mind
about what to do. I saw him looking all around our little
camp, from Clem's rifle over to Doof's, then down to my
.44; maybe he even saw that lady's barrel. He turned in the
saddle, looking back toward the river, maybe figuring odds.

As much in pure bluff as anything, I said, "May be seven
of you out here but I will guarantee three of you will never
see Kanesville again if you touch a trigger. That's a Texas
promise."

The paunchy man settled his dark eyes back on me.
"You are dumb to get involved in this, Texas boy. Where's
the ignorant New Mexico sheepherder?"

"Stay around. He will be here soon enough. There is four
with him." I spit casually into the grass to show I was very
relaxed. I was not. Had a dragonfly gone past my nose, I
would have shot and rolled.

Deep-socket eyes chock full of meanness, Mr. Shacklett
finally said, "Tell him you'll never make it to Loup Fork.
That's a Kanesville promise. Nobody is going to stomp a
member of G. B. Minzter's family and get away with it.
Dave didn't come all the way from Philadelphia just to get
stomped."

Clem said, rightfully, "Dave messed with Bert Pettit's
best goat. . . ."

I said, "Never mind. I will tell the drover."

Mr. Shacklett looked around again at our little campsite and then nodded for the other six to start riding with him and this they did for about a hundred feet as I sighed with great relief; then they turned and went straight into the sheep, yahooing. Those poor woollies, goats, and dogs began to scatter every which way.

In a few seconds, twenty-five hundred or so sheep were running in fright before seven big, twisting, turning horses. Legs were being broken as woollies went down. Then I heard a shot and Mr. Shacklett himself spun prettily out of his saddle and bounced hard on the prairie, white hat flying.

That stopped their little show right away.

Thinking sure Clem Epps had done it, I looked over and saw that Mrs. Dessery kneeling on the wagon seat, bonnet off, sighting a rifle I did not know she had. She let off another whining shot and then Doof grabbed the gun from her.

"Why did you do that?" I yelled at her.

She did not even bother to answer me, just kept watching as the horses milled around Mr. Shacklett. Those boys were surely surprised and kept looking back toward us, worried we might shoot again.

I went over to her and she finally said to me, calm as deep well water, "You weren't doing anything, Mr. Carmer. You're young. You'll learn to meet force with force."

Still surprised, I said, "Mrs. Dessery, why did you not just shoot over their heads and scare them?"

"That is not how to stop things," she replied, with a smile. "And I only winged that man, Mr. Carmer."

We watched them put Mr. Shacklett back on his horse like a limp sack of oats and ride off northeast in a hurry.

The African giant took great pleasure out of that surprise shooting. He and that tiny woman laughingly jabbered in French about it. But Clem and I felt betrayed. Women should not be shooting unless called upon to do so.

We all got up on mules, summoned Cho and the two dogs we had, and went out to round up the sheep. Four had broken legs for Will Pless to work on.

It took us almost an hour to get the woollies back into a nervous circle near the wagons, dogs doing the bulk of it, as usual. I have often wished that dogs could handle steers. They cannot.

Just about then, the final woollies came scampering up with the other two dogs herding them along, Hector in the lead. Behind those woollies trudged Drover Pettit, Salvador, Pless, the fat cook, and the girl with her dog, Rufus. I had nothing against that dog except he was useless.

Soon as the girl got close, d--ned if she didn't jump up and down and shout, "Glory all! Hallelujah! Sacramento City, here we come!"

Then that Mrs. Dessery added her two cents. "Hooray! Hooray! We should celebrate our departure."

Celebrate? I looked at Clem and he at me. Before it was too late, Drover should send them both straight back across the river was my idea.

As he came up I said, "Could I talk to you?"

He nodded. I took him over by the big wagon where Clem was and told him everything that had happened. Mr. Shacklett getting shot and so forth. Celebrate?

"G-d almighty," said Drover, hardly believing it.

Clem said, "Drover, I am not one for women shooters on a trip like this. It's dangerous."

I quickly agreed. "Neither am I. Those two could get us all killed."

Drover nodded strongly and went over to them. "G. B. Minzter is going to come after us for sure now. I advise both of you to go back home while you are still alive. This soon ain't going to be no place for women. I promise I'll get the money back to you in time for that court date."

"Never," said Mrs. Dessery, firmly.

"We will not go back," said the stubborn girl, face set and feisty. "We are staying with these sheep. They are ours. If you're afraid of G. B. Minzter, you go back." Sassy as could be.

Addressing her directly, Drover asked, "Did you happen to know that your auntie here killed a man this afternoon?"

The girl looked over at her auntie in total surprise.

Mrs. Dessery quickly protested, "I did not. I just winged him."

"Suit yourselves an' die," said Drover.

The women put their heads up like colts full of p--s and ginger and walked away toward their little red wagon. They were the most stubborn, uppity women I'd ever met.

# 2

Now, to say a few things about myself, and how I think, over and beyond being a fool for ever getting myself involved in a Taos poker game with Bert Pettit. I will say it as strong as I can—*I had no use for sheep then; I have none for them now.* They savage a range. In fact, the only time I was ever around woollies was that fateful summer of 1852.

I do brag a lot about being the first authentic American cowboy. That is my greatest fame, duly recorded by the Texas Historical Society, see Volume I, page 11, under the name *Clay B. Carmer, Rancher, Del Rio.*

I am that Clay Butcher Carmer and I was born to poverty on a frontier farm near Ysleta. I was more or less on my own after the age of thirteen when a Ranger gunned my Daddy out in the pigpen. Folks think all Texas Rangers are good people. That is not so. Some are thieves and murderers and I have had a special bullet waiting for Ranger Caskey since 1842. He shot my innocent Daddy one morning when Mama and me were in Ysleta buying yard goods. I was the one who found Daddy blown away in the mud and hogslop, and had nightmares over that gruesome sight for years. Daddy was not gunned down because he was a bandit. For all to know, he was shot because he told on Caskey, who had gotten drunk and killed a mocking boy no older than me down in Fabens. Ranger Caskey then jumped across the Mexican border. Let someone tell me they sighted Ranger Caskey and I will be on my way across the Rio.

As to the cowboying part, *vaqueros* started teaching me about longhorns, which were roaming wild all over south Texas, when I was about ten, and I finally took a bunch north for sale in 1851, which was, of course, long before the War Between the States; long before anyone ever heard of General U. S. Grant and General Robert E. Lee; long before anyone ever heard of cowboys.

Drover said, "You take the two o'clock watch with that wiggle-tail."

"Why me?"

" 'Cause you're closest her age. She's also got a warm eye for you an' mebbe you can talk some sense into her."

I had to laugh long and hard.

My nice loving sisters back in Hudspeth County and over in Uvalde, both churchgoing mothers, were polite, reasonable women with no blades to sharpen, no tricks to play. Maybe Iowa-bred women are different?

Now, I did have to admit she did not look too bad for fourteen and was beginning to blossom fast. Marrying age already, she would ripen within the year and she would surely put some poor man through pain and misery in not long a time, adding her baggage to his. But I would do what I had to do and keep my distance. I was and am an honorable man.

Being tuckered, I went to sleep long before the wolves began to howl. Yet it seemed no more than an hour when it was 2:00 A.M. and Fat Charlie was shaking my shoulder. He handed me a shotgun.

Will Pless was routing that girl out of the red wagon at the same time.

Packed in a tight circle, the woollies were lumps of white in the darkness, with the two wagons on opposite ends; four dogs spread almost equally around, tents the same. Pless and Fat Charlie shared a tent; me and Salvador had one; Doof had one to himself, Pless claiming he'd rather sleep with smelly Fat Charlie than with the African giant, of whom he was afraid. Drover had his own tent. Clem's bedroll was in the big wagon and that's where he stayed.

Still half asleep, the girl stumbled down holding a buffalo robe, dog Rufe with her. Heavy-eyed, she asked a dumb question, "What do I do?" That dog of hers was yawning, already laying down. Worthless.

"Sit right here and stay awake," I advised.

Pless had given her the shotgun. A rifle is no good for this type of guarding. Scatter shot will not do much good at fifty feet, but it sure scares the hairs off a prowling coyote or wolf. Looking at me groggily, she huddled down in that big robe and I thought, oh, oh.

I went on around to the big wagon and kicked at chars of wood in the campfire. Fat Charlie had left me some steaming strong coffee and I had that. Clear sky peppered with stars, the cold was fierce that April morning, I remember. Shotgun steel was icy even though I was wearing gloves.

Though there were a few lonesome, pesky wolves this near to Florence, they were not much of a worry, we had been told by the Indian agent. Those sheep dogs could pick up animal scent in their sleep, I do believe. Whether or not they could always smell a human crawling upwind was something Drover was not certain of. He was betting Minzter would ride in at night, if at all.

Nothing was moving out there that I could see and the dogs were quiet, but around three o'clock that girl's shotgun went blamming off, and heart in mouth I ran around to where she was, beating Drover, in his long johns, by only a few steps.

"What'd you see?" he asked, wide awake, eyes darting.

She was looking off into the darkness. "Wolf!"

"Dogs bark?" he asked me.

"Nope. Not even hers."

"You hit that wolf?" he asked the girl, suddenly suspicious of her and rightfully so.

"Maybe."

Her dog was three feet away, sitting up, nipping fleas. Wolf out there and even that dumb dog would have been raising back hairs, I believe.

"Which way did you see it?" I asked.

She pointed and I walked out near fifty feet. Nothing. Everybody else wisely went on back to bed.

I got a lantern out of the big wagon, lit it, and went back to look close for wolf tracks. None there. Then I went back to the girl, curious about what animal she said she shot.

Just about where she'd been sitting I could see that the dirt had been scuffed up good and something gleamed down there. I put the lantern closer and saw where scatter shot had hit the ground. I kneeled down and smelled burnt gunpowder.

Lifting the lantern so I could judge her face, I said, "Went to sleep and just about blew your foot off, did you not?" I had caught her flat.

Gazing up at me, she did not answer, as criminals usually do not.

I advised her, "Stay awake next time or there may be worse than a wolf."

She stared at me in the lantern glow and said, "You do your job, Clay Carmer, and I'll do mine." That was her only defense. Deceit was her game.

New coffee was boiled an hour later and then we rolled, Cholula's rich milk sloshing around in the butter churn beneath the red wagon. The churn was located next to the hanging grease bucket and chicken coop. Those complaining hens had not laid an egg since we left the Dessery yard and I could hardly blame them. Walking behind the wagon at sunup, I could see them lurching around in there.

First there was Drover on Rinaldo, way ahead, then the red wagon with that Mrs. Dessery at the reins, girl walking beside it; then the goats; next was me and Abber Doof; back about midway on either side of the sheep was Will Pless and Fat Charlie; then behind the sheep was the big wagon, Clem Epps up, and beside it walked Salvador Baca. Every time a wagon wheel took three hundred sixty turns we were a mile ahead. The dogs never stopped moving along the whole length of sheep. I suppose it was a grand sight to see, that big blur of white going over the grassy plain.

No more than three or four wagon trains had departed this early, so the trail was not all eaten off, rutted, and littered the way it would be in a few weeks as more trains rolled. One was about four miles ahead of us and we could see its white tops bobbing along. Nine or ten thousand wagons followed us that year, I am told.

Right behind us was a Mormon train with a lot of Britishers and behind them was the "Richmond Company," organized out of Virginia, with at least fifty wagons. Trains were crossing the Missouri every day.

I had looked at the guidebook in the big wagon. There was nothing much ahead until we got to Fort Laramie, in Wyoming Territory. Loup Fork, the river Mr. Shacklett said we would never reach, was ninety-odd miles ahead, joining the lazy Platte. Eighty miles on past where we reached the Platte was "Last Timber," only tree visible for two hundred miles. I had never seen flat, treeless land like this.

But the mules had an easy time pulling the wagons and there wasn't much to trailing sheep, either. The dogs and goats did all the work. The woollies sometimes spread from walking thirty to forty abreast to seventy or eighty, then the dogs would tighten them up.

I quickened my steps, passing the red wagon, doffing my Saltillo hat to the ladies, and went on up to where Drover was sitting half asleep on Rinaldo, cigar stub cold in his mouth.

"When do you think Minzter will come after us?" I asked.

"Not sure he will." He yawned.

"But if he does . . . ?"

"Tonight, tomorry night. He won't let us get no more'n twenty, thirty miles away, if that far."

"Drover, this thing got out of hand, did it not?" I said as we plodded along. That was my thought.

Drover shook his head in dismay. "Never have I had such a run o' bad luck. First I come here at the beck an' call of a dead man. Then they lied about the sheep. Not ten thousand but three. I lose my best goat an' Minzter's nephew gets stomped. D–n them women, anyway. I'm too trustin' an' good-hearted for my own good."

Drover was quiet a moment and then said, "We'll put them women to bed tonight an' all of us stay up. No matter how many he sends, they can't come down out o' no trees or hills on this plain. Hard to sneak up on us."

We did not stop for breakfast until about eleven o'clock, putting the sheep to water in a creek and letting them feed during "nooning" when we ate. The mules were let off harness and put on picket ropes to nibble in the new, thick grass. Goats and dogs went free, as usual.

## 3

We stopped toward late afternoon and cut out most of the woollies, sending them on northwest with two of the dogs and Salvador Baca. Drover went with them, finding a hollow off the trail so they'd be safe for the night. We kept just enough sheep so if anybody was hunting us they would not have any trouble spotting where we were in the darkness. Drover wanted Minzter to come in and get it over.

Just before sundown, Rinaldo came cantering up the trail and mule skinner Epps was quick to ask Bert Pettit if it might not be a good idea to ride back to the Mormon camp for men with rifles. They were about three miles behind us now, easily visible. People usually helped each other on the trail.

"Nope," the drover said. "Our fight, not theirs."

"So be it," Clem answered, unafraid.

We had not made more than twelve miles that day; still near the Missouri, so it would be easy for Minzter or who-ever he sent to catch us. This time, with Mr. Shacklett shot up, nobody believed they would be content just to scatter sheep.

"But that gives me another ideer," said Drover. He turned to the girl and that Dessery lady to say, "I'm sendin' you two back to that Mormon train to spend the night. You'll be safe. I was thinkin' today they might try to burn these wagons. Don't want you sleepin' in them." He was being very nice about it.

As might be expected, Mrs. Dessery quickly replied, "I appreciate your concern but I won't hear of that plan. I am a frontier woman and you are not sending us anywhere."

It was a repeat of yesterday and Clem Epps slapped his leg and cackled, in his usual way.

"I'm certainly not going to the Mormon train," said the girl.

"You may need all the guns you can get tonight," said Mrs. Dessery, a true statement.

"Well, your own funeral," Drover said to them. "Just don't get in our way."

"Mr. Pettit, that's the last thing we'd ever do," she said, a statement he had heard before.

He threw a skeptical look at her and went about prepar-ing for the night. "Clem, take all those mules 'bout two miles away from here an' hobble them. Same with the goats. If we leave 'em here, they can be shot."

About then, we pushed the wagons tongue-to-tongue on

a north-south line to concentrate rifle fire. Drover's days of scouting and Indian fighting and his time with General Winfield Scott in the Mexican war was duly called upon now to save our lives. It was evident he knew what he was doing.

As total night came down, we were all sprawled underneath the wagons, eating soda bread and buffalo jerky, rifles ready. About three hundred sheep were mounded behind us to say that we were not some innocent Mormon train.

About eight, when the dark lightened, stars out, Drover said to me, "Clay, go on up the trail 'bout a quarter mile an' find you a spot an' jus' lay down an' wait. See what comes an' how many."

Though I did not particularly want to go, I said, "All right." I had no army training. I was not a scout.

He went on, "But get back here before sunrise. I don't want you out there alone after that. Don't shoot 'less you have to."

I got my knife out of the big wagon and walked about a quarter-mile east, and then got down on my belly by the trail in six-inch grass. Thankfully, bugs had not come out as yet, spring night chill still holding the plains.

As I lay there in the cold damp grass waiting for who knows what to come along, I was more than ever wishing I had just taken my longhorn money and gone on back to Texas rather than that side trip to Taos. I could have lost at poker in San Antone just as well without ever meeting Drover Pettit and his mangy sheep.

As I listened to some wolves talk back and forth, I thought some about my boyhood. I thought about old Celestino Esquivel, who had taught me to be a cowboy, the most noble profession there is anywhere on earth.

The Esquivels had a *hacienda de ganado* on the Rio and

I went over to that cattle spread. Maybe I was nine. Eyes sparkling, Señor Esquivel laughed. *"Muchacho,* every Mexican boy who wants to be a *vaquero* starts in the *pollo* yard. You catch a rooster with a loop of string. Then you learn *la reata,* the rope. You learn to ride. Burro first. Then an old horse. And in time, you meet the *ganado,* with horns spread seven feet and eyes of fiery red. . . ."

As I lay there shivering I could not help but think of that sweet Texas heat and those brassy skies; those fine four-legged saddle animals God put on this earth to save boot leather and blisters.

About midnight, I think it was, I heard some snuffling nearby and eased my knife out, saying to myself, "Mr. Wolf, just come right on and I will leave you mouthless."

Whatever it was, was coming from the west, not the direction of the Missouri. I got up to a squat and waited, ready to do some fancy cutting. The snuffling kept up.

A few seconds later, down the trail came an animal, but it was not no wolf. I could tell the way it walked. It was that worthless dog belonging to that girl from Iowa. It came sniffing up to within an inch of my nose, tail wagging, and I said to it, "You are one lucky dog. You come near losing your throat. Now get on back to those wagons. . . ."

I had no sooner got that out but there was a whisper, "Clay, Clay . . ."

Oh, my G-d, I thought. *It was her!* It was her, without a doubt.

She came up quickly and knelt down beside me. "I knew good old Rufe could find you," she said, breathing hard.

"What are you doing out here?" I asked, none too gently.

"I knew you'd be lonely and I brought you this buffalo robe."

I said, "Girl, you are plumb crazy and you could get killed out here. Something may come up this trail any minute. Does Drover know you are gone?"

"He's asleep," she said. "They're all asleep."

That was just fine, I thought. I am freezing and they are sleeping.

"Drover said the dogs would wake them up if anybody came. He doesn't think anything will happen until sunup."

So why was I out here alone in this wet grass? "Is that right," I said, none too nicely.

She said, "Take this. It's cold out here, isn't it?"

Yes, it certainly was and I gratefully took the robe. I said, "Well, thank you. Go on back, now. Drover can be wrong, you know. Minzter's timetable may not be on the same clock as Drover's. They could ride up here any minute."

"I'll just stay a while," said the girl. "Anything comes this way, Rufus will warn us."

On past performance, I would take no bets on that.

Dead silence fell upon us. The only sound on that whole plain was wolf conversation to the north. There was not the slightest breeze blowing, which made it even colder.

"Would you like to talk?" she asked, coming over to sit beside me without being invited.

I had no idea what to say to a fourteen-year-old female at midnight. She had never been to Texas and we had nothing at all in common. I said, "I will answer any questions."

I guess that was fine with her. She asked, "You speak Indian?"

"Nope, just Spanish."

"Well, *ne-ko-ma-puk-a-chee keo-sauqua-sepo-kiou* means

'the pony has run away across the dark river.' That's in Iowa tribe."

"Is that so?" I asked.

"Yes, it is," she answered. "Now, do you know anything about prairie birds?"

"I do not." Birds of any kind did not interest me very much.

"Well," she said, "you'll see bobolinks, rose-breasted grosbeaks, red-shafted flickers, dickcissels, and sometimes a yellow-headed troupial along here the next few weeks. Just ask me about them."

I said I would. I wondered if any of them were eating birds. I did like roasted quail.

She said, "I also know quite a lot about snakes."

Well, I did know something about snakes myself. They can start a stampede was what I knew. I shot them on sight. I looked over at her. In the starlight I could see her face, serious as a Baptist preacher's.

"We'll have to watch out for the massasauga rattler, the banded rattler, and the prairie rattler . . ."

Rattlers was rattlers as far as I was concerned, never mind the names, and this was the d--ndest conversation I had ever had with anyone past midnight.

I do estimate that that Iowa girl talked on until after three o'clock A.M., at which time I said, "You better go on back to those wagons. I got a hunch that things will happen in an hour or so, or less. . . ."

Without argument, she departed, along with that dog, so she could be reasonable on occasion. As she left she said, "I'm glad that we had a chance to visit, at last. . . ."

There was not much for me to say but yes. She had brought me that blanket. I added, "Wake them others up.

It will be getting light in not long a while. I thank you for that buffalo robe."

Yellow was showing on the top edge of a roll of low black clouds to the east when someone started coming my way up the trail, on foot. I could see him faintly outlined, just a shape, moving slow, looking out for something. Could be an innocent Mormon from the train back there, out early hunting rabbits, or could be one of Mr. Shacklett's boys of yesterday.

I rolled over another three or four feet from the wagon track, staying on my belly, grass barely covering my shoulders. Good James Bowie was coldly in my right hand. What a lot of people do not know is that most all of Texas Jim Bowie's namesake knives were made in England. Mine happened to be a fine Sheffield blade, suitable for shaving, toothpick, whittling, or other things.

On came this mysterious man and I could see that he had a rifle. But ten feet closer I could also see he was no innocent Latter-day rabbit hunter. He was a horse rider on foot, scouting as you please this chilly, shadowy dawn. Looking for Drover Bert Pettit and his sheep people, to be sure.

I decided to let him pass and come up behind him soft-like.

Eyes straight ahead up the trail, he was squinting as he came by me, probably seeing a white blur of sheep up the track. I let him go by about five feet, then moved on him, grabbing him from behind and laying that sharp Bowie up against his windpipe. I had my left forearm around his neck, down low; right hand holding the knife just over it, tip of the blade just under the edge of his right jawbone.

"Drop that rifle," I ordered, and he did so. "Now, just

stay very still so this sharp blade does not do more than nick you."

He wisely decided to do so.

About my size, maybe about the same age, he was wearing a big hogleg on his right hip, but both hands were safely out in front of him like he was begging for bread and water.

"Now, kick that rifle away," I ordered.

He did so but got the sudden foolish notion to go for his gun while he kicked, throwing back his head to try and butt me. He hit my right elbow and pulled away to the left. I thereupon moved back a step as his hand went to his belt and brought James Bowie, of Sheffield, England, skimming along his skull, over his nose, punching through his left cheek and stopping with a crunching noise on his lower teeth. Had it not been for those solid molars the blade could have gone on down to his navel.

Mostly he did all that cutting to himself by moving his head. Lucky for him it was not deep, but blood did spray into his eyes and that surprised man just stood now, docile as could be.

To get my pity, he said, "You cut me! You cut me! My mouth is fillin'!"

"D--n right I did," I said. "I did not stay out here in cold grass all night just to be shot by you. You made it worse by moving."

Whimpering, he put his head down so his life's liquid would drain out and not drown him. "I will die," he said, in a gargling, whimpering voice.

I hate whimperers and asked, "Where are the others?"

"Do something for me," he said.

"You tell me where the rest is, and how many you got, and I may help you."

He just stood there trying to hold his hands over that gash that went from right earlobe to left jaw. Truly, he was a mess. I could not even tell much what he looked like.

"Please help me," he pleaded. "I think I'm gonna go down."

"Just tell me how many and where," I repeated.

He spit out a lot of blood and gargled, "Fifteen, 'bout two miles back."

"On horses?"

He nodded and went down to his knees in the prayer position.

"Minzter with them?"

His head shook a firm and likely truthful no and I believed him and decided to help him.

I went around behind him, pulled off his dirty wool jacket and ripped his shirt, buttons flying. Wadding a piece about the size of a biscuit, I told him to stick that in his mouth to stop the bleeding inside. Taking the rest, I bunched it up and told him to hold that over his face gash. I was being very brotherly to that evil stranger.

After I kindly wiped the red out of his right eye, I made him stand up on his own two big feet and told him to start out for his Kanesville friends. I even pointed him in the right direction.

In a high, whiny voice, he said, "If I pass out, I'll bleed to death."

I said, "Mister, you got no more than a quarter-inch cut there, but you are going to have one fine scar cheek to cheek and right over your nose. Your grandchildren will ask about it for years. Now I have this to say to you: Tell your *compadres* that we will be waiting. We are dug in under them wagons and will shoot every last one of you out of your saddles. Now, get along."

Holding his gashed face with both hands on the rag, he stumbled away in the dawn gloom, whimpering softly.

Not feeling at all sorry for him, I retrieved his rifle and six-gun and took off at a trot for the sheep camp as thin light began to spread.

About sunup, a single rider came from the east and stopped maybe six or seven hundred yards away. I suspect that he had a spyglass and looked us over, not liking what he saw. No one could blame him for that. We were tucked under those wagon beds and with eight rifles could pick off two or three easy as shooting November persimmons every time they rode by. If they tried it on foot, we would get even more. There was just no place to hide in that grass.

But they were still tempted and about nine o'clock another one came out to look at our wagons tongue-to-tongue and got a little closer, whereupon Drover said, "When I count three, put a little lead in his direction." So eight rifles let loose at him.

He rode on off and Drover said, "Let's get the mules an' roll."

If those trains behind us, with all their hungry stock, ever caught up and passed us, they could eat the grass alongside the trail down to a chigger bite.

Just in case we had visitors, both wagons tailed the sheep now and Salvador had the woollies bunched up instead of strung out.

I sat in the back of the big wagon and kept a sharp watch toward the east.

# 4

I had nothing more to do with that girl for the next two daybreaks. She stayed awake on watch, I do believe. I checked her twice.

On we went. Still no sign of the Kanesville boys and we were ferrying sheep across the Elkhorn, which was running swift even though the snow melt had not begun north of us to much extent. That Mrs. Dessery said there was likely still ice on the Niobrara.

Now, the Elkhorn is not nearly as wide as the Missouri and we had the wagons plus most of the woollies crossed by three o'clock when it came time for me to go over again on a longboat with the girl and Fat Charlie. We had about eighty sheep on board that trip; another eighty or ninety still left on the east bank with Salvador and one dog.

High wind had commenced during the night and was still whistling over the plains in the afternoon, causing a cold chop on the river. Oarsmen were having a lot of trouble and the sheep were nervous as gusts exploded against the boat side.

I was looking toward the other bank when I heard that girl yell and saw her bobbing in the water; floundering, being swept along. Dimpled Fat Charlie was just standing there, watching her; doing nothing. Heavy jacket pulling her under, she was yelling for help. Maybe she could not swim? She had talked a lot that night but nothing about swimming. She had not said, "I can swim."

So I jerked off my boots, Saltillo hat, and jacket and jumped in after her, letting the current carry me along. That water was icy that April day and my breath sucked on down to my toes. Fortunately for her, I am one of the few Texas cowboys who ever learned how to swim and I struck out after her, finally getting a good grip on that short hair, knuckles right down at her scalp, and went kicking on over to the bank. Her face was pasty indeed.

When I had caught my breath, I asked her what had happened.

Soon as she caught her own, she said, "I was standing beside Charlie Quarry. I guess a ewe bumped him hard and then he bumped me overboard."

She went on off to the red wagon to get dry and change her clothes and I went to the boat landing to get my boots, hat, and jacket. Fat Charlie was there. That is exactly what happened, he said. A ewe bumped him and he bumped the girl. "I'd of jumped in myself but I can't swim," said the man from Reunion. Reasonable enough. Swimming does not come easy for everyone.

A little later the girl came to me to say thanks, and gave me two pills. Though nobody had asked her to do so, she had taken over all doctoring. Sometimes I thought too much.

"What are these?"

"Compound cathartic pills so you don't get sick. They will sweep your liver and clean your bowels."

I thanked her kindly. The pills tasted terrible, but the worst thing that could ever happen to you on the trail was to come down with croup and fever.

At supper, the girl came over and sat down beside me, which was all right, I first thought. I was beginning to thaw a little with her. Then she said very earnestly, "Did you ever hear about that Iowa tribe saying—if you save someone's life, that person is yours forever?"

That statement was not all right with me. Not at all! It

scared the h--l out of me and I almost spilled my tin of beans. I got up on my feet and said, "I have never heard of that and do not want to hear of it. I am a free man."

There in the orange twilight, she looked at me with great intent. "Well, I am yours forever." She was dead serious, I could see.

I said, "You are not going to trap me that way. I do not want you even for a while. You are too young and inexperienced for me. You brought me a buffalo robe two nights ago and I got you out of the river today. We are now even." With that, I walked away.

She called after me, "Clay, that is a Pottawattamie saying."

I didn't care a burro's behind what it was.

Soon, we were trudging by the mile-wide and inch-deep Platte, a dreary, meandering river of shifting sandbars. In Pawnee country, the sluggish Platte was enough to put you to sleep in broad daylight and that's what Drover often did on Rinaldo. We would have to follow it hundreds of miles.

5

On the eighth day, which I tell about now, there was a blue-black prairie storm at dawn, the likes of which I had never seen in Texas or New Mexico. With no mountain range in Nebraska to break up the storms, they travel over the flat land like the wet devil hisself was steering them.

Thunder bellowed over us, clapping like cannon; lightning made the plains blue-white in flashes. Just after daylight, the air became cold and rain slanted down, roaring at us. The flat land turned into a churning brown sea and tents blew down.

Whinnying and bucking, mules strained against picket lines as lightning shot out of the densest folds. After flash lightning was forked lightning; then chain lightning. Sheep were down and smoking, burnt by a blue charge, first losses on the trail. Then they stampeded, running before the dark storm, which was drifting northwest.

I had been in a dozen cattle stampedes, hooves pounding and horns clicking, wall-eyed cows gone crazy with fear. There is nothing quicker to cause terror in a cowboy than a thousand storm-scared steers. You stay with them until they drop, then sing lullabies to them until they snore.

Sheep is different, not so dangerous, but spooky just the same. Aside from the bells on the lead ewes, they run without a sound, bunched together, and move in waves, like wind washing through a wheatfield.

The storm lasted until eight o'clock, when ice needles hit us, and then there was a bright streak of red sky on the eastern edge. Soon, the prairie began to glitter with hundreds of colors as the sun broke through what was left of the inky blue clouds.

As we quieted the mules down and got ready to go out and hunt sheep, I said it was the worst storm I had ever been in, including lightning that killed a horse and cowboy over near Jarales. Clem Epps said it was by no means his worst. Hail the size of quail eggs hit him near Bent's Fort, raising welts an inch high on his mules.

We found the first bunch of sheep grazing about two miles away in soggy grass, as calm as if no storm had ever hit. They began to follow Cho, a dog pacing behind. That girl, Will Pless, and Charlie Quarry took them on back to camp as we spotted another bunch about a mile away. Steam was coming off their backs as the sun mounted. The last bunch was to the north and we had them all safely back to camp by noon.

Not much in either wagon was dry. Mrs. Dessery and Clem Epps had spread everything out. Bedding, clothes, tents, all was soaked. So Drover decided to stay until next morning and we spent the afternoon skinning and butchering three dead ewes. Nine had been killed, but there was no way to keep all that meat.

Along about five, when I was scraping out ewe skins, Drover came up with Clem to say, "Walk a ways with us." He had a funny look on his face.

After we were up the trail about a hundred yards, out of earshot, he said, "I been robbed. Had six hundred fifty in Dix notes and gold eagles in the trunk. Trail money. It's gone. Nothin' in that sack now. I opened it to dry it out . . ."

Clem said, "No one but me an' them women has been near that wagon today, I swear it. Will and Charlie come back with the first batch o' sheep, along with the girl, but then they went off again."

"Well, the women wouldn't steal it, would they?" I asked. Vexsome they were but not thieves, in my opinion.

Drover said, worriedly looking back toward camp, "That's wool money to get us across. Pay ferries, buy supplies in Laramie. We split it up before we ever left. They still have their half. They checked on it a few minutes ago."

"When did you last look at the sack?" I asked the drover.

"At the Elkhorn, when I paid those ferrymen. I put it right back into the trunk, under my street clothes."

"Ferrymen see you?" I asked.

"No, they'd gone on back to the boats by the time I put the sack away."

"Anybody standin' near the back of the wagon?" Clem asked.

Drover rubbed his knuckles on the back of his heavy neck, frowning, trying to remember. "Fat Charlie, Doof, Salvador. They brought the last batch of sheep over after you went in after the girl, Clay."

It wasn't likely any stranger had gotten past the dogs at night; one of us was always on watch in front of the wagon. Clem slept inside there every night. No doubt someone on the sheepwalk had robbed the "crossing" money.

I asked Drover what he planned to do.

"Bide my time."

Mr. Shacklett had not made good his promise of shooting us up and we arrived safely at Loup Fork, where that river joins the lazy Platte, on the eleventh day.

What I haven't said so far about the Loup is that its bed is almost pure quicksand. There are sandbars, between deep channels, that look firm but are treacherous yellow liars.

Ducks had been flirting along that river all day, honking and coming in to feed, and I had seen that girl's dog eye them joyfully. The girl remarked that there was nothing closer to his heart than to retrieve a shot duck. She said much time had been spent in Iowa ponds teaching that dog how to perfect its instincts. That was well and good, I thought, making him useful for something.

About three o'clock, when Mrs. Dessery and the girl were hitching the mule team to the red wagon, getting ready to be ferried across, Salvador, down by the water, pulled a trigger and a fat mallard spun down to a sandbar. That was all that dog needed—the shotgun sound and the sight of a spinning duck coming to rest. Headed for midriver, he took off like his rear end had been dipped in turpentine.

Sorry to say, he did not get there. Six or seven feet from the slippery bank he mired down and began to struggle. High panic in his bark, he was up to his haunches and sinking.

The girl saw him about the same time I did but was a lot closer. She slid down and tried to take a step to reach him. Suddenly, she was in to her waist herself, sand sucking her straight down.

By the time I got there, Salvador was on his belly, feet remaining on the bank, and was stretching for her. "Stay still," I yelled to her, and grabbed Salvador's feet. He finally got her by the collar.

Helpless to do anything, we watched as the dog went slowly under. I will always remember his brown eyes. They were pleading and filled with terror as he looked at us. Then he was forever gone and only small bubbles remained on the yellow sand.

As Salvador pulled her from the muck, the girl's eyes were a lake of tears and her chin quivered, but she was tough enough not to let it out. Salvador put his arms around her and held her as her body shook. I felt genuinely sorry for her that day and told her so.

The elephant had arrived and it would be more than two months before it went away.

# 6

There was not enough wood left anywhere on the prairie in 1852 to patch up a keg hole, but dried buffalo dung burns just as good. Smokeless, as well. Mrs. Dessery politely called the chips, in French, *bois de vache*, or cow wood. I asked her to spell that and she did so. She made much better bread than Fat Charlie and before beginning her baking would look up over her specs and say, "Would someone please gather me some *bois de vache?*"

Over the next weeks, I must have gathered a ton of *bois de vache*.

On this particular late afternoon that is exactly what I was doing, gathering buffalo dung after a dry drive of about nine miles. We were camped near a tiny stream and I was about two hundred yards up from where the woollies was drinking when I came upon Will Pless around a bend pouring something into the water.

Curious, I asked, "What are you pouring, Will?"

Startled at first, the man from Leavenworth then said smoothly, "Oh, jus' some stuff that has gone bad." He kept bottles of milky-colored sheep medicine in the big wagon.

From what I also knew, you do not pour anything bad into fresh water. You pour it into sand and scuff it over.

We had been losing a few sheep at a time to what Will called "poison water," stagnant pools of it alongside the trail, though Salvador said we should not be running into that problem as yet. Way on ahead was many alkali pools and plenty of poison weeds, bad country for unsuspecting animals. So far we had dropped about a dozen to bad water.

I took my sack of chips and went on back to camp and there said to Drover, "Maybe you ought to find out what Will Pless was dumping upstream."

In a while, he did that. Will repeated what he had told me—sheep cure gone bad. "I just plumb forgot I was upstream," said Will. "I was all turned around."

That was reasonable enough, but Drover said, "You

know better, Will. Dump it in the dirt where sheep can't get at it."

Will said he would do that in the future.

Next morning, even before we got the coffee fire going, we saw some sheep belly-up and bloated, eyes fogged over; swollen tongues blackened. I counted seven and Salvador stooped by one ewe and examined her in lantern light. *"Veneno,"* he said.

The girl was up and about and asked, "What does that mean?"

Before I could answer, Drover said, "Pizen," face grave in the soft light. He added, "It didn't come from no trail pool or weed."

Remembering what had happened the day before, I ventured, "Will Pless?"

"Don't know," Drover said. "How can you tell that these sheep were the first ones downstream from where he poured. Pizen dilutes in not long a time."

"Why would he do it?" the girl asked, puzzled too.

In a moment, Will Pless himself walked up. "Look at these sheep, Will. I think they've been pizened," said the drover.

While we stood and watched, Pless examined them in the widening dawn light. "Yep," he said. "Maybe that worm medicine I dumped yesterday did it. Smelled something awful. How many are down?"

"Seven," Drover told him.

"I am sure sorry," said Will. "I just wasn't thinking when I emptied that bottle." He seemed genuinely sorry. "What can I say?"

Drover said, "Well, you made an honest mistake."

The tall, skinny Kansan nodded and went over to get his coffee mug.

But I noticed Drover taking another long, thoughtful look at those dead sheep. A little later, as we marched out on the trail again, another ewe keeled over.

As Drover passed by me on Rinaldo to take up the lead, he paused to say, "After while, go back an' tell Clem to say he has axle trouble. Tell him to drop that big wagon way back jus' before noonin'."

So about nine, I slowed down, falling back, let the band of sheep pass me, then fell in beside Clem, who was walking for a while. Salvador was spelling at the reins.

I stayed back there for another hour, then mounted a mule and rode to the head of the column, telling Drover everything was set. We reversed course, Drover shouting to everyone as we passed, "Keep goin'. There's a crick up ahead an' we'll noon there. We'll catch up soon's the wagon gets fixed."

So the column kept going, except that Salvador climbed up on my mule to double back to where Clem had stopped.

We were soon unloading the wooden case of big bottles that held the milky worm medicine. One bottle was missing and we knew where that one had gone. Drover opened another and passed it to Salvador. He sniffed it several times, touched a drop to his tongue, then said, *"Veneno."*

Quickly, corks were pried out of all the rest. They were all poisoned.

Drover stood back to say, "Worm cure don't go bad 'less you mix pizen with it. I think Will Pless meant to kill off all these sheep."

"Why?" I asked.

Drover lit his cold cigar stub and puffed a few times. "My guess is that Will Pless took some money from G. B. Minzter."

I remember Clem Epps saying slowly, "I sure do think we ought to go back right now an' shoot him on the spot."

Drover shook his head. "He'll do somethin' else. We'll catch him an' take care of him."

We capped all the bottles, putting them back exactly the way they were in the case, and then placed the case back near Drover's oxhide-covered trunk, wedged with ground cloths and tenting, the position it was in before nooning.

Then we slowly rode back to the sheep camp by the creek, green wagon following.

Will Pless greeted us by calling out, "Got it fixed?"

Drover answered. "Runnin' smooth now, Will."

# 7

I woke up, knowing something was wrong. It was nearing full light and I had not stood my two-to-four watch; Fat Charlie had not come to rout me out. Crawling out of the tent, I looked around in the flat gray light. Sheep were up and grazing; dogs taking care of them, as usual. I went down to the red wagon and the women were still asleep in there. Then I turned and looked back toward the big wagon. *The mules were gone!*

Clem usually picketed them in good feed a hundred feet or so from his wagon. From chewed grass and mule dung I could see where they had grazed. I could also see where their ropes had been slipped.

I yelled for Clem to wake up, then ran on down to Drover's tent. Hearing the yelling, he came out on hands and knees, saying, "You sure?"

"They are gone," I said.

"Rinaldo?"

"Every one."

Drover's face had disbelief all over it as he pulled his pants on. "You sure they didn't break loose? You can't see 'em anywhere?"

"Nope." Even in that gray light, you could see a dozen mules bunched together two miles away.

By now, everybody was up. Everybody, that is, but two. It was Clem Epps who said, "Where is Will and Fat Charlie?"

I ran down to their tent and jerked the flap open. Their bedrolls were gone and so were they. I yelled that fact out to the rest.

Drover came over and looked in, then kicked their tent down in a rage, cussing them. Steal a horse, mule, or oxen on the trail and you have messed with someone's life. There were pieces of frayed rope up on "Last Timber," upon which had hung three horse thieves. No trial.

All of us gathered around a few feet from the flattened tent and Drover said, "Hosses, 'less we catch 'em, this sheepwalk is over. They got a four- or five-hour start on us . . ."

Mrs. Dessery piped up, "If we don't catch them, can't we keep the sheep here and send back to Kanesville for more mules?"

"We can do that an' lose two weeks. All these trains behind us'll pass by an' we'll have to go two miles off the trail to get good grass. I aim to catch 'em," Drover said.

Will Pless being a thief or worse was not much of a surprise, but Fat Charlie being in cahoots was. It was hard to figure the dimpled cook being in with sheep poisoning and mule stealing.

Drover said to me, "Clay, get a saddle rifle an' we'll go

back to that Mormon train right behind us an' either borry
or buy two fast horses."

Back there, they were walking everything from cows and
oxen to horses. When we had seen them at the ferry landing, they even had turkeys.

Salvador said, *"¡Yo quiero ir! ¡Will Pless es para mí
mismo! ¡A ese quiero!"*

*I want to go. I want Will Pless for myself.* They had
argued.

Drover firmly shook his head. "Ain't but two of them,
ain't but two of us goin'. . . ."

Salvador pleaded, *"A ese cabrón Pless déjamelo."*

*Let me have that b-----d Pless.*

Drover replied in Spanish, "No, you, Abber Doof, and
Clem stay with the women. Mebbe this is more'n mule
thieves at work. . . ." Then he told Mrs. Dessery that we
would need a hundred dollars in case the Mormons would
not lend us horses. She went off to get it.

A few minutes later, each carrying a saddle rifle, extra
ammunition, and the spyglass, we started east over the trail,
walking as fast as possible. In a few minutes, Drover lagged
behind. After about a half mile on, he said, "You can go
faster'n me. Take this money an' go on ahead. Get us some
horses an' come back an' get me."

Having twenty-odd years on Bert Pettit, I went at a good
trot up that trail and got to the British Mormons just about
when they were ready to roll wagons. Looking me over, the
wagon master said, "Say, young man, aren't you the one
with the lot of sheep up ahead?"

I had to admit I was.

I said, "Major, this is a true emergency," explaining
about the theft of our mules.

"My word," he said. He was a roly-poly man with a big mustache, and a monocle.

"Can you lend us two fast horses?"

He cleared his throat. *Lend* did not set very well with him. "We really need our—"

"Will you sell us two horses? I have a hundred in eagles."

He muttered and mumbled some more, then said, "All right, young man. Fifty dollars each, with saddles, and if we see them again I shall buy them back at ten dollars each." No wonder the Latter-day Saints got rich.

Thanking him, I picked two horses, a sorrel and a blackie that didn't look too bad, then saddled them with two of the worst beat-up U.S. Cavalry saddles that I had ever seen, neither of them worth two dollars, and was on my way.

Drover had made a mile since I had left him and he was very glad to see me. He climbed on the sorrel and we were off again, soon circling away from that Liverpool train.

The first three that we passed had not seen Pless or Charlie, but the commander of the fourth one, a Captain James Gainsford, of Lexington, Kentucky, said, "They rode in on us about daylight. Two of them, all right. One tall an' one fat, an' offered to sell us ten of those mules for four hundred dollars. I was tempted. On about five hundred miles from here when these animals start wearin' down, I'll probably wished I'd of bought them. . . ."

We thanked Captain Gainsford, who had a good-looking train, and went on east in bright sunshine and mid-May heat.

Distance is deceiving on the plains, so tricky that six crows at high noon can look like a party of men standing six feet tall. Heat distorts everything, making movement where there is none. As far as we could see, clear to the horizon, wagon tops were shimmering and bobbing in a snaking white line. If Pless and Fat Charlie were sticking close to the trail, trying to peddle those mules, we would come on them without much warning. Riding by the on-coming wagons, we were staying over to the right-hand side of the trail.

About eleven o'clock, there appeared in the distance about a dozen "crows" off to the right side of the trail. We kicked those horses ahead and closed to within a mile of them, then looked through the spyglass.

"Will and Charlie, d--n them," muttered the drover. "Will's up on Rinaldo. Let's switch over to the other side."

So we crossed ahead of an oncoming train and got on the left side of the trail, keeping close to the wagon tracks so if Will or Fat Charlie looked back all they would see would be wagons and walkers beside them; the few people who were riding horses or mules.

Going against the wagon traffic, we just loped along, making sure the rifles would slide from the saddle holsters. Drover said, "Soon's we get opposite them, we'll cut on across." That way they would not see us until we were on top of them.

About eleven-thirty, we were finally across from them, though hidden by a Conestoga. The thieves were certainly not looking to be caught. Mules strung out behind them on ropes, Will and Fat Charlie seemed to be in no particular hurry. I expect they were sizing up each train as they met it, waiting for one pulled by mules instead of oxen.

Holding his Navy Colt in his right hand, reins in the left —me the same—Drover said, "All right, let's get 'em. Don't hit no mules," and we went galloping across ahead of a wagon, oxen team swerving as we passed, lady driver with eyes bulging.

Drover shot Will Pless prettily off Rinaldo before the Kansas man ever saw us coming and I aimed squarely at Fat Charlie between the eyes but missed and got his shoulder as he was jumping off his mule. He started running, tugging at his holster at the same time. He went back the other way, tried to scramble past that rolling Conestoga, dropped his gun, and I heard him yell. Charlie had reached at the wrong time and a wheel had gone right across his wrist.

# 8

Deciding to make an example of Fat Charlie and have him hung at Fort Laramie, we put him up on a mule, tying his feet so he would not fall off. His big white belly was flopping out this noontime as we had used most of his shirt to bandage the hand and wrist. Head down and bouncing, chin hitting his chestbone, he looked weak enough to die already. I had just grazed his shoulder so that wound did not amount to anything. The wagon wheel had done the damage to him.

So far, Fat Charlie had not said a blessed word to us; had not pleaded for any mercy. I think he was surprised that Drover just had not shot him and left him by the trail.

However, I was not sure he would make it to the sheep camp, much less Fort Laramie. I said to Drover, "I can put a tourniquet on his arm and stop that bleeding. He is losing a lot." It was dripping.

Drover answered, loud enough for Fat Charlie to hear, "You can do that whenever he tells me what he knows."

The wheel had crushed his wrist and Charlie was truly a

sorry sight, bloodstain on his shoulder; big bloodstained bandage wrapped around his right hand.

"He will never make it," I said.

"Up to him," Drover replied, in a loud voice. "I must say I won't dig his grave. Any man who steals another's transportation don't deserve no grave."

Will Pless, newly down in h--l, had just found that out. Drover had lassoed a rope around Will's ankle and dragged him about a mile off the trail for wolf and buzzard bait.

Drover looked back at Fat Charlie to say, in a loud voice, "He is nothin' more than a miserable prairie dog an' don't deserve to live to sundown."

Hearing all that plainly, Fat Charlie suddenly began to sniffle and whimper. There is nothing worse than a whimperer, even a wounded one. It is the worst sound on earth. Fat Charlie was a prairie dog, without doubt.

Suddenly outraged by it all, Drover jumped off Rinaldo and went back to Fat Charlie, grabbing his mule's headstall with his left hand. With his right, he grabbed Fat Charlie by the greasy hair and yelled at him. "Tell us what happened, Charlie, or I swear I'll blow you away before we ever make camp."

It was a traitorous tale he had to tell. He and Will Pless had indeed been hired by G. B. Minzter to do us in one way or another. Hundred dollars each. Stealing the trail money out of Bert Pettit's oxhide trunk was Will's own idea. Mules as well as sheep were to be poisoned, but then Will Pless decided to steal them instead.

"Where is that money?" Drover roared at Fat Charlie, still holding him by the greasy hair.

"I don't know," whimpered Charlie, eyes rolled way back in his pasty head. "I swear it. He hid it somewhere along the trail." Then Fat Charlie disclosed something I never ever would have expected. "Will tol' me to push that girl over the side into the river but make it look like an accident."

Charlie was an attempted murderer. Just the same I put a tourniquet on his upper arm and cut off the blood. He had talked and that is what we wanted.

When we got back to camp and told everyone what had happened and that we intended to make Charlie pay his dues at Fort Laramie, the doctor's daughter promptly said, "There is no way he'll ever make it unless we operate on him."

At that moment, Fat Charlie was over underneath the big wagon on a blanket, moaning and groaning. The girl and Mrs. Dessery had looked at the mashed wrist.

A conference was then held. The hand and wrist had to come off and the girl volunteered to do it.

I said to her, "You are only fourteen and have no business doing amputations."

Without pause, she said back to me, "I am going on fifteen and saw my Daddy do four or five. Twice on arms. He left a stump about four inches below the elbow . . ."

Mrs. Dessery spoke up. "I want no parts of this," and then she jabbered to Abber Doof in French to let him know what was going on. Then she announced, "Mr. Diouf wants no parts of it, either." They walked away.

Throughout all this, I noticed that Fat Charlie had quieted down and was listening closely to us. I think he found it hard to believe what he was hearing. A fourteen-year-old girl was going to be his surgeon.

"I will put him to sleep and he won't feel a thing until tonight," said the girl.

Charlie finally piped up weakly. "Do you have to?"

"Yes, we do," firmly said the girl, looking at him direct.

"Well, that settles it," said Drover. "Off it comes."

She said she would need hot charcoal powder, a lot of hot water, some whiskey, and strong men to hold Fat Charlie down just in case he did not go all the way to sleep. With strong Abber Doof out of it for his own reasons, that left the drover, me, Epps, and Salvador as holders. I was not looking forward to the operation.

Then Salvador did a nice thing. He volunteered a pint of *mescal*, which is Mexican liquor strong enough to melt varnish, that he had been saving for emergencies. Knowing what was going to happen to him, Fat Charlie drank the whole pint in six or seven swallows. While all this was going on, I built the fire up; started water heating.

Once again I asked that girl if she really knew what she was doing. "Positively," she said, and went about gathering her doctor tools out of the red wagon.

A tarpaulin was spread and soon we carried drunken Fat Charlie over to it and laid him out so the girl could put him to sleep with spirits of nitre and chloroform. Though I did not like the smell of the latter, I have to admit all this was very interesting. When Charlie did not moan or groan when she punched him in the belly with a needle, we knew he was ready for it.

Soon she cut off what was left of his wrist and said, "See, I am clamping these arteries . . ."

I did not look. I was holding a leg.

"My Daddy, up in Beulahland, would be proud of me this day."

She talked throughout the whole thing.

"See, I have a nice flap here."

Drover said, "I am sure going to have to tell Jarramilla about all this. . . ."

"Twenty-five, thirty stitches ought to do it," said the girl.

I still did not look up.

A little later, Drover said, "You do stitch well."

A little while after that she said, "Now, we'll pack this good-looking stump in the hot charcoal powder and let him wake up."

At that moment, I let go of Charlie's leg, got to my feet, and walked away, knees weak, feeling funny inside. I was cut out to be a cowboy, not a doctor.

I must say that Fat Charlie Quarry was surely a subdued mule thief when he woke up and looked at his new stump.

We rolled the next morning at four A.M. and during the day passed the Liverpool pilgrim train, dropping off the two horses and those no-good cavalry saddles, getting back twenty dollars from the Mormons.

For five days, Charlie Quarry moaned and groaned in the back of the big wagon, claiming he was too weak to walk because he had lost so much blood. He was, however, going to be able to face the army hangman at Fort Laramie.

Mrs. Myrtle Dessery became the number one cook, which was all to the better. We had not been fed so well since leaving Kanesville. Fat Charlie getting his hand under a wagon wheel had some benefits. On the sixth day, Drover made him get down out of the wagon, ordering Charlie to walk behind the last of the sheep, so Clem could keep an eye on him. In that position he had to walk through sheep droppings as part of his punishment. Drover also gave orders that no one was to talk to him and that he had to eat his meals alone.

I must say that the girl had done a good job. His stump was healing nicely, though it was still very red and had charcoal discolor in it. He kept a sock on it most of the time since it was still tender.

As the days went by, Charlie tried to help Mrs. Dessery as much as he could with one hand—scrubbing pots, mixing soda-bread dough; stirring soup. Without use of ten fingers, work was not easy. He was also losing his paunch and actually looked better than he did before the amputation. His double chin was almost gone and I thought there might be some hope for him.

I still had not forgiven that man from Reunion for what he had done, but I did go to Drover to say, "Is it not about time we let Fat Charlie come and eat with us?"

"It will never be that time," said Drover.

It got so that I would not look at Fat Charlie Quarry so that I would not have to feel sorry for him.

# 9

The weather was hotter, drier each day, as we got closer and closer to Wyoming Territory, leaving the grassy plains. With Will Pless gone forever, we were now losing sheep to ordinary alkali pools. Rattlesnakes were out along the trail; hissing vipers and toads aplenty. White wolves and mean mosquitoes were around.

Now in the heart of sandy buffalo country, we had seen signs of them all the way. Chips and thousands of bones bleached out for years; whitened skulls and winding trails and wallows where they had rolled and scratched. Despite that, the animals were scarce. Once there had been millions on these plains, but by the time we passed through the skin hunters had killed off most of them. Early Mor-

mon trains and now the gold rush wagons usually drove
what was left farther from the Platte.

Because my feet were hurting something terrible, itching
between the toes as well, I rode in the big wagon beside
Clem Epps for a long while.

He said, foxily, "I saw you talkin' to that girl yesterday.
She was holding your hand. She sure has an eye for you."

I said, "Well, she better take it off me. I am too old and
experienced for her kind."

"Is that so?" he asked, still foxing me.

"Yes, it is," I said. "Let me tell you what happened in
Santa Fe last year. It involves girls. After I sold them longhorns I went to a honkatonk where they have tables and
booths. Must have been twenty girls there. They had a
piano player and some of the girls sang dirty songs I had
never heard before. They did not have much cloth on their
arms or shoulders and they did not have regular skirts that
went to the floor. They had little pants up above their
knees. I was told they were 'tights' and I got a big sweat
just looking at them."

Eyeing me close, Clem asked, "You in a table or in a
booth?"

"Booth," I said. "And after a while one come over and
sat down and asked me, 'Where you from, boy?' I told her
I was from Sleeta, Texas, and she said, 'I'm Lucille, buy me
a drink, pretty Texas boy.' So I bought several and after a
while that sweet-smelling girl took my arm and put it
around her waist. I had never done that before in my life.
Put my arm around a strange girl's waist. Then she started
whispering some things into my ear."

"Like what?" Clem asked, with eagerness.

"Oh, like saying she wanted to cuddle me. Then she
took my head in her hands and kissed me square on the

lips. I like to sent my hat up into the air. I felt my legs straightening out. She did it three or four times . . ."

"And then what happened?" asked Clem.

"She began kissing me and pushing her knee against mine at the same time. I got up and shouted and jumped around on the floor and she told me to sit down and said some more things. Then she asked me how much money I had, again calling me 'pretty curly-haired Texas boy' . . ."

"An' you tol' her?" asked Clem.

"No, I did not. I was drunk but I had that cow money safe in a sack tied just under my belly button. Well, she started chewing on my ear and feeling around for my money at the same time. When she found that sack, she began to unbutton my pants right there in the booth and that did it. . . ."

Clem asked what it did.

"I ran right out into the street, got my horse, and rode to Touse."

"An' lost your money to Drover?"

I nodded, having thought a lot about that. I would have had considerable more fun losing it to Lucille and never would have had to walk across the nation.

We began to look for snow-topped Laramie Peak, ten thousand feet up in horned-toad country, with parching air and mountain distances that cholera did not like. Colorings of the land turned to yellows and faint greens; there was more flaking sandstone.

Soon we departed Nebraska, entering Wyoming Territory and on the second hot day of June, I went to a hilltop that looked across a stream where the Platte and Laramie rivers join up. In the distance was Fort Laramie, with adobe walls fifteen feet up. Big grassless bluffs were on either side of us and behind them rose black hills, the Laramie Mountains.

About two miles from the fort we stopped and set up camp, aiming to stay several days, buy some supplies and do some other transacting.

Very first order of business was to rid ourselves of Charlie Quarry and have him hung. I now had some mixed feelings about that. He was now like a sinner who had taken to the Lord and I was not sure he should be strung up even if he did steal mules.

The girl went with Drover and myself up to the army post to be a witness on the attempted-murder charge.

Charlie, no longer fat, pants sagging, looked like a sorrowful, wet drooping rag as we marched him straight to the office of the fort commander, one Captain Percy Wiggins, of Illinois.

Old Bedlam was the officer's building at the fort and Captain Wiggins held out in there. That day there must have been five hundred noisy overlanders camped near the fort and another thousand silent Indians scattered around, mostly in tipis. They were Sioux, I was told. I did not know one tribe from another.

Drover said to Captain Wiggins, "This one-handed man is a mule thief, also an attempted murderer, an' we are turnin' him over to you to be hung right away."

Captain Wiggins was a red-faced man who had fought in the battle of Bad Ax. "I don't want him," he said swiftly, surprising us. "We don't hold courts here unless they are military. Is this man a deserter? Then I can do it and quickly."

That had never occurred to us. Drover turned to Charlie. "Are you a deserter?"

Charlie said, "I'd never do that, Drover. I was never even in the army."

Drover shook his head in frustration and again addressed the Illinois captain. "You mean to tell me that the United States Army will not hang a rotten mule thief?"

"So long as he does not steal U.S. property is what I mean. If we tried and punished every thief along this trail, that's all we'd be doing night and day."

Drover tried something else. He turned to the girl. "Tell the cap'n what this prairie dog Charlie Quarry did to you."

She had also been feeling a little sorry for one-handed Charlie, I do believe. I had seen her talking to him on the sly. She said, "Well, it was a few weeks ago at the Elkhorn and I . . ." She hesitated. It was not so easy with Charlie standing right there beside her, looking pitiful.

Drover demanded, "Tell the cap'n, tell him!"

"He tried to murder me," she blurted out, not looking at Charlie, who was now hanging his dimpled head, the picture of a found sinner.

"How?" said the drover, like a lawyer.

The girl sighed. "He pushed me into the river."

"Can you swim?" asked the drover.

"Not really," said the girl. "I can float."

Captain Wiggins turned to Drover. "Why didn't you just shoot him on the spot?"

"I should have when we caught him," Drover admitted. "Now that I know the U.S. Army won't have anything to do with mule thieves, I should have shot him like I did the other one, Will Pless. I made yet another sorry mistake on this sheepwalk."

Through all this latter part, Charlie just stood there head down, eyes tightly closed. It occurred to me that he might be praying.

Finally, Captain Wiggins addressed Charlie Quarry with exasperation, making him lift his head and open his eyes. "Why didn't you run away from these people? I would have."

Charlie replied like a man pleading to a sympathetic judge, "Where could I go, sir? The first five days after they cut my hand off I was too weak to run. . . ."

"Cut your hand off?" said the captain, blinking.

The girl said, "He crushed it under a wagon wheel. . . ."

"Go on," said the Illinois captain to Charlie.

"Now I am too far away from home to run, an' no other wagon train'll take a one-handed cook. . . ."

"Hmh," said the captain.

Feeling another sure defeat, Drover asked Captain Wiggins, "What do we do with him? He is like a leech now an' not pullin' his weight."

The captain's answer was not very satisfying. "Just don't leave him here. We have enough riffraff already."

With that, we left famous Old Bedlam with Charlie Quarry following us like a lost lamb. Going back to camp, Drover turned on him angrily to say, "Charlie, you better d--n sight learn how to use that stump better'n you do."

Well, I knew he was trying. I had seen him try to skin a rabbit by holding the elbow of his stumped arm down on the rabbit's head. Charlie was unlucky in that he had lost his right hand instead of his left.

Relieved that he was not going to be hung, Charlie promised he would try harder and tagged behind us eight or ten feet. He was walking. We three who had come to prefer charges were riding.

We were now fully stuck with Charlie Quarry. That was plain.

The morning after that, before the dawn bugle blew at the fort, off we went into the desert, circling around sleeping overlanders and Sioux tipis. Up we went gradually through sand and sage and prickly pear. On by wolf-picked skeletons of oxen and horses.

To me, this was more like good old Texas cavvy trail. If I shut my eyes and opened them, before me would be a rumbling bull instead of miserable sheep. Bellowing, cussing everybody, he would paw up some red trail dust and throw it over his swollen neck, snorting and looking for trouble with fiery eyes. Oh, I was getting so homesick for Salt Basin.

Coming back to earth, those miserable sheep stirred alkali powder with every step. My lips soon split in the sun, dust caking in cracks; eyes turned red and itched. The girl looked into her doctor book and gave all of us zinc sulphate compound. That helped.

Driving up out of New Mexico with sheep, Drover had made this mean section of Wyoming before. "Here on, it is bad country for sheep, man, an' mule alike. Bad water, black laurel, death camas, an' locoweed off to trailside. . . ."

After ten days, we bid farewell to the Platte. More and more, we knew we were in elephant country.

# 10

It was nearing sundown, and we had just gone past Independence Rock, about a hundred seventy miles out of Laramie, when Drover came back along the sheep on Rinaldo and said to me, with a long, suffering sigh, "Clay, go on back an' find that d--n wiggle-tail before dark."

"Where did she go this time?" I asked.

My unhappy voice just about told it all. More and more, she had gone off by herself. Exploring, she said. Just got up on a mule and took off for an hour or so no matter how much Drover complained.

He nodded back toward the great rock. "She got a hammer an' chisel from Clem an' said she was goin' up there to Independe Rock to carve her name in. I tol' her fifty thousand people already done it an' it was a waste o' time. She tol' me it was historic an' said even John Charles Fremont cut his name up there in '37. I tol' her it was way too late. . . ."

All of that did not surprise me the least. The last weeks even that Mrs. Dessery could not always control her.

I expect that Independence Rock was about the most famous trail landmark of all. Half-mile long, almost two hundred feet high, it looks like a giant turtle with the legs tucked into the sand and the head pulled back into the shell. Nearing the Continental Divide, nearly half of America crossed, it seemed to overlanders that the trip was nearly half over. So a lot stopped there, put their names down, the date; maybe the name of the wagon train company, either with tar, paint, or chisel.

"We'll keep goin' on another hour," said Drover, trying to make up time we had lost.

Straight ahead Devils Gate split the horizon. By hour's end, he would cover no more than two miles, if that. The sheep and mules were tired after trekking all day. As a matter of fact, so was I. And I usually got stuck with bringing her back, which she resented mightily. Drover never sent Salvador or Abber Doof after her; Clem was always busy driving mules. So I got stuck.

Dropping back to the big wagon, I picked up a mount

and set off for the granite rock, which still had a few minutes sun on top, being that high up. Everything around it
was already slipping into shadows. Overlander campfires
were dotted all around the base. The girl had no business
up there by herself this time of day, a fact that Drover
recognized and worried about.

It took me a few minutes riding around the base to find
her mule and then locate the crawlway where she had likely
gone up. I went up at that spot, too, and on top had the
grandest view of the whole trip. I stood there for a few
minutes in the cool twilight just looking either way. A few
white tops of prairie schooners were still bobbing along to
the east. Most had pulled off the trail into circles on either
side, and fires burnt there, too. Even in the dimness, I
could see ten or twenty miles to the east.

In the other direction, I could see the white blur of our
sheep as they raised a dust cloud along the Sweetwater,
headed for Devils Gate. I was wishing I had come up earlier to see it all in daylight.

Almost everybody had left the top of the rock, going
back to their wagon trains, but there seemed to be a few
people way up ahead, almost the full length of the half
mile, and I started that way, cussing the girl to myself.
Why had she waited until late afternoon?

The sun dropped out of sight and I knew I had maybe
fifteen minutes until it was black night on top the rock.
Hurrying along, my boots went over hundreds of names,
but I had no time to read any of them. Clem had told me
that on a July day in '50 there was an unbroken column of
wagons stretching east from "the rock" for five hundred
miles.

I heard some men's voices up ahead. Laughing, whoop-
ing, and hollering. Most likely, they were rowdy drunk. It

was easy enough to buy a jug of whiskey at most of the trading huts along the trail past Laramie. In the dimness I could not make them out but could sure hear their voices carrying in the dead quiet. They sounded eastern.

Busting through suddenly was a long, terrified scream. Female, I was sure. I began to run, pulling the .44. Then there was a shout, "Hold that little b---h!" More laughter. I cocked the gun and kept going, finally spotting them as the female kept screaming for help.

"Don't" and "Oh, please don't" and "Help me!"

Then I saw them. Four of them getting ready for some twilight gang rape. Three were kneeling and one was standing up. The kneelers were holding someone down and not having an easy time of it. It did not take much imagination for me to know that it was that foolish Carlisle girl. Once too many times she had gone off exploring.

As I moved on up, one of the men kneeling down yelled, "J---s. Howard, hurry up for G-d's sake. She tried to bite me." Then they all laughed.

She was writhing around on that rock, struggling with them.

In the dimness I guessed they were greenhorns, maybe about my age, full of whiskey and meanness. You could usually tell the greenies because they had fancy faded uniforms. I got within ten feet of them, and being occupied with the girl, they had no idea I was there.

Howard had his boots off and was half out of his pants, balancing, one foot still in his right pants leg, when I took aim and shot him in the right hip, which faced me. He yelled in surprise and pain, spinning down, while I shouted to the others to stay on their knees, hands on the rock.

I moved up closer to them, kicking the one nearest me,

sending him flat on his face. "You raping b——s, you even blink and you are dead," I said.

Clothes ripped off, the poor girl was now clutching herself, trying to cover herself. On her side, she was drawn up into a protective knot, sobbing. I said, "Susan, it is all right. You are safe now."

In the gray light I could not see how much she had been hurt, but I did not want her out there naked. They had seen all of her they would ever see. I kicked another in the ribs and told him to take his buckskin shirt off and hand it to me.

Tugging it off, he held it up, then began to vomit from fear and bad whiskey.

Still on her side, still clutching herself, still terrified, not sure of anything, she suddenly had trouble breathing and began to gasp. I shouted to her, "Get up and come over here behind me." Two or three times I had to yell that before it sunk in, then she came over on her hands and knees in a crawl that I hope never to see again. She went sideways like a crab.

Soon as she got behind me, I passed the shirt back to her.

The man I shot had passed out or died. There was a red stain on his johns from his waist to his knees. The other three greenies were quaking, wondering if they were going to get it next. None of them had guns. When they climbed up they probably left them in their wagon. Only greenies would do that.

I said to them, "You better get your friend to a doctor. I think that bullet went on through his groin."

Their jug of whiskey was a few feet away and I moved to give it a kick, sending it crashing. Pottery shattered.

Then I said to the girl, "All right, we are going to leave

here. You are safe now. When I tell you, start walking back toward the crawlway. I will be right behind you. . . ."

I was hoping she could walk. I still could not see her face; whether or not she had taken a beating.

In getting ready to leave, I said to the greenies, "I ought to shoot every last one of you. I am tempted to do it. . . ."

I only had one question to ask the girl: "Did they do it?"

I turned a little to look at her. Face hidden, her head shook me a no. She was trying to shrink herself inside the shirt.

One man raised up. "We had too much to drink . . ."

Hard as I could, I slapped the gun up against his temple and he sprawled out flat; then I hit the other two along the skull for good measure. At that, they were lucky. Most others would have killed them, but I am kinder than most.

"We can go," I said to the girl, and she started off in front of me, hiding her face; shaking all over. I came up beside her, put my arm around her for support, and that is the way we went to the far side of the rock and the path down it, to where the mules were waiting.

At the campfire, everyone stood up immediately when they saw the girl in someone else's shirt, with no boots, hiding her face. Mrs. Dessery ran over and took her off to the red wagon. We could hear sobbings and hysterics from there.

In the dawn, I was standing beside Drover when the girl came over to say thank you. We could barely hear her. Her face was drawn and stricken, but I could not see any marks on it. She looked twenty years older.

Bert Pettit's blue eyes examined her at length and then he said, "Time to roll, Hoss. Let's move the sheep out."

Her chin quivered and there were tears to be seen, but she nodded. She was quite a girl, I thought.

Just ahead was Devils Gate, where the Sweetwater had cut a chasm four or five hundred feet deep through stonebound high hills. Beyond that was slowly climbing wilderness until we got to South Pass, seven thousand feet up, where we would go from the Atlantic Slope to the Pacific Slope; where peaks, in the distance, made white sawtooths against the sky; where river waters flowed west, not east.

# 11

The girl barely talked at all that day, just walked by the front wheel of the red wagon, keeping thoughts to herself. At supper, she sat far away from us, with Mrs. Dessery, as if she was tarnished in our eyes. But the next day, at nooning, she said, "Would you take a walk with me, Clay?"

I said I would. She was not her old feisty self at all. In the daylight I could see no bruises or cuts, but she looked lifeless. Something was in her eyes that I had not seen before. Maybe she could not believe anyone would do that to her. It was worse, I suppose, because she had always been so sure of herself. Cockiest girl I had ever met to that point.

That day we were nooning by a freshet creek that had deep crystal pools and brown rocks; some pines bending toward it casting shade now and then. Prettiest no-name creek we had seen for a hundred miles.

We were going slowly along it, saying nothing, when she stopped and turned to look square at me, kind of searching my face. "Do you want to know what happened up there?"

"Yes, I do."

None of us men had asked, but we had all made some

guesses. I had shot a man because of it, not that I was at all sorry.

She said, "Well," and stopped, her eyes directed past me up the creek.

I had known this girl for two months, but I suppose I had never really looked close at her. She had upset me so much that I had no time for that. Now I did look at her. She had pretty hazel eyes and her skin was clear except for a few freckles down from the bridge of a good nose. She had a nice full mouth and a good set of teeth. I know she washed her hair a lot because of all the dust. On second thought, she was likely as pretty as anything I had seen in Texas.

She started off again. "Let's keep walking."

I said that was fine.

". . . I'd thought all morning about going up on the rock. I could see it ahead and all the guidebooks had talked about it. I wanted to put my name up there, where I was from, and the date. My Daddy had wanted to do this, make this crossing, and I had to have our name up there. . . ."

Drover could not understand that, but I could. Once I had carved my name on a tree in the Doña Ana.

"I got down on my hands and knees and began to chisel, not realizing it would take me so long and I wasn't paying much attention to who was around. I knew it was getting dark but I thought I could at least do my name, then ride back in the morning and finish it . . ."

She stopped walking and took a long, deep breath.

"You want to sit down?" I asked.

She shook her head, still avoiding my eyes. ". . . I had finished the *Susan* and had chiseled in the *C* when I heard some men behind, laughing and hollering. Just having a

good time, I thought. I would mind my business and they'd
mind theirs . . ."

Her voice changed pitch and there was a wait.

". . . but one said, 'Hey, boy, cut my name in, too.'
From eight or ten feet I guess I might have looked like a
boy kneeling down. I had on those boy's pants I'd bought
at the fort . . ."

In that twilight, it would have been easy to take her for a
boy, I expect.

". . . then suddenly they were all around me. I kept my
head down and kept chiseling, then one said, 'Well, this
boy's name is Susan. How about that? That's what he's
carvin' in the rock. Or are you a boy?' They had been
drinking a lot. I could hear it and smell it . . ."

That pure cold water was rushing by us. Everything was
peaceful and quiet.

". . . I didn't answer them, Clay. Then he said, 'I tell
you, we got us a pretty white girl up here tonight.' I stood
up then and held the hammer . . ."

She took another deep, deep breath.

I said to her, "I do not need to know all this, after all."

"I have to tell you," she said. ". . . The man nearest me
said, 'Susan, my name is Howard. I am sure glad to know
ye.' He had a funny accent. And even though they were
drunk, I thought they would talk a minute, then go on
about their business. Then that Howard said, 'Look at
them chest apples she's got. I tell ye we just might have
some fun with Susan tonight. . . .'"

I repeated, "You do not have to tell me any more."
What difference did it make now?

". . . When he said that, I said, 'Don't come any
closer,' and drew back on the hammer. Then he grabbed
me and took the hammer away . . ."

She stopped on the pathway and turned to the creek so that her back was to me. ". . . and then they ripped my clothes off and pushed me down . . ." Her voice started to break. ". . . that's when I started screaming. Before you got there, one man touched inside me . . ."

Looking at the back of her head, I said sharply, "I do not want to hear any more." I should have gotten there sooner. Should have killed all four of them. What I should have done then was taken her into my arms. I did not.

We finally sat down on one of those big brown rocks by a crystal pool and she was silent for a while, then said, "You know, Clay, I never thought it could happen to me. No one ever threatened me that way. There were all kinds in Kanesville but not a one ever touched me."

There were men and men, I thought.

"I didn't even think to take my gun up there. It was in the red wagon."

"Maybe you were lucky it was."

Lost in thought for a while, she frowned and shook her head. "I knew how babies were made when I was six, but my Daddy never talked about anything like this. . . ."

I felt foolish sitting there beside her, nodding like I understood; not knowing what to say. So I got up and went down by the pool. Dozens of brownish-green crawdads four to five inches long were scurrying around on the sandy bottom, running between rocks; biggest ones I had ever seen. Much bigger than the ones we had in the Little Pony or Mosquito. I said, "Hey, come and look at these 'dads. Biggest I have ever seen. . . ."

She came down and stood beside me.

I said, "They are real toe-biters, I would bet."

She laughed and said, "They look it."

It was good to hear her laugh.

"You ever get bit by a crawdad?" I asked.

She said she had not, and I told her the only time they would ever bite was when you got a toe under a rock where they lived. "You got no business sticking your toe in their house is how they feel, I expect."

She laughed again.

Except for the rush of water, silence came over us as we looked down into the pool until I finally worked myself up to say, "None of us know exactly what to do. We know you got hurt bad and we are all sorry for that. . . ."

There were suddenly some tears around her eyes, but her teeth were locked and she nodded at me in a fierce fighting way.

Then I said, "In the famous words of Drover Pettit, I think we will be needing to move some sheep soon. . . ."

As we started walking away from the no-name creek, she said, "Take my hand, please, Clay. . . ."

I said I would and did. No harm to that.

After a while there was a soft laugh from her. She said, "I was just thinking. A woman back in Kanesville, Frenchy Moll, told me to show you some flesh. But she didn't mean it the way you saw me the other night."

# 12

As we left broad South Pass, Green River Valley stretching in front of us for miles, off to the right was Rocky Mountain snow peaks, something I never reckoned on seeing in my lifetime. Air was cool and good there, but we did not travel far that day, stopping near Pacific Springs to graze the animals, letting them drink water from what became the Colorado.

Next day we went on to Little Sandy and then found more good grass six miles away the following afternoon. Drover was letting us dwindle and dawdle and fiddle along, resting the livestock, letting them fill their bellies in the coolness. Ahead was one long piece of misery.

About noon, he said, "Hosses, we'll leave here in three hours an' walk all night. Best you fill every keg an' canteen. No creeks for forty mile an' I'm not stoppin' till we're finished the cutoff."

Back in country he well knew, he was talking about Sublette's.

We rolled at three and soon there was a fork in the train. To left went on down to Fort Bridger and Salt Lake City; to right, Sublette's Cutoff went west, then joined the north trail up to Fort Hall. After that, it was south and west into Nevada Territory.

At sundown, big gray wolves started howling on either side of the trail, just waiting out there to come in and kill sheep. Carrying shotguns instead of rifles, we tried to look through the shadows and see them. Hanging forty or fifty yards out, they were just waiting, as twilight went to darkness.

Many times we had walked at night on the prairie for a few hours, last-minute driving for good campground and grass, but now this was hills and rock and rutted dust trail in the blackness. One step was on flat ground, the next a foot down in dust. Rocks bigger than cannonballs littered Sublette's road.

Mules and sheep were skitterish; even the goats and dogs were nervous. Wagons creaked and clanked, slamming up and down. The rear axle on the big wagon began hollering for grease and I could hear it all the way to the head of the column.

The gouged-out trail, chewed up by thousands of wheels —frozen during winter, thawed in spring, turning to caking flourlike dust in summer—had steep banks in places and I fell down twice in no time at all, tumbling once thirty or forty feet, lucky the gun did not go off. Then the moon came out and things got a little better.

I walked beside that girl for a while. Dust from sheep hooves was so thick that it hung in the air like smoke and there was not a bit of breeze to blow it away. It rose into the night sky like a brown cloud. The girl had a rag across her nose and mouth. To her credit, she did not once complain.

I picked her up several times, proud of her. No one talked.

Once I drifted back to the big wagon and saw that Abber Doof's face was no longer black. Clem Epps, riding that wagon seat as it lurched around, was getting it worst of all, almost smothered in fine dust. Salvador spelled him now and then.

By midnight, nine hours along the way, the sheep had turned dingy brown, dust clinging to new wool. They were crying out for water. The mules echoed the cries with guttural whinnies. We stopped and Drover rationed out drinks to the mules, dogs, and goats, and us two-footed creatures. There was not enough for the woollies and they bleated pitifully in the still night, smelling what they could not have. There would be another fifteen hours before they could drink at Green River.

Throughout the night the wolves attacked, no matter how many times we drove them off. A half-dozen times I saw a wolf grab a terrified ewe right behind the ears and drag it away into the shadows, not able to get a clean shot at it. By dawn, when Drover finally found a sparse patch of grass, with a little dew on it, letting the woollies graze for a while, we had lost an estimated twenty.

More asleep than awake, we had bread and coffee, rested for an hour, then drove on until midafternoon, when the sheep sniffed water ahead and broke into a wild stampede.

Drover yelled, "Let 'em run," but they would have done that anyway. They pounded the last mile to Green River under a cloud of dust, having gone twenty-four hours without water.

Looking around after we reached the banks, I saw that Mrs. Dessery had climbed down from the wagon and was leaning against it, dazed. Even Drover was out on his feet. We drank from the cold river, then washed up. Even though we were exhausted, Drover forced us to go another four miles upstream for good grass. There, we collapsed and slept about ten hours, only the dogs to guard the sheep.

# 13

Waking up well past dawn, I took my first long look at where we were. Green River sat in high bluffs with the snow-covered Rockies in the distance on one side; pine-patched mountains on the other. The cold salmon river sliced through the brown rock bluffs.

On the morning of the second resting-up day there, I noticed that Charlie Quarry was not up and around to start breakfast. After Fort Laramie, he had been allowed to eat with us, though he was not spoken to very often. But he had pulled his weight lately, so to speak, doing much of the cooking again; learning how to do things with his stump. He said it was not so painful when he touched something with it. Clem had made a leather sock to fit nicely over it.

Charlie had been sleeping on a bedroll beneath the big wagon. Always first up before we rolled, he had been trying to make up for past sins. I went over to him. Still on top his bedroll, he looked sick. "You all right?" I asked.

"Hot 'n' cold all night," he answered. "Got a fever. Bad headache. Sure felt bad yesterday, too."

As soon as I saw the girl up and around I asked her to take his temperature.

Hundred and one, she said.

Clem Epps came around. "You got a rash?" he asked Charlie.

Charlie nodded and pulled his shirt up. Red dots were all over his chest. "They started breakin' out on my hands yesterday."

Clem frowned. "I think Charlie has the Rocky Mountain ail. You better tell Drover."

"What's mountain ail?" I asked.

"Spotted fever, that's what it is. Tell Drover."

The girl dug out the medical book and we read this:

Rocky Mountain Fever, also known as Spotted Fever, usually begins with a red rash on the hands, wrists, and ankles, then spreads to the trunk of the body. Headaches, pains in the back and joints are common. High fever is usual. Delirium and coma can occur. Death may result. Delirium, the "typhoid" state, rigidity, and coma usually precede death. Severe cases last up to three weeks. When fatal, death occurs eight to seventeen days after onset. Treat with quinine, if possible. Reduce fever with cold baths and cloths.

Drover listened and then inspected Charlie Quarry. "He's got spotted fever, all right. Say your prayers, Hosses. . . ."

We walked away to have a conference, at which Clem said, "You get it from drinkin' snow water."

Drover, the old mountain man, disagreed. "D——t, Clem, no one knows where it comes from. I've drunk a lake full o' snow water an' have never had it."

The girl said, "I'll get some quinine for Charlie."

Drover advised, "Don't waste much on him 'cause he ain't worth it."

The girl said to him, with some sting, "Doctoring is equal, preacher or thief, is what my Daddy said."

Drover said back, "Now, you listen to me. It don't strike jus' one. It can take a whole train down. Last time I went through the Rockies I met up with trains that had a half dozen die. It's almost as bad as the cholera. It makes you so weak you can't stand up for days. If we lose Charlie Quarry, we haven't lost anything. Save the quinine."

"I have to take care of him," the girl insisted.

"Why, that jay popper tried to kill you," Drover shouted, within earshot of Charlie.

The girl stood her ground. "I know. He will still get quinine."

"I agree," said Mrs. Dessery, and that was that.

Drover glared at them both and said, "We're leavin' tomorry. If Charlie can't travel, I'll leave him here with you. I'm not holdin' up on his sorry account."

"He'll travel," the girl declared.

Salvador and Abber Doof had the sheep off grazing and Drover, snorting to himself, went out to check on them. I helped Clem work on the big wagon, which I much preferred to tending sheep.

Several times during the day I checked on Charlie, as did the girl. She gave him more quinine in late afternoon and the temperature stayed level, but the rash had spread all the way to his ankles. His breathing seemed harsher by sundown when the sheep came home.

After that march over Sublette's, none of us was up to snuff and there was not much said about anything, including spotted fever, that night at campfire. We were all a little scared of what was in that doctor book.

The next morning the girl went to Drover before breakfast to say that Mrs. Dessery now had those same rose-colored spots all over her wrists and forearms. Having had chills during the night, she said her legs and shoulder muscles were aching. We had an epidemic going, and the sheepwalk was stalled.

Drover asked, "Does that doctor book say anything about burnin' all the clothes an' blankets?"

The girl said it did not.

Having known Drover since the summer past, I had never seen him frightened of anything. He was now. G. B. Minzter was a fly to be swatted compared to the mountain ail.

About midmorning, Drover mounted Rinaldo and rode the four miles back to the ferry landing and settlement to find a doctor. He found one, a falling-down drunk, and rode back alone.

Charlie Quarry was much worse off than Mrs. Dessery. I have since learned that women are always tougher than men when it comes to anything but knifings and gun wounds. Charlie's fever was higher this day and I helped the girl, changing a damp cloth on the head of the man from Reunion every hour; making him drink water every so often. She tended to Mrs. Dessery.

Meanwhile, Salvador and Abber Doof had the sheep about two miles away. Whatever was happening to us humans, the animals could not have cared less. What they wanted was good feed and good water. Both were to be had at Green River.

Drover told me to keep helping and forget about the night watch, but I did not sleep very well near Charlie. He rasped all night long. Several times I got up to change his warm forehead rag, dipping it into the water bucket. I do not know how much he slept.

In the morning his eyes had a too bright cast to them and he did not look to be improving. He mumbled he would be "all right," but I had my doubts.

After breakfast the sheep were trailed off to graze, Drover and Salvador taking them while Doof stayed in camp to help out. He stuck his head into the red wagon three or four times to check on Mrs. Dessery, jabbering to her in that language they both knew.

Along about noon, Drover Pettit came walking slowly back to camp, weaving a little. He sprawled out inside his tent and the girl was soon giving him quinine. She now had three patients.

That evening there was another parley down by the river. The girl had said there was not enough quinine to go around. I told Salvador what was going on and we tried to make Abber Doof understand.

Clem ordered, "Don't give no more to Charlie!"

The girl looked over at me. I said, "I guess I agree," not believing that Charlie would live, anyway.

Quinine was given to Mrs. Dessery and Drover that night. None to Charlie Quarry. Next morning, he asked me about it, saying he needed some, and I lied, "It has run out, Charlie." This many years later, those words haunt me now and then.

The next five or six days go together in memory for me. They did not seem to end. I constantly went between

Drover's tent and Charlie while Salvador and Abber Doof took care of the woollies. Clem Epps did the cooking.

I said to him one night at campfire, "Suppose we get it? What happens if we five get it?"

"Be a lot o' dyin'. It's happened before."

We all had the same food, the same water. Why the fever took one of us and not the other could not be explained.

On the morning of the eighth day I knew Charlie Quarry was dying. His breath heated the palm of my hand, harsher than ever. He knew what was happening. As I bent over him he whispered, "I won't make it, Clay."

"Sure you will," I said, "drink a lot of water today."

From his cracked, parched lips came another whisper. "I want everyone to forgive me."

"We did that long ago, Charlie," I said. I had, at least.

Next day, Charlie went into deliriums and began calling out, "Rachel, Rachel . . ." over and over again. He had never mentioned her before. Wife, maybe. Girlfriend? He was naked under his blanket, and I kept him wet, pouring buckets of water over him. I sat by him in mud.

That day was one of the worst, I recall. Fever had drained Drover entirely and he crawled in and out of his tent only to meet nature's call. Once he passed out and I carried him back. Though Mrs. Dessery seemed to be improving steadily, the weakness had her in its grasp, too.

About two o'clock, the deliriums departed Charlie Quarry and as the book predicted, coma set in. About five he stopped breathing. I put my ear down to his heart and there was no beat. So I pulled the wet blanket up over his head, feeling ninety years old.

Clem said, "We did everythin' we could."

Clem knew that was not true. *The elephant had come to Green River.*

We buried luckless Charlie Quarry the next morning, a very pretty morning. White clouds drifted overhead and butterflies spiraled around. I doubt the dimpled man from Reunion had been in a church in twenty years, but that made no difference. Salvador, the only one of us beside Abber Doof who made much of religion, did the sign of the cross over Charlie and said some Catholic words to the sky.

Rocky Mountain spotted fever had one more of our sheepwalk to claim. Two nights after we buried Charlie, I woke up feeling warm around my ears. My shoulders ached. I did not even need to light a lantern and look for spots on my arms. I could feel them.

I lay there, getting hotter by the hour, thinking about the quinine that we did not have. I was sure this was Charlie's revenge for not sharing the medicine; for my lying about it. As daylight came on, I thought to myself, Clay B. Carmer, you are a goner for what you did.

My fever went up fast. After that first day it shot up. On the fourth day, I remember the girl sitting beside me and saying, "Your temperature is a hundred and three. You are cooking."

I was. I said to her, "I am a goner. Just let me be."

She said, "I won't hear of that. You are going to help me break this fever. You have to help me fight it."

I repeated, "I am a goner. Just let me be."

She said, "I love you, Clay Carmer, and I'm not going to let you go."

Burning up, I just wanted to die in peace. I managed to say, "Do not harass me with that love talk when I am on my deathbed. Just let them know in Sleeta."

It was then that I went into strange deliriums and I do not remember anything else until I woke up a day later with very bad rope burns under my armpits. To this day, I have the scars.

# PART III

# To Conquer a Texas Cowboy

Keep not your kisses for my dead, cold brow;
The way is lonely, let me feel them now. . . .

From *If I Should Die To-night,*
poem by Arabella Eugenia Smith
1845–1916

# 1

In the midmorning, I, Susan D. Carlisle, sat by Cowboy Clay Carmer changing the wet cloth on his curly head every half hour or so, saying encouraging things to him. Nearing the top of life's hill, he'd either crest it or he'd linger up there and fall back, like Charlie Quarry. His burning bright green eyes opened and closed turtle fashion. Now and then he'd look at me, almost in pure panic.

I said to him, "You pretty Texas boy, I can't let you die. *I will not let you die!* I love you more than anything on earth. I love you more than life itself."

Hearing that, he tried to get up from the bedroll under the big wagon, hit his head on the hounds, which connect the front axle to the rear axle, of course, and fell back, seeing stars, I imagine.

I said, "Save your strength, pretty Texas boy."

He just moaned.

Leaving him for a few minutes to climb up into the red wagon, I quickly covered *all* the fevers in the medical book. The cure was the same for each one, whether it was the breakbone fever or the Rocky Mountain kind: *Reduce the fever, then let the patient rest.*

I went back to beneath the big wagon and knelt down by him to announce, "Clay Carmer, you are going into that river and stay there until your fever is all gone. Do you hear me?"

His look was as blank as unrisen dough. So those words did not panic him further and that was all to the good.

For those who did not overland, the current in cold Green River was boiling swift, but the gravelly bottom was firm where we were camping and it didn't drop off for quite a few feet. So long as the Texan didn't thrash around on me and get away, he'd be fine. However, I still worried that he might plunge loose and go spinning down the river like a dead fish, ending up in Flaming Gorge.

I told Clem Epps of my fears. He knew what to do. He got a maul and rope out of the big wagon, then drove a stake deep into the bank, tying one end of the safety rope to it.

Thinking they might be interested, I told both Auntie Myrt and Drover what I was going to do, and Drover said, "I'd like to see that."

It was the same with Auntie Myrt, who was rapidly recovering. They were still weak, but she left the red wagon and he left his tent to come out and sit on the bank. Auntie Myrt made use of her red and white Bondurant parasol.

Next, Clem and I dragged the cowboy over the dirt to bank's edge. He mumbled all the way and the look of panic had come back into his feverish eyes, but he was too weak to resist.

Sitting there, a paler, thinner Drover asked, "Are you sure this is gonna help him? He looks poorly to me. This may kill him."

Auntie Myrt, always the wise one, commented, "Or it may cure Mr. Carmer."

That was pure Giddings Carlisle, M.D.

Clem frowned as I stripped my patient down. I said, "Why, I've seen plenty of privates before. His don't look any different to me."

Clem said, "They aren't, but I'm not sure Clay'd want *them* lookin' on." He thumbed back toward the audience.

"He'll never know," I said. "He'll weigh thirty pounds less with these clothes off, and remember, we have to heave him back in."

Clay Carmer's face and hands were sunburnt, I already knew, but I now noticed that the rest of him was as white as the inside of an apple. Nor did I know until this moment that his legs were a little bowed. Nothing too bad, but I had seen better knees.

After tying the line around him, we slid him out into the current, letting him play like a hooked salmon rippling out to midstream. He let out a big, long "Ahhhhhh," sucking in wind down to his vitals as his hot body went fully into that snow-fed stream.

Auntie Myrt yelled from the sidelines, "That is encouraging," and that it was.

Standing thigh-deep, I held firmly on to the rope and let the frigid water flow totally around him. After a few minutes I noticed he was beginning to breathe more regularly instead of with big gulps. Observing him closely, I could see that the red, tense look in his face was also beginning to slowly depart. His eyes were closed and he wasn't moving, but I was sure he was alive. Dr. Giddings Carlisle was again looking down on his daughter with great approval.

I maneuvered the rope, which was secured firmly under his armpits, so that his nose and mouth stayed a few inches above the water. He was washing on a line under his jaw and by his earlobes. It took a few minutes to develop the skill to keep him on even keel.

Drover said, in amazement, "In all my life, I have never seen a treatment like this."

Auntie Myrt likewise seemed impressed. "Neither have I."

Though shivering and shaking myself, I kept him in about ten minutes and then Clem Epps helped me haul him back up on the sunny bank, letting him rest awhile.

I bent over him and asked into a pearly ear, "Do you know what I'm doing?"

Those green eyes were rolled back in his dripping black curly Texas head, and he was shivering in the hot sun. His jaw was quaking and his teeth were knocking together, but he made no reply. He was, however, very much alive.

Holding his hand, I said forcefully, "True love will conquer all."

Still wobbly, Drover rose to his feet and came over. He looked down at the naked cowboy. "Well, he ain't dead at least."

"He is far from being dead," I said.

As long as he shook and shivered the way he was doing there was a lot of life left in him. I said, "Clay Carmer, twice more and we'll chase that fever of yours away forever."

Looking down too, Clem observed, "I think he'll quit the fever jus' so he don't have to go back in there. . . ."

There was something to that, too.

"Well, look here," said Clem, with a cackle. "His dingleberry has jus' about disappeared."

I looked and happily agreed. Shriveling was most always a welcome medical sign, according to Giddings Carlisle, M.D. O, the wonder of nature.

After the next time, he seemed to be able to focus his eyes when I said to him, tenderly, "My darling, we have the spotted fever on the run."

Mouth hanging open, he nodded weakly and I thought

that was another very good sign that we were beating the crisis.

Nonetheless, I dunked him in once more and took his temperature again. It was now ninety-nine. I said, "We have won," and his green eyes seemed to say, *Thank God.*

With that, Auntie Myrt and Drover Pettit went back to their bedrolls to rest and Clem and I dragged the cowboy back over to the big wagon, dressed him in dry johns, and settled him under the quilt.

As any good doctor will do, I stayed with him until he went to sleep. The only minor damage done to Clay Carmer by this treatment in the Green River were rope burns.

Later, I was told by a better-qualified physician that I had risked pneumonia. Well, you can't lick Rocky Mountain spotted fever with halfway measures. *Meeting emergencies was what life was all about.*

Over the next days, while Clay gathered his strength and mentally patched himself back together, I often sat by him under the big wagon—having wrapped the hounds in cloth so he wouldn't bump his head—and we talked of many things. I think he now recognized my worth. It was Clem who explained to him how the hemp burns got underneath his arms. Not me.

He talked a lot about cows. He told me that he thought people were going to start eating beef instead of pork and mutton and that the cattle business was going a lot further than hides and tallow. Clay was deeper than anyone thought. He said his ambition was to get a *ganado rancho* in southwest Texas and run a hundred thousand longhorns.

Looking him straight in the green eyes, I said that my ambition was to be a slinky Paris-type wife, about which Sweet Frenchy Moll had talked.

On one of those days, I said of him, to Auntie Myrt,

"That's the man I intend to marry once we get to Sacramento City and then we will live in Sleeta, Texas."

There was a considerable wait and then she said, with firmness, "Not so long as I'm your legal guardian."

"I'd like to know why not?"

"Because you're going back to Kanesville with me and go to that new college in Davenport that Judge Tuttle mentioned."

"Oh?" I said, alerted to a sudden change in her thinking; a taking charge of my life.

"You married Mr. Dessery when you were fifteen, didn't you?"

"I did."

"Wasn't it a good marriage?"

After another considerable wait, she said, "It could have been better."

Anything can always be better and I dropped the subject for the time being, knowing full well that true love always finds a way.

We stayed by the Green River another three days while my curly-headed patient recovered, then Drover got up on Rinaldo to say *"Adelante,"* and we trailed the sheep downriver to another price-gouging ferry. Run by a Frenchman, of course. He was alarmed when fierce-looking Abdou Diouf began speaking *parli Français* to him, telling him what a gouger he was. My Auntie Myrt put Abdou up to that.

We continued westering.

## 2

There are some people in this world who cannot resist continually scaring others with foreboding talk. Drover Bert Pettit, of Taos, was forever one. By now, he'd certainly warned us all of the infamous Humboldt Sink, Forty Mile Desert, and the elephant.

I said, "I'm well aware of what we face." I was also thankful we had only three hundred miles to go.

"You'll see," he said, in late July.

I said, "After all that has happened, I don't think you need to scare us further."

"I'll let it lie," he replied.

I thanked him for that.

We soon began going along the winding Humboldt in high heat, through crusty sand and parched sagebrush. Burnt mountains were on either side of the sluggish river. Heat was the enemy, searing down on us. We moved before dawn each day, camping in early afternoon by the river, wading out to cut salt grass for the livestock. The bottom was too mushy to let the animals wade in.

The calendar was now pressing us, though I tried to pay it no mind. We'd lost those three weeks by the Green River and certainly wouldn't arrive in Sacramento City before early September. One morning, as we plodded along in that furnace of Humboldt Valley, I asked Auntie Myrt, "What are our chances?"

"Slim," she said.

Even if we got a ship departing San Francisco by mid-September, hurried across the Isthmus of Panama, and were lucky enough to catch a boat right away for New

Orleans, then go straight on to St. Louis and Kanesville, the chances of standing before Judge Tuttle, money in hand, by November 2, were now less than slim.

Auntie Myrt added, "In truth, I hope that somebody has already shot, or will shoot, Mr. Minzter." That, of course, would be the ideal solution. But people that you most want shot always seem to go free.

And I was also learning that *hope* is a very dangerous word. I'd *hoped* that we'd be safely back in the Big Muddy in mid-October.

My auntie went on, "I should have asked for an extension until December first."

*Should have* are also trap words, I was learning. *My Daddy should have never borrowed money from G. B. Minzter; Farmer Kinchlow's dam should have stayed in one piece.* Not thinking it through, I said, "We can send a letter from Sacramento City."

"We *should have* sent it from South Pass."

It was very depressing to think that we'd gone through all this pain and strain just to be defeated by the calendar. Yet there was no way to travel faster. The mules were already weak from heat, as were the slogging sheep. They looked at us each day with accusing eyes as we trailed along the desolate valley floor.

There wasn't a single good thing about the Humboldt. White-hot heat all day, mosquitoes all night. Trying to feed on scrub willows, the mules whinnied dusk to dawn from insect bites and in the morning we could see blood streaming from their sides. Wool protected the sheep, but they dodged their heads all sleepless night to shake off swarms that were thick enough to snuff out candles. We humans suffered under buttoned raincoats, blankets over our faces. Better to sweat than slap.

Even before we reached the Sink, stretches of burning sand began to tell a tragic story. Wagons had been abandoned and stench came up from both sides of the trail. Carcasses of mules, oxen, and horses were roosting places. Staring at us with red eyes, buzzards went back to picking at rotting remains, not even bothering to flap up as we went by. Mixed in with the decaying livestock were human graves.

During late afternoon, August 8, we cut the last available saw grass and stuffed it into the wagons to provide mule feed for the Forty Mile Desert drive. And then, on the purple evening of August 9, we stood fearfully at the edge of the Sink, at a point where the river, after shallow pooling, simply disappeared into muck and sand. It was like that river had started down to the center of the earth. Far into the distance were blue humps of the Sierras.

Nodding in that direction, Drover said, "Ten mile beyond here is a sloo. Water was in it last year but mebbe we won't be so lucky this year. We'll make that in the mornin' then drive on in the afternoon an' through the night. Twenty mile beyond the sloo is a hot spring. . . ."

Salvador Baca spoke up and Drover answered him in Spanish. I asked Clay Carmer what'd they said. "We'll lose mules. Already, three can't make it."

Three did look like they were on last legs. Their ribs were carved. When they weren't pulling, they stayed in one spot, heads down. Strength sapped. They did not want to live. I kept my eyes away from them.

"God help the weak," murmured Auntie Myrt, staring out across the baked waste of Forty Mile Desert.

Then Clay Carmer walked ahead of us along the north edge of the Sink. Winter runoff water had long ago dried in the fierce sun. He came back to say, "That is pure powder out there now. I sank down to my knees."

"Hope the wind doesn't come up," said the drover.

We left an hour before sunrise, moving into the white alkali fields. Fine ashes drifted up in the shallow darkness, hooves stirring up the dust. It floated ten or twelve feet up and fell slowly back.

Before we'd gone a mile the fine powder was choking us. Sheep baaed in the stillness. Mules whinnied and coughed. Only the goats and tough dogs were totally silent.

We made no more than a mile an hour.

Clay Carmer crossed through the sheep to say to me, "Suck on this bullet. It'll stop thirst."

As the sun came up, blinding as it spanked off the alkali fields, I didn't know which was worst—the lead taste or the thirst.

By midmorning, one mule had dropped. Salvador and the other men pulled it out of the traces and got it to the side of the road for buzzards to feast on.

Around noon, another mule dropped and Drover put Rinaldo with the team to keep the green schooner moving.

Ahead of us, desert shimmered and floated. Mirages, which I'd never seen before, brought green mountains a tantalizing half-mile away. Then a lake glistened invitingly before us and white dust devils, swirling tubes of alkali, danced across the sands. Alkali in my hair and up my nose, thickly coated on my lips, I went along mechanically, hoping we'd soon stop.

Hidden under the roof of her bonnet, Auntie Myrt rocked silently back and forth on the seat of the red wagon as the mules struggled on. Clay Carmer walked beside them, popping a long whip, yelling at them hoarsely.

About two o'clock, we reached the slough and the animals finally got a little moisture after ten miles of baking. Humans crawled into the shade of the wagons. We sat under there in the hot sand; puffing, eyes bloodshot, lips bleeding, saying nothing to each other.

But the dried lake was behind us, as were twenty or so dead sheep, and two mules. Another keeled over and died in its tracks two hours later. After it was dragged to the side, Drover came over to squat by the red wagon. "We'll leave the big one here, an' go on with jus' your wagon."

By now, there wasn't much in the big one and we'd have extra mules to get us across the Forty Mile.

Nearing five P.M., after we'd emptied the battered, faded green Caster-built; after we'd filled every keg and canteen with alkaline water; after we'd fed the mules with some salt grass, Drover forced us back on the trail. To stay another day at the slough was to lose more stock. It was so hot that just to touch any part of the wagon was to get a burn.

That night of walking never seemed to end. Sounds were the muffled pad of hooves, creak of the red wagon, and wheezes of breath. Sheep were no longer even baaing.

No one talked.

Finally, to our backs the horizon became yellow and gray, then red, and the sun edged up just as we reached the hot springs, on the side of a low, rocky ridge. Boiling water spouted up ten or fifteen feet from fissures, then flowed into a small steaming pool.

The sheep ran for it, but the first few there screamed in agony as they took mouthfuls. The water was scalding.

Drover yelled for everyone to dig holes.

For the next hour, we hacked deep into the clay and sand, then poured buckets of water in for cooling, so the animals could drink.

If ever there was a big piece of bona fide hell, it exists

here on earth near those hot springs of Forty Mile Desert. Not a blade of grass. Not a cloud in the light blue sky. Only lizards scurrying around and rattlers hiding in scant shade. Yes, it was elephant land.

How Mrs. Myrtle Dessery survived at her age, I'll never know. The sand got worse after we left the boiling springs.

It stayed bad until Drover shouted, "Truckee ahead!"

We could see a line of tall cottonwoods on the horizon and the sheep broke into a weak trot to stagger on to that beautiful cold river. Thanking the Lord, we picked up a little speed ourselves and finally spread-eagled into the rushing water. Even Auntie Myrt climbed down and dunked herself, bonnet and all.

The grass was green and sweet far back from the river and we stayed by it three days to rest. The Truckee twists and turns through high-walled canyons, but there was coolness and fresh water. Even when the rocky turns were so tight that we had to unhitch the mules and skid the red wagon through sideways, it was heaven compared to alkali drifts. The sheep walked the Truckee with ease, crossing and recrossing the shallows.

At last, driving up a steep trail, we mounted the Sierras, finally going through a pass near what Drover called Donner Lake. Eventually, there was a crude sign in the pass that said CALIFORNIA, but I was too tired to even hallelujah.

Going over the steep, slippery west slope, over rocks as big as a house, we had to lead the mules and sheep down a narrow side path and then snub the wagon with a rope wrapped around a fir to keep it from crashing loose. Cordelle it. The brakes wouldn't have held.

It was here, in a green eagle's-nest snow-peak setting, on a sunny Tuesday afternoon, that the elephant was seen for the last time. Indian Myrt, Salvador Baca, and myself had taken the sheep down and then Salvador went back up to lead the mules down.

Drover, Abdou Diouf, Clay Carmer, and Clem Epps were cordelling the wagon over the rock face just about the time we arrived. Salvador went over to help them, but I thought it best to stay out of the way. I'd seen wagons cordelled on Missouri bluffs and it was not a job for females, I'll truthfully admit.

Not twenty seconds after we'd arrived on the scene, the rope broke with a loud pop and spray of hemp strands. The red wagon crashed on down and there was a muffled scream. I ran to the bottom of the rock face and saw that the wagon had lodged up against a tree but in its path was a body, and I knew who it was without a second glance. Clem Epps.

Then the elephant went away.

# 3

Mr. Tapps, a somber man in a round-top hat, long black coat, and black tie, a buyer for Simpson's Wholesale Provisioners, said, "They ain't in very good shape."

"Two weeks on this grass, an' they'll fatten right out, an' you know it," Drover replied.

We were camped at Elk Grove this September morn, twelve miles out of Sacramento City, having trailed along the American River after coming safely down out of the Sierras.

"Any worms?" asked Tapps.

"Not a one," said Drover proudly.

"Prices dropped way down since you were here last," said Tapps, weaseling us.

"How far down?"

"Oh, I gave eight dollars a head last week but these beaten-up sheep ain't worth seven."

My heart dropped.

"These are fine sheep, an' you know it," protested Drover.

"Gold boom is long over," said the somber sheep buyer. "You're too late. You got the peak last year."

I finally spoke up, addressing Drover. "Maybe we can find another buyer?"

Drover gave me a bleak look and they walked on, circling in and out of the band. I was trying to count in my head— eight times 2,400, the sheep that had survived, was $19,200. After the drover took his cut, on a losing proposition at that, I'd be lucky to end up with $4,000.

I walked away from them and on back to the campfire. I said to Indian Myrt, who was seated there with Clay Carmer, "The price is way down."

"How far?"

"Less than eight dollars a head."

Even if we hadn't lost more than two hundred on the trail, plus twenty that we'd butchered, I still couldn't have made the fifteen thousand plus interest to pay off Minzter.

Indian Myrt saw how crestfallen I was. "You tried hard, Susan."

Yes, I had done that, but the rainbow I'd walked up so nobly had turned out to be a bridge of mud.

Soon, I was summoned back to fireside. Drover had returned, minus the Simpson company buyer. He said to us, "We're gettin' ten a head."

That was a pleasant surprise and my spirits soared up again.

"There's six thousand in wool on those backs, I told

Tapps." He looked from me to Indian Myrt. "You'll not get a better deal."

I asked, "Did you tell him yes?"

Drover nodded. "There's some sheep comin' up the San Joaquin in a few days. If they're better'n what we got, the price will drop another dollar or so." Then he squatted down and did some figures in the dirt. Finally, he lifted his head to say to me, "Hoss, your share is eight thousand seven hundred and thirty, an' I'm bein' kind."

"That you are," said Indian Myrt, no slouch with figures herself.

What could I say? It wasn't his fault that gold miners didn't need as much meat as in '51. With the boom over, up to ten thousand greenhorns had already gone home, pockets empty.

Drover added, "I know that leaves you short to pay off Minzter but I've got my own expenses. . . ." He had to pay off Abdou Diouf and Salvador Baca, and finance the trip back to Taos as well as earn some profit.

I was no charity case, as yet. I also said, in language Drover could understand, "I have that ace in the hole. Uncle Roblett Chauncey Darden." Though he'd never written to me, I was certain he was still in Sacramento City.

Indian Myrt looked over at me. "You know, I have been sitting here thinking about him."

Well, I'd been thinking of Uncle Roblett, off and on, ever since we'd lost those three weeks at Green River. A loan, not charity, was what I needed. In memory of his late sister, Uncle Roblett should give me every consideration. Furthermore, I was prepared to put up my house as collateral for that loan of about $12,000 cash. If I lost the house,

he'd get his money back with interest. How could he re-
fuse?

"The sooner we see him, the better," I said. It was then
about nine o'clock, as I remember. Now that the sheep
were sold, I was figuring we should be on the steamboat to
Panama within three days. All we needed to do was take a
long tub bath, buy some new clothes, and head south.

Indian Myrt agreed and I turned to Drover to ask,
"Where is that J Street?"

He explained that First, Second, and so forth ran parallel
to the river levee, and alphabet streets like J, K, L went
crossways. "J Street is the biggest one, 'bout a mile long.
You'll find it easy."

"We'll just go from one end to the other and ask people
for Hudnut & Darden's," said Indian Myrt.

As we were walking toward the wagon to spruce up, I
said to her, "Maybe we should go to a clothes store first. I
surely don't want my Uncle Roblett to see me like this." I
was clad in little more than tatters.

"I think you'll be better off if he sees you this way, fresh
from the trail, worn out. All gussied up, he won't really
believe you need the money."

That was something to consider, though I'd long set my
mind on him seeing me spicy and pretty as could be. "Do it
later," she strongly advised. "I'll wager he's seen a lot like
you just off the trail."

So we washed up, fixed our hair a little, and hitched up
two of the mules to the empty wagon, and then we were off
to Sacramento City. I must say that the flat wide road from
Elk Grove was the best I'd ever seen. And on it that day
was considerable traffic headed for the mines. Light-spring
open wagons with four or five seats across; now and then a
six-horse stagecoach, jammed with miners. Destination

signs were on them: HANGTOWN, CHICKEN THIEF FLAT, MOKELUMNE HILL, CHINESE CAMP, ANGELS CAMP. We waved, of course, but they paid little attention to us. Women in the goldfields were no longer a novelty.

Just after we jangled past Sutter's Fort, by now a ruined place inhabited by bats and moles, weeds growing in the courtyard, flagpole toppled over, poor Sutter having departed to a farm after the gold seekers had plundered his property, Sacramento City came into view impressively.

The high levee ran all along the river, with steamboats and tall-masted sailing ships tied to it, and the wide streets were chockablock with wooden buildings and houses, painted white and trimmed in green. There were also a few blocks of brick buildings. People thronged. St. Joe was the biggest city I'd ever visited and Sacramento City was fifty times as big.

Though tempted, we went past the Alpha Bath House (warm and cold shower baths), and turned into J Street, deciding to proceed on foot. We hitched the mules in front of another bathhouse, BIGELOW'S—WARM SHOWERS FOR LADIES AND GENTLEMEN—where a man was hanging up a sign and I asked if he knew where Hudnut & Darden's General Store was.

"Hudnut's is two blocks up the street. Don't know that there is a Hudnut and Darden here. Who is Darden?"

Well, that was odd. I thanked him and along we went, walking by buggies, horses, and carts. The sidewalk was laden with people of all descriptions and strange national flavors. I think I saw some Kanakas from the Sandwich Islands, later to be known as Hawaiians, and some Malays.

Then suddenly, over a one-story-wide building, was a sign, HUDNUT'S—THE UP TO DATE GENERAL STORE. Smaller signs directly over the wide doors said, TEAS & COF-

FEES OF SUPERIOR EXCELLENCE—EXTRACTS, HONEY, DRIED
FRUITS—HARDWARES OF ALL DESCRIPTIONS—TOOLS AND
NAILS AND SHEET TIN.

Nowhere appeared the distinguished name of Roblett
Chauncey Darden. Perhaps he had sold his interest in that
store to open an even larger one. So, up the two steps we
went to inquire inside for the whereabouts of my Uncle
Roblett. Perhaps he was a silent partner.

I asked a stockboy, "Is the proprietor in?"

He pointed toward an aproned man with a bountiful
belly, wearing wide suspenders and a bow tie. His cheeks
were apple full and he looked jolly. Going up to him, I said,
"I am Susan Darden Carlisle, and this is my guardian, Mrs.
Myrtle Dessery. We're from Kanesville, Iowa."

"Good morning, ladies," he said affably. "Iowa is a long
way away. What can I do for you?"

"I'm seeking my uncle Roblett Chauncey Darden," I
said. "I was told he was your partner in this store."

Mr. Hudnut's face changed from bright day to darkest
night. "Who told you that?"

"He wrote that to my late mother."

"Liar," shouted Mr. Hudnut, "even if he is your uncle.
He is a scoundrel! He clerked for me here two years ago
and stole more than he sold."

I was stunned, completely taken aback. The mental picture of my Uncle Roblett that I had long treasured turned
to rotten dirt. I hardly knew what to say. Finally, it was
Indian Myrt who found her calming voice. She said, "Perhaps it is the wrong Roblett Chauncey Darden to which
you are referring."

"Chauncey is it?" rasped Mr. Hudnut, with full depreca-
tion. "I hope there is only one miserable Roblett Chauncey
Darden in this entire world and you'll find him down at

Hardin's Exchange, near the levee. Good day, ladies." Mr. Hudnut's face was florid from the exertion of thinking about my uncle.

My knees felt perilously weak as we left Hudnut's General Store. My face was milky white, I'm sure. Nothing worse can happen to you than be told a revered kin is just a common thief.

"Susan, have faith," said Indian Myrt, though I knew her own had been shaken down to her shoe snaps.

We retraced our steps toward the levee and saw a sign that said THE ELEPHANT HOUSE, SACRAMENTO CITY'S MOST FAMOUS HOTEL. It sat on the levee and looked rather tawdry. Near it, however, was another sign, HARDIN'S EXCHANGE. And if our spirits were down while talking to Mr. Hudnut, the bottom of the earth plunged to infinity when we recognized what Hardin's really was—a bustling, noisy high-class gambling hall.

We stood outside a moment, and then approached closer. Through the wide-open doorway we could see a huge bar, and rich pictures not unlike the one in Frenchy Moll's. Piles of refreshments were to be seen, and a brass band was playing loudly. All sorts of gambling was going on in that splendidly decorated hall, from three-card monte and roulette and faro to thimble rigging. The place was already full of greedy gamblers, though it wasn't much past noon. Such was the depravity that boys of no more than twelve were trying their luck. The only women we could see in there were plainly "keepouses." They were courting around bearded men who carried pokes of gold dust. I whispered, "I can't believe my mother's brother works here."

Just then a fairly respectable-looking man was departing Hardin's and coming by us, so I addressed him. "Sir, being ladies, we do not wish to go in there but we are seeking a

man named Roblett Chauncey Darden and would appreciate it very much if you'd point him out for us."

"My pleasure," he said, tipping his derby hat. He had a
diamond stickpin in his cravat.

He went back, and we watched as he made inquiry at the
bar. We saw the bartender point toward a man who was
standing at the *thimble rigging* table. This man was in his
thirties, I estimated, and did indeed look spicy. Yes, he was
handsome, had a mustache, and undoubtedly was of great
interest to the "keepouses." We saw one deliver a big kiss
to his cheek, since it was a slack time at his table.

I exchanged a look with Indian Myrt. Disgust was on her
face. Just then the gentleman came back to say, "That man
is Roblett Chauncey Darden. May I be of further service?"

"Thank you, no," I said, and he tipped his hat and went
on his way.

We stood for a little while and watched my uncle. There
wasn't a worse or more crooked game anywhere than thimblerig, played with a pea under shells of one sort or another.
You guessed which shell the pea was under and you seldom
won. Thimblerig was always the sharper's favorite swindle
on riverboats and here I was, witnessing my only uncle
engaged in that practice. This was a sad moment and thank
goodness my late mother wasn't here to see her brother.

Later I was told that Hardin's was tame compared to
earlier gambling halls such as Round Tent, where "un-
masked depravity" occurred, and The Stinking Tent,
named for its roof, a smelly sail from a whaling ship. Well,
Hardin's appeared to be wilder than the Ocean Wave, of
Kanesville.

Leave soundly sleeping stones lie untouched was again
my motto, even if it meant losing my house. I said to Indian Myrt, "Shall we go?" and off we went, knowing it

would be a long time before I could wash the ne'er-do-well Roblett Chauncey Darden out of my mind. I had not the slightest desire to even talk to him.

We walked a ways, past interesting stores and shops, still stunned, and then Indian Myrt wisely said, "Let's go have a soda and relax."

That was Mrs. Myrtle Dessery at her very best. We went to a nice hotel, sat in the lobby restaurant and had two glasses each of Daniel's Mint-Flavored Soda, and felt much the better for it. Then we walked around a while longer, just to see the great city, going along the levee now, and soon passed another gambling house. It was an open shed, built partially on cinders. Stacks of burnt lumber were nearby and the smell of crisped wood was in the air. Obviously, it had burnt down the past week and here it was, defying defeat, already in business again. Fires and floods were part of Sacramento City, it seemed.

A shill with an eastern voice, raspy and caustic as always, yelled to us passersby: "Win your fortune here. Quadruple your money . . . free food . . . free beer . . ." His raspy voice hung in the air, and Indian Myrt, frustrated as I, said offhandedly, "Oh, how I wish I could expertly gamble."

We both stopped and stared at each other. As much as I hated gambling, loathed gambling, despised gambling, I found myself saying, "Drover knows how." Cowboy Clay Carmer and the late Clem Epps were monuments to Drover's expertise.

Mrs. Dessery glanced at me, thunderstruck as well by the offhanded thought. "You said that he lost on the *Pyle* . . ."

"He did that time. But Clem Epps told me he doesn't often lose."

We stayed dead-still on that sidewalk by the levee for a
few minutes, looking square at each other, this out-of-the-
blue conversation so spontaneous as to be a miracle.

"If he could just triple it, not even quadruple it," I ventured.

"If he loses, we're not much worse off than now," she
said, thinking it through. If we went back to Kanesville
now with only five thousand and some, the house would be
lost anyway. *There was a possibility, a slim possibility* . . .

The trip back to Elk Grove, with twilight descending,
was more or less silent. We didn't even notice Sutter's Fort
as we jangled by.

# 4

Everyone was around the campfire.

I said to all of them, "I must be truthful, gentlemen,
even though it hurts. My uncle Roblett is a sharper, and I
was told he's also a common thief. He was never a partner
with Clarence J. Hudnut, just a clerk. So he is a liar. Now
he is a thimblerigger at Hardin's Exchange."

Indian Myrt said helpfully, "I've never known a family
that didn't have some black sheep."

"Everyone can't own a store an' be rich," said Drover,
who was also being helpful.

"I've known a few good-hearted sharpers," added Cowboy Clay Carmer.

"He may not even be a sharper," added Drover.

All of that might or might not be true, but I had to
change the subject. There was not much time to waste.
Looking Drover eye to eye, I said, "Would you please take
five thousand of my sheep money and try to triple it?"

Bert Pettit's bushy eyebrows went up. "Hey an' hoot, you said gamblin' was evil."

"I've changed my mind."

Indian Myrt chimed in, "It was my idea, Mr. Pettit."

He shook his head. "Too risky. I could lose all of it."

"I won't hold you responsible," I said. "It's the only way I know to save my house."

"Do it for her," urged Clay Carmer, and I looked at him with gratitude.

"I haven't had my fingers on cards in four months," Drover said. "I am rusty."

"Sometimes that is better. Luck will run your way," said the cowboy from Ysleta.

Drover scanned around, feeling the pressure. We were now a "family," one for all, all for one.

"Please," I said.

He sighed. "All right, Hoss, I'll try, but I want a paper signed sayin' I ain't responsible if I lose every dime." His blue eyes riveted on Indian Myrt and myself. "You both sign it, an' I don't want no female tears if I lose, which I can easily do."

"We'll sign it, and I promise no tears," I said.

"Another thing," he said, "I don't want the two of you lookin' over my shoulder in 'Frisco. I'll take the five thousand an' tell you when an' where to meet me, winner or loser."

"What do you mean?" I asked, having a chilling second thought. He could abscond.

"I just said it. I don't want you two followin' me aroun' to poker tables, checkin' up on me. Hoss, you did that on the riverboat an' I didn't appreciate it at all."

"All right, we'll abide exactly by your rules," I said, with misgiving. I trusted Drover ninety-seven percent, but there was always that loose three to cause worry.

The next morning, the buyer from Simpson's Wholesale appeared on schedule with cloth bags of gold eagles and counted out our money, a total of $24,000, bringing along his own Kanaka herders, two dogs, and a single Toggenburg goat that Hector and Cholula viewed with great suspicion.

Soon, bearing up under a touch of sadness, I saw my sheep go trekking up the road to Sacramento City, bells ringing for the last time. I had gotten to know those noble animals pretty well over more than a year's time and now their final fate was the slaughterhouse. I did not wish to dwell upon that.

It was a sad morning in other ways. I said my gratitudes and good-byes to Abdou Diouf and Salvador Baca, two of the finest overland trail companions that any Iowa girl could ever have. They got misty-eyed and so did I. Then I said good-bye to the dogs, goats, and even the surviving mules. We'd gone through a lot together.

Finally, Clay Carmer brought the faded red wagon up for the ride to Sacramento City. I sat on the seat beside him for the twelve-mile ride into town, and we talked of many things. Drover and Indian Myrt sat in the back, discussing how the country would change when the railroad came through.

We had to wait awhile for the river steamer *Senator* to load for the trip to San Francisco and I walked slowly along the levee top with Clay Carmer. At one point, I swung around in front of him to say, "Though we have a few years difference, I am deeply in love with you, and will be forever. I want you to think about that in the coming months. Now, before we part I want you to kiss me square on the lips."

He did so, and it felt very good. I'd never had a better kiss in my life.

After that, I took our few remaining possessions out of the red wagon with WALKING UP A RAINBOW barely visible on its side, bidding it a fond farewell. No vehicle had ever been more faithful over creek and mountain, plain, bog, and alkali desert, than that Caster-built. Drover would sell it for what he could get.

I had one last minute with Clay Carmer, asking him to kiss me again because the first time felt so good, and then the *Senator* blew its departure whistle. We soon followed Drover Pettit aboard for the six-hour trip to 'Frisco. I stood on the stern waving good-bye and blowing kisses to Cowboy Clay Carmer as he stood on the levee. Clay was headed back for New Mexico with Drover, then on to Texas. I soon joined Indian Myrt and Bert Pettit in passenger seating. Drover was already dozing, my bag of gold eagles between his thighs. He looked scruffier than the first time I laid eyes on him, that disgraceful beaver hat and animal-skin coat having had two thousand more miles of wear and tear on them.

## 5

Before a nodding Drover went off to sleep sitting up, I asked if he could recommend a nice safe clean hotel for us in San Francisco. Why not try Mother McAdoo's, his boardinghouse of the previous stay. Visiting sheep and cattlemen often lodged there. Well, I'd had my fill of sheep talk lately.

So, as we steamed downriver in the 750-ton wooden side-wheeler, I began a lookout for someone who might have knowledge about suitable hostelries. Finally, I saw a portly man in a frock coat and tall silk hat. Approaching him, I said, "Sir, I'd appreciate it very much if you could recommend a safe hotel for us," nodding toward the yawning Mrs. Dessery.

He stood up and bowed, intoning with a slight Irish brogue, "May I say it's a pleasure to serve you. My name is William X. Fitzgerald. I'd recommend the Wentworth House, on the Clay Street side of Portsmouth Square."

Five hours later, as the *Senator* paced across the sparkling bay, I found myself almost speechless, something that did not occur very often in my early teens. On the skyline in either direction was the gold rush city, four or five stories high. Drover had awakened, as had Indian Myrt, and the latter shared my openmouthed awe.

Tall masts of once proud ships were everywhere. "That's Clark's Point," said Drover. "Them windjammers been rottin' there three years now. Captains an' crew jus' jumped ship to go diggin' an' never came back." There must have been three hundred, forlornly strapped together. Some were burnt to the waterline.

The *Senator* soon docked at the foot of Pacific Street and we filed off into foot traffic of miners, Sydney Ducks, jolly tars, harlots, bucko mates, gamblers—lowest riffraff of the entire world. Eighteen-passenger omnibuses careened along; rattling drays, handcarts, delivery wagons. Horsemen picked their way up the muddy street on which a streetcar line was being built. From auction houses and saloons came brass-band music. Boys no older than ten, puffing cigars, darted around, hawking wares. Screech and din was high.

About then we saw a huge machine, spewing fire, smoke, and steam. Drover said, "That's the famous Pacific Vaporific, a steam paddy, eating the hillsides for landfill." He added that land was needed because the city had grown from three hundred to thirty thousand or more in three years.

*Pacific Vaporific.* I made mental note of that. The Missouri bluffs could use one of those.

As we went toward the hotel we passed a pony having its right forehoof polished at a bootblack stand. The waiting owner was engrossed reading a newspaper, long, stringy hair tied beneath his chin so that his face was in a brown wreath. The pony seemed aloof. No one was paying much attention to that memorable scene and Indian Myrt murmured, "There is stark insanity in this town." I couldn't help but agree.

Plastered all over the streets were big placards advertising the weekly bull-and-bear fight. Vaguely, I remembered Drover telling me about that ridiculous event. Imagine anyone attending!

At the door of the Wentworth House, Drover instructed, "Meet me outside the El Dorado tomorry night at ten."

"That's where you'll gamble?" I asked.

"Don't know. May try 'em all. Parker House, Bella Union, Verandah, Aguila de Oro . . ."

I was suddenly uneasy. "I do hope you'll remember that it is *my* money you're gambling with."

He replied, "Hoss, I'll treat it as my own," which made me even uneasier. Then he went on to that sheepman's boardinghouse on Bush with five thousand dollars of mine.

I did not know how to take his last remark and said to Indian Myrt, "I'm tempted to follow him."

She said, "Either you trust him or you don't. Which is it?"

Despite his gallantry after Independence Rock, I had trouble answering that, and we forthwith entered the

Wentworth House, presenting Mr. Fitzgerald's card and acquiring a nice room on the third floor. Still worried, no sooner had I put down my valise when I said, "I wish we were staying at Mother McAdoo's so we could keep track of him."

Indian Myrt advised, "What is done is done."

Such advice is not always easy to accept, but there were other pressing matters. As soon as we took hot baths and changed chemises, we went along to the Pacific Mail Steamship Company, about six blocks away. In line in front of us was a well-dressed middle-aged man who was receiving a lot of attention. The clerk fawned over him. When he'd finished his business, he stepped aside, smiled cordially at us, and departed.

"Know who that was?" asked the clerk, slyly.

We admitted we hadn't the slightest.

"Henry Gladly. Mr. Henry Gladly. He's famous here. We had an awful problem with rats and mice. They came in on ships from everywhere. We had brown rats from Persia; white, pink-eyed rats from Batavia; vicious black rats from New York and Boston; blue rats from Chile. Then Mr. Gladly solved it by trapping two thousand cats in New Orleans. He brought them here in cages, hundred to a cage." Turning half sinister, the clerk laughed. "Now we have the fattest cats in the world."

I looked at Indian Myrt and she at me. We did not join in the sinister laughter. Pink-eyed rats from Batavia; blue rats from Chile? There was indeed something very queer about this city, and we quickly bought two tickets to Panama, booking passage three days hence on the *SS Oregon,* a Smith & Dimon side-wheeler.

The desk at the Wentworth House had sent us to Madam Ressac's to acquire new wardrobes, and I was immediately bedazzled by what was in that store. Never had I seen such finery, and it was lucky that Indian Myrt spoke such fluent French. That language was soon flying all over the shop. So we had an "in."

Unfortunately, the Madam's prices were too high and we finally outfitted for the voyage home at Mrs. Cole's Millinery.

It was then very close to five o'clock and I said to Indian Myrt, thinking about the night ahead, "I'd like to go over to Mother McAdoo's and wish the Drover good luck on his gambling. Bush Street is down that way four or five blocks."

"Why didn't you wish him good luck outside the hotel? You made a pact not to follow him."

Pacts are made to be broken. "I had other things on my mind," I said. Such as money.

"He'll think you're checking up on him," she warned.

So be it. That was exactly right. "I can't help what he thinks."

Bush Street turned out to be almost as scruffy as I imagined Sydney Town would be, and two inquiries took us to a three-story narrow blue-and-white-trimmed wooden house from which hung a sign MRS. MORDECAI MCADOO, ROOM AND BOARD. Up the steps we went, and pulled the bell cord. With the opening of the door, corned beef and cabbage and potato smells rushed out and before us was a barefooted woman who weighed at least three hundred pounds.

Wearing what is known as a muslin "wrapper," she was the biggest "Mother" I had ever seen. She shouted, "I have stopped taking female boarders. Forever!"

I said, calmly, "We don't need rooms, Mrs. McAdoo.

We are looking for Mr. Bert Pettit, of Touse, New Mexico. He's a sheep drover—"

"Well, he isn't here," she yelled, and slammed the door.

We stayed a baffled moment, then began retreating down the steps as the door opened again. It was Mother McAdoo. "He came here three hours ago but I wouldn't let him in. Last year he had a fight in my parlor over a poker game. Broke a table, two chairs, and my umbrella stand."

I wasn't much concerned about the fight. "Did he win that poker game?"

"No, he didn't. He seldom does."

Lordy, I thought. He was a loser, after all. Could it be that Clem Epps and Clay Carmer were just bad players? "Where is he now?"

"I have no idea," yelled Mother McAdoo. "I hope he goes to Miss Puckett's and gets shanghaied. He always has a few before he gambles." The door slammed again.

"What does that mean?" I asked Indian Myrt.

"Don't know. Shanghai is in China, I'm positive."

We went straight back to the Wentworth House and luck was with us. Standing in the small but clean lobby was Wm. X. Fitzgerald, engaged in conversation with a tall, distinguished gentleman who looked as if he should have been wearing an officer's uniform. He was slim, ramrod straight, and had a crisp white mustache and modified muttonchop sideburns. I went up to them and addressed Mr. Fitzgerald, begging his pardon for the intrusion. "We're the ladies from the *Senator,* the ones you directed to this fine hotel," I said. "We need your help again."

He bowed, as usual, saying, "May I introduce Colonel J. W. Wentworth, the proprietor, formerly of the First New York Volunteers, and second cousin to President Millard Fillmore."

Colonel Wentworth bowed, too.

I was impressed and had guessed right. The only thing missing about the President's second cousin was a dashing uniform.

"Now, how can we be of service?" asked the politician.

Quickly, I told them some of the story about our reason for being in San Francisco, and the apparent disappearance of Drover Pettit. I said, "Mrs. McAdoo mentioned something about 'Miss Puckett' and being 'shanghaied.' Could you gentlemen explain that to us?"

They looked at each other in some alarm and Colonel Wentworth said, "Well it is not a pleasant thing to tell ladies from Iowa, but in this city certain individuals operate to supply crew members to ships, whether or not that person wants to be a crew member, five dollars per live body. Miss Puckett is one such individual, a depraved and toothless woman who runs a saloon. There are others such as big Mrs. Bronson, who runs a boardinghouse on Stewart Street; Shanghai Kelly; and six or seven more. Miss Puckett's place is on Davis Street."

"Should we go there to look for him?" I asked.

"I'd say not," said Wm. X. Fitzgerald. "Even though not a strand of your golden hairs would be harmed, I myself would be afraid to go there without six or seven strong men."

"What happens at Miss Puckett's?"

Colonel Wentworth told us. "It grieves me to say it. Men are lured to these places by loose women. They are then drugged with rotgut laced with opium and dropped through a hole in the floor, waking up at sea. These terrible ships often go as far as Shanghai, China, and that is why the practice is known as 'shanghaiing.' Mother Bronson just hits them over the head with a horseshoe wrapped in a stocking, but Miss Puckett uses knockout drops. Then down through the trapdoor. They prey on strangers such as Mr. Pettit."

Now that I'd heard how this worked, I doubted very much that Drover Pettit would fall prey unless he was drugged. I had no idea whether or not a loose woman could entice him. Oh, how I wished we'd brought Cowboy Clay Carmer along.

"How much money did you say Mr. Pettit was carrying?" asked Mr. Fitzgerald.

"Five thousand dollars of mine and I don't know how much of his own."

"That is target enough," said Colonel Wentworth, shaking his head.

"Where are these dangerous places he might go?" Indian Myrt asked. That Navy Colt hogleg of hers was upstairs and loaded.

"Besides Miss Puckett's, in Sydney Town there is Hell Haggarty's Goat and Compass," said Mr. Fitzgerald.

"There is also the Boar's Head, the Fierce Grizzly, Cowboy Mary's, and the Magpie," said the colonel, "just to name a few. Every place in Sydney Town is a dive."

I was remembering each saloon that he mentioned, storing them for later use. Recruiting five or six strong men was out of the question, and we couldn't pay for them, anyway. But if Wm. X. Fitzgerald was correct in saying that the murderers and thieves and even "shanghaiers" would respect our ladyhood, as he'd said earlier, then there was little worry.

Colonel Wentworth said, "Let us hope that he's a sensible man and doesn't go into those places."

I replied, "Yes, let us hope that."

We thanked Mr. Fitzgerald and Colonel Wentworth for

their good advice and went on up to the room, needing to plan the night's search. Indian Myrt said, "Before we get involved in this, isn't it possible that Mr. Pettit is well capable of taking care of himself?"

I said, "Look what happened to him in Kanesville. He got innocently involved with G. B. Minzter."

Indian Myrt nodded and said, rather tartly, "He also got involved with you. Innocently."

Ignoring the tartness, as well as the unfairness of that statement, I nodded back. "So he isn't as experienced as he looks and talks, and I'd certainly hate to see him go to Shanghai."

Soon, the plan was to visit Miss Puckett's and the places in Sydney Town, looking for Drover. If we found him, we'd lightly say, "Well, we were just sightseeing these famous places and . . ." Supper could wait, though it was already dark. There was a moment of discussion over weapons. Indian Myrt thought the Navy Colt was firepower enough and refused to let me take the point 31 Presentation.

Outside, we hired a carriage and driver—a small but muscular man in at least his fifties. His name was Raymond H. Johnson and we learned he was formerly a carpenter from Los Angeles, the first native-born Californian we'd met. Not many exist. He was wearing a blue woolen cap and took it off to expose curly dark hair. He had a pleasant, trustworthy face.

I said, "We'd like to go to Miss Puckett's, on Davis Street."

He gasped, saying, "Ladies, that place—"

I said, "I know, I know, but my poor father may have been enticed there. We have to save him." I winked slyly at Indian Myrt when I said "father."

"And this is your mother?" asked Raymond H. Johnson, nodding at Mrs. Dessery.

Before Indian Myrt could reply, I smiled at him. "We all have one."

He nodded and said, "I see, but Miss Puckett's is a terrible place and often dangerous."

I said to Indian Myrt, "Open your pocketbook and show him."

She did so, and he saw the hogleg nestled in there against a sachet-scented lace handkerchief. "I see," he said, and soon popped the reins on the back of his big gray horse. Off we went into the deepest of depravity looking for Bert Pettit.

# 6

There is a great difference in appearing ladylike and womanlike. The "bar keepouses" and "demonidestes" of the world could always be womanlike but seldom ladylike, so our very lives depended upon instantly appearing like ladies, "flower of American womanhood," as Wm. X. Fitzgerald had put it.

I will therefore say exactly what we were wearing that night for protection: Indian Myrt had on a rust-colored taffeta with shirred sleeves and high-neck lace collar and fetching bow. The bodice came to a point in front, and the full skirt was over three petticoats and a hoop. Her triangular shawl was of Indian cotton, and her straw bonnet, flared at the front, had cloth lilacs on it. There was no mistaking Mrs. Myrtle Dessery for anything but a lady, with her auburn hair in a neat bun.

For myself, a Scotch-plaid floor-length taffeta, with a

straight-line bodice, and scalloped ruffles on my sleeves, told who I was. On my head was an ivory-colored straw bonnet, a wreath of tiny painted wooden flowers on the crown. My shawl was of cashmere.

Outside Miss Puckett's, Raymond H. Johnson asked us if we'd like him to be escort inside and I replied that we'd welcome it. So, he anchored his gray horse and accompanied us. A tipsy man was coming out of the saloon as we were entering and he fell over backward in surprise at the sight of us. So I knew that our mode of dress was working.

Dimly lit and full of stale whiskey smells, Miss Puckett's was a long bar, some crude chairs and tables and a piano player in a peaked felt hat, not much enticement for any man, one would think. But then we saw the gaudy "demonidestes" lolling all around. The place quieted down, just from guilt, I think, as we stood inside the door, two unmistakable ladies.

The men we saw were of all kinds. There were miners in red flannel shirts and wide-awake hats, trousers stuffed into their boots; Chinamen in purple-figured silk jackets; and Mexicans in serapes, with rows of silver buttons down the outside of their pants. Most looked glazed-eyed, though the miners did now and then say a toast—"Here's all the hair off your head" or "Here's another nail in your coffin." The piano kept playing.

Raymond H. Johnson whispered, "There she is," and I knew he was talking about Miss Puckett. Just then she turned around and I received the shock of my life. I doubt she was even thirty, and she didn't have a tooth in her head, so her lips and chinbone were separated by only a half inch or so. Her mouth turned sharply down at the corners, but somehow she was managing to hold a shaky cigarillo between her gums. I whispered to Raymond H.

Johnson, "She's taken too much calomel. That mercury'll do it every time."

Miss Puckett frowned at us, wondering what we were doing there, I'm sure. She was wearing a long, form-fitted red gown that exposed a lot of her ample bosom. Not a sign of a corset. I whispered again to Raymond H. Johnson, "I can't see my father in here but I'd certainly like to see her trapdoor." I truly wanted to see how she carried out her shanghaiing.

Ever so slightly, he shook his head. He seemed nervous. There must have been thirty occupants in there, male and female, and they were all staring at us. I began to wonder if Wm. X. Fitzgerald had been correct in saying we'd never be harmed. Raymond H. Johnson advised quietly, "Let us go," and we did an about-face out into the fresh, foggy air.

In quick succession, we then went to the Boar's Head, the Fierce Grizzly, Cowboy Mary's, and the Magpie, all of the same depravity. Not a single sign of the beaver hat and mothy animal-skin coat belonging to Drover Bert Pettit, but something dramatic did occur in each place we visited. As we stood just inside, looking around, some of the tough men at the bar saw us, then broke down and sobbed. We reminded them of the good women they'd left behind in "the States." In fairness to them, some men, under the influence, will cry over card tricks.

I said to Indian Myrt, "We'll try one more, Hell Haggarty's Goat and Compass." The fact that *goat* appeared in the name of the establishment might have been an inducement for Drover to visit.

Raymond H. Johnson said quickly, "I don't think you should go to Haggarty's."

"Why not?"

"It's a true cesspool," he said. "Worse than anything

you've seen tonight. I'm sure your father would never go to Haggarty's. It is *the* home of the Ducks."

I said, "Well, you don't know my father."

For those who did not visit San Francisco in the fifties, Sydney Town, located up and away from the foot of Pacific Street and on back toward Telegraph Hill, was named for the large city in Australia. Doing the U.S.A. a lot of dirt, the Australians wanted to get rid of all their worst criminals, so they were conveniently put aboard ships and dumped on San Francisco. The latter was too busy hearing gold clink to pay attention to what was landing. In came the convicts like flotsam on a foul tide.

Raymond H. Johnson went on, "You're liable to meet Jack Dandy, or Dab the Horse Thief, or Singing Billy . . ."

I said, "We're not afraid of them. We'll mind our business of finding my father."

"You may meet Adelaide Alice or Canberra Kate . . ."

Indian Myrt spoke up. "They are human beings just like we are."

That wasn't altogether true, but off we went to Hell Haggarty's, which was lit up in front by pine-knot torches. Shadowy individuals were moving all around and then we saw a white goat just by the doorway, attended by a dark-faced man in a brown robe with a turban on his head.

Raymond H. Johnson said quietly, "That's Haggarty's famous African mascot goat, Noobie. It likes cav-ee-are."

Indian Myrt explained, "French, for fish eggs."

Lordy. I wondered if Hell ever kissed his mascot goat like Drover Pettit did.

In we went, and unlike in the other places, the shouting men paid no attention to us whatsoever. In the fiddle-playing smokiness, there was a girl with orange hair dancing up

on a tabletop and she wasn't even wearing a handkerchief.
If I live to be a hundred, which is doubtful, I'll probably
never enter a place as depraved as H. Haggarty's. Almost
any of the men present would have qualified as Dab the
Horse Thief.

As we scanned around for Drover's keg head and scruffy
hat, avoiding glances at the rotating girl with orange hair,
two of the "demonidestes" advanced on us with no good
intentions. They were looking us up and down as if we were
last week's trash. Maybe they were Adelaide Alice and
Canberra Kate? At this point, carriageman Raymond H.
Johnson was of no help. He'd separated from us by about
three yards and was watching what was going on atop the
table.

These female individuals, both with enough makeup on
to paint the *Prairie Queen*, came up close and the tall one,
who had puffy eyes and wore a necklace of seashells, said to
her companion, "Whaddya reckon, these lydies come to
see us boongs?"

Wm. X. Fitzgerald had said the men wouldn't harm a
golden hair of our heads, but he had made no mention of
the female species.

Indian Myrt, with her usual diplomacy, said, "Good evening to you, we are here to locate someone."

"Oooooooweeeee," said the short one. A small red velvet
cap graced her kinky yellow hair. "Their cobber ocker
strewd the path, whaddya reckon?"

Whatever did that mean? I had thought Australians
spoke English.

Then the tall one began plucking at the little wreath of
wooden flowers on the crown of my bonnet, at which point
Indian Myrt made her move. She opened the pocketbook
and let her right hand caress the Navy Colt. She then

brought the pocketbook up close to the tall one's nose and said, softly, "Lay a hand on that girl and your scalp will sail across San Francisco Bay." It was done in perfect Drover style.

The tall one glanced down at the point 36 and her hand fell away from my bonnet. That Australian floozie had no idea that the ladylike Mrs. Dessery was packing a hogleg. We then collected Raymond H. Johnson from his obscene gawking and proceeded toward the door.

Just as we were leaving, a fierce-looking huge man with a shaven head and great black curving mustache ran after us. Raymond H. Johnson breathed, "That's Hell Haggarty himself."

Hell said, "Lydies, lydies, don't go . . ."

Indian Myrt replied coolly, "We've seen quite enough, Mr. Haggarty."

Whether in Kanesville, or Sydney Town, people like Hell Haggarty and G. B. Minzter clearly yearned for the finer things in life.

"Where to now?" asked Raymond H. Johnson, relieved, I think, that we had finished the search for this night.

It was nearing nine o'clock, but seeing all the depravity in action had left us with not much appetite to eat at a restaurant like Delmonico's, which I dearly wanted to attend. I said, "Can you take us someplace for something light? A nice place for a change?"

Raymond H. Johnson said instantly, "A refreshment house, W. L. Winn's Fountainhead of Luxuries. Ice creams; confections. The fairest of the fair go there, only ladies and their natural protectors."

After all we'd been through, a sweet and cleansing W. L. Winn's was exactly what we needed. "By all means," I said.

Winn's was all that Raymond H. Johnson had predicted,

and we invited Mr. Johnson to join us at the table, though a few people looked askance at us entertaining the driver. He did politely take off his woolen cap. We had our fill of confection and I wish I could say the evening with Raymond H. Johnson ended on a pleasant note. It did not.

Outside of Winn's, I asked how much we owed and without blinking he said, "A hundred and forty dollars."

I was stunned. I said, "That is robbery."

He answered, "My fee is seventy dollars an hour."

No wonder he quit being a carpenter. I said, "You didn't say that when we hired you."

"You didn't ask me," he answered. "And I'm usually given a twenty-dollar tip. After those terrible places I took you, I deserve thirty dollars tonight."

In Kanesville, you can rent a horse and buggy for a month for thirty dollars.

Indian Myrt said, "Pay Mr. Johnson. We didn't ask him, that's true."

I paid him, reluctantly, but made a mental note that San Francisco carriage drivers were never to be trusted. The only tip that Raymond H. Johnson got was the dish of ice cream at Winn's.

It was about ten as we walked toward the Wentworth House and I said to Indian Myrt, "We should try once more to contact Drover." I knew we'd be going by the El Dorado. All of the city's best and biggest casinos were on Portsmouth Square, which was on our route.

She sighed, "Susan, I'm very tired."

"Just one," I pleaded.

She gave in and we went to the El Dorado, the rendezvous spot with Drover for the following night. My reasoning was that he might now be studying the poker players, checking them out, so to speak. I simply wanted to remind him of my deep interest in his activity.

The El Dorado, newly constructed the past year, made the Ocean Wave look like a muskrat trapper's shack. The walls of the large, square, thickly carpeted casino were covered with paintings that would have made Sweet Frenchy Moll blush deep purple—various women in various abandoned poses. The furniture was elegant, and there were pyramids of dazzling crystal. At one end was the raised orchestra platform, draped with bunting, flags, and colored streamers. At the other end was the huge bar, behind which were fine mirrors nearly the size of G. B. Minzter's. Down the middle were all the gaming tables, piled with bags of gold dust, nuggets, silver and gold coins, chips and checks.

Pale and thin, the dealers and croupiers were impeccably dressed in black and white, thin of chest with steady eyes and steady hands. Nonetheless, I saw the bulge of their derringers in their waistbands. Those little guns only shoot two yards but throw a ball of lead the size of a baby's fist.

Beautiful women, gowned in low-cut silk, were at the roulette tables, spinning the wheels. Their steady surveying eyes would have chilled cut glass. "French mam-zelles, I'd say," said Indian Myrt. One was smoking a thin, long cigar.

Suddenly, I had the feeling that Drover would be way out of his class in here. There were fully as many "dandies" as there were miner types. Not many scruffy types at all. Drover was nowhere to be seen.

Just then, a good old American female voice from "the States" said, "Susan Carlisle, whatever are you doing here?"

We swiveled our heads in total surprise. Coming toward us was "Aimee," of the Ocean Wave, Kanesville, Iowa. She was holding a tray in front of her revealing green dress, which was decorated with little gold flashes. Well, I wouldn't have been more surprised if the Blackwells had ridden in on Gabriel and old red Samuel.

"What are *you* doing here?" I asked.

We went through that kind of conversation for almost a minute. I told her of our overlanding with the sheep and the current mission, and she said she'd fled Minzter to begin a new life in San Francisco, taking a ship from New Orleans; crossing hazardous Panama with her little boy by mule and canoe; then another steamer to this city by the bay. I learned then, for the first time, her full name. Polkinghorn. Violet Polkinghorn.

Mrs. Myrtle Dessery always looked down on the "kee-pouses" and "demonidestes" such as Violet Polkinghorn, but in this case I believe she recognized a woman of value despite her profession. Not many women would cross Panama alone, and perhaps without a gun. At any rate, Indian Myrt was cordial, saying, "Good evening, I've heard about you."

Incidentally, the little boy was sound asleep on a spare roulette table in a back room at that very moment.

Violet could not linger too long without taking an order, so I decided on a ginger pop and for Indian Myrt, Violet recommended a "specialty of the house" called a Tom and Jerry, invented by the El Dorado bartender, Professor Jerry Thomas. We watched it being made. It was quite spectacular.

When Violet came back, I quickly told her of our search for Drover. She said, "You've been looking in the wrong places. Only the professionals play poker and they play in back rooms. He may be in a private room at the Oregon

House or the Verandah. He could be in a room at the Bella Union or Aguila de Oro. Maybe even here. I'll check."

I described him as being quite "unique" in dress so that she couldn't miss him. The beaver hat was always a telltale. A little later she came back to say he wasn't at the El Dorado. She also advised, "Tell him not to play poker in this city. Every sharper from New York City and Philadelphia west is here now and they'll take his money in no time. Playing in Touse and Santa Fe doesn't fit him for this town."

I thanked Violet Polkinghorn for the good advice and we departed the El Dorado about eleven. I attempted to extend our search to the Parker House or Aguila de Oro, but Indian Myrt flatly refused, claiming exhaustion.

With the additional worry of Bert Pettit facing sharpers across the table on the morrow, or worse, having already faced them and lost, sleep at the Wentworth House was not easy to attain. Whistling, snorting, grunting Indian Myrt did not help. Nor did people on either side of us. Snores went through the thin walls of that room like lead baby-fists.

# 7

Dawn came in rainy, matching my mood, and though for breakfast we could select from beef and venison steaks, pork chops, fried trout, veal cutlets, calf's head, and fricasseed oxtail, as well as hot rolls, toast, and brown bread, I just could not work up an appetite.

Throughout most of the morning we slopped around San Francisco streets looking for Drover. By then, I was thinking he'd lost all my money and could not bear to face me;

or he'd just absconded with it. We even went back to Mother McAdoo's to see if, just by chance, he'd dropped by. "No!" she shouted.

This city of excitement by the Pacific, a place I'd long dreamed of, was turning into a sad and treacherous pile of mud, thanks to the elusive Bert Pettit. I was down to asking various carriage drivers if they'd seen a man in a tall beaver hat.

Even the lobster course at Delmonico's, on O'Farrell Street, under candlelight and on spotless linen, did not lift my spirits. Tears not far away, I told the headwaiter that I'd once thought of being married there. He said, "Madam, we are not open for marriage, but wedding supper is another matter, complete with champagne and music. . . ." I was too "down" to discuss it further, Clay Carmer not being my priority this night.

We departed Delmonico's shortly before ten P.M. and arrived outside the El Dorado promptly at the appointed time. Even this drizzly night had not deterred the gamblers. The casino was full and boisterous. The hundreds of lamps cast a warm glow inside the elegance. From the orchestra platform came a fast polka. Indian Myrt and I took up station.

Nearby was a stocky man dressed in a black suit, bow tie, and bowler hat. We barely glanced at him, since it is not appropriate for ladies waiting in front of a gambling casino to eye male bystanders. We kept a watch for a beaver hat proceeding toward us.

After a few minutes, I said to Indian Myrt, with a sigh, "Well, I should have known better. We'll likely never see that man again." My five thousand was as good as gone.

I'd barely gotten it off my lips when the stocky man

stepped over, playing his dirty trick, saying, with an inward grin, "Hoss, don't we have business to attend to?"

It was Drover Pettit, all right, foxing us. I couldn't believe what I saw. He was clean-shaven, and dressed as a gentleman. His hair was cut; his shoes were shined. He had clearly taken several baths. I said, "You don't look like yourself."

He said, "I am not driving sheep at the present time."

Mrs. Dessery spoke up, a smile in her voice. "I think you look handsome, Mr. Pettit," said she.

In the shock of it, I almost forgot our mission. Then it hit me. "Did you play poker?" I asked.

"Nope."

I almost sank to the planks with relief. I said, "We were warned last night about all the sharpers in town. We looked all over to tell you."

Drover said, "I checked out a dozen games and I wouldn't have bet a Texas two-dollar bill in any of 'em. Sharpers is right."

I said, "Why don't we go inside and have a meeting? I have a friend in there who will tell us what to play."

"Hoss, I already bet that money," Drover said, surprising me again.

"On what?"

"On General Scott."

"Who is General Scott?"

"He is a grizzily bear who will fight a bull named El Tornado tomorry afternoon at two P.M. in the bullring at Powell and Vallejo."

I was stunned.

Drover went on, "Last night at the Graham House I met a Spaniard from a place called Mad-rid, an' he kept talkin' 'bout this bull, El Tornado. I got four-to-one odds."

"And you bet all my money?"

"Plus two hundred o' mine."

I was speechless and don't think Indian Myrt knew exactly what to say either. She finally asked, "Is that bear named after General Winfield Scott, Old Fuss and Feathers?"

"The same," replied Drover. "Fought the British at Chippewa, was wounded in Lundy's Lane; was in the Aroostook war an' a national hero from the Mexican war. I served with him at Chapultepec. He's now runnin' for President of the U.S.A. on the Whig ticket. . . ."

Indian Myrt said, "He is illustrious, isn't he?"

"That he is," said Drover, wiping some drizzle off his face.

I was dumbfounded. What did all that have to do with the bear? I said, "I can't believe you bet my five thousand on a dumb animal."

Drover said defensively. "The odds are better'n any poker game. General Scott was trapped up at a place called Cimarron, which is known for fierce bears."

"Has he ever fought a bull before?"

"Nope. That's why I picked him to win. Not having fought a bull, maybe not having ever seen one, he won't be afraid of it. In addition, I'd always bet on any 'General Scott.' I have a deep affection for that soldier."

I asked, "Drover, is there any way of canceling that bet? Could you tell that Spaniard you actually were betting for a young and innocent girl from Iowa who might lose her house and home if she doesn't win?"

Drover shook his head, "These gamblers from Mad-rid wouldn't excuse their mothers from a bet."

Things seemed to be going from bad to worse. I asked, "Who is holding the money?" I had learned that much about gambling from my Daddy. Make sure the holder wouldn't be the stealer.

"The Adams Banking and Express Company. They do it for one percent. That Spaniard put up Peruvian piasters, moidores, rupees, Maria Theresa dollars, Dutch florins, *perros gordos* . . ."

My mouth was open. The Spaniard had unloaded all the freak currency in the land on me. It's a wonder he hadn't dumped in Javanese coins from Batavia.

"What are moidores?" I asked.

"Portuguese money.

"*Perros gordos?*"

"Fat dog Messican dollars."

I didn't want to hear any more.

He said, "I have to be going. I'll meet you tomorry at twelve-thirty at The Wentworth an' we'll go see the fight." He tipped his bowler hat and went into the El Dorado.

I said to Indian Myrt, "I think I'm going to be sick." I could feel the lobster and chocolate ice cream coming up.

That second night in San Francisco was one of the longest in my entire life. Snoring sounds, all different pitches, went on hour by hour. I finally got out of bed and sat by the window, tears rolling down my cheeks.

How could I have ever become so unlucky as to meet Bert Pettit? He'd almost gotten me killed several times crossing the country, and now he'd led me to an insane city where steam paddies operated, where ponies had their hooves shined; blue rats scurried around and white goats ate caviar; bulls fought bears. Moidores! *Perros gordos!* Agony was drilling at me.

Being so expensive in gold rush days, two dollars each, eggs were not on the hotel menu, but I ordered two, soft-boiled, anyway. That and some dry toast was all I could stand the next morning.

Then about ten o'clock we made our way to the bullring. I wanted to see General Scott, upon which my house was riding, in living person. I hoped he was eleven feet tall with fangs the size of stalactites and claws as big as rutabagas. I hoped he'd look mean enough to chew oakwood.

However, we saw El Tornado first. A huge, brick-colored bull, he was chained in a pen at the edge of the ring, being fitted out with steel tips on his horns. The tips were about four inches long and appeared to be sharp as spears. El Tornado was certainly not happy with what was going on. He was snorting and pawing earth already. Ten men were struggling to hold him.

Indian Myrt didn't help matters by saying, "That's the biggest, meanest bull I've ever seen."

I asked a boy who was sweeping off the stands where I might find General Scott. He pointed across the ring to a chute. We went over there and found the unattended steel cage containing the bear from Cimarron. He was a big lump of long brown hair at the far side of the cage, sprawled out, slumbering. I yelled at him to wake up, with no results. Then I found a rock and bounced it off his head. He raised up, gazed at me groggily, and went right back to sleep. What sent me into complete despair was his face. With a kind, gentle, even cuddling countenance, he didn't even look like a grizzly bear. Even worse, he was slightly cross-eyed.

Now I knew why that Spaniard from Mad-rid was giving four-to-one odds. Frankly, I doubted General Scott could lick my late beloved dog, victim of Loup Fork quicksand.

# 8

I had chills and a slight fever and tried to diagnose myself, thinking I might have a delayed case of spotted fever. Yet there was no telltale rash on my hands and arms. Nonetheless, I took a dose of ipecac, which the hotel desk provided, and went straight to bed.

I was in that prone position at twelve-thirty when Indian Myrt said she had to go down to the lobby to meet the drover. I said to her, "I've never felt worse in my life."

"Drink a lot of water," she said, offering little sympathy.

Water would not cure what was wrong with me. I decided to make no comment about where she was going or why. I had no desire to think about the slaughter at Powell and Vallejo nor that nameless Spaniard with his freak money, and my certain loss.

I stayed in the bed—thinking, thinking. No wonder I was ill. If you considered everything I'd gone through in thirteen months, beginning with Mead's Meadow—the liening of my property by G. B. Minzter, the historic crossing of the sheep, attempted murder by Charlie Quarry, Humboldt Sink, Forty Mile Desert—it was little wonder I was moving rapidly toward the grave. Body weakened; nerves frayed. I must have fallen into tortured sleep sometime between one P.M. and two because about two-fifteen, I was awakened to shouts in the street: "The bear won! The bear won!"

Quickly, I got up, dressed, and went down to the desk to check the calendar. It was now September 14, and we'd leave on the morrow. There was an outside chance, just a chance, that we could make it back to Kanesville by November 2. Fifteen days to Panama; four or five across the isthmus; eight more to New Orleans; another twenty or so to Iowa via St. Louis, if all went well.

I returned upstairs, undressed, and got back into bed, awaiting Indian Myrt to surprise me, giving her that little joy. I pretended to be asleep as she burst into the room, saying excitedly, "General Scott won! General Scott won!"

I bolted up. "He did? I can't believe that!"

She was all wide smiles. "Yes, he did, Susan. You won the bet!" The joy and surprise worked.

"Oh, my," said I.

She quickly closed the window, then sat down on the edge of the bed, lowering her voice. "That fight was fixed," she said. "Never tell anyone."

I promised. "I never will."

"When Mr. Pettit came to get me, we went straight to W. L. Winn's to buy a gallon of vanilla ice cream. You know how bears like sweets."

I nodded.

"Then we went to a provisioners and Mr. Pettit bought a pound of cayenne pepper, and a butter paddle. After that, we went up an alley and he mixed the pepper into the ice cream. With that accomplished, we went on to the bullring and about twenty minutes before the fight Mr. Pettit went down to where General Scott was located and asked the Kanaka who was from the Sandwich Islands if it was all right to give the ice cream to the bear. The Kanaka said he didn't care, so Mr. Pettit gave General Scott that entire gallon."

"Where were you all this time?"

"In the stands waiting for him. He came up and sat down and then the fight started. It lasted less than two minutes, Susan. I've never seen anything so destructive as that bear. I think he believed the bull slipped him all that cayenne. He looked like the Pacific Vaporific when he went raging after that bull, breathing fire. He took El Tornado by the nose and swung him around, then threw him up into the stands. It took twenty Mexican cowboys with ropes to get General Scott under control, at which time we left."

Miracle of all miracles, my house might be saved, thanks to Drover and General Winfield Scott. I said, "Has Drover gone to collect the money?"

"No. He doesn't think it's a good idea for us to keep it here tonight. He said we could get it on the way to the ship tomorrow."

That sounded reasonable.

"Do you feel any better?" she asked.

"Much better," I said. My chills and fever seemed to have gone.

We invited Drover out to victory supper that night and ate at Tortoni's, another good place for a wedding party. After the meal, the first I thoroughly enjoyed in San Francisco, we invited Drover to accompany us to the American Theatre to hear Elisa Biscaccianti, the coloratura soprano, but he decided to go to the Bella Union for a little faro.

On the dot at ten o'clock the next morning we met Drover at the frock-coated Adams Banking and Express Company on Montgomery Street. He said, "You have your choice of money. I suggest you take Dix. Gold eagles would wear you down."

Yes, gold was too heavy to carry, and we were going back to the sane part of the nation where Dix, by virtue of the Banque des Citoyens, of New Orleans, was just as good as gold.

Indian Myrt nodded agreement.

The Adams bank thereupon gave Drover twenty thousand in cash, my winnings, less two hundred in holding commission. Drover then began to count my share and stopped upon reaching $14,800. I said to him, "You only invested two hundred, so my share should be much more."

The keg-headed man from Taos looked at me and replied, "Hoss, I said I'd triple your money. Not quadruple it. I'm takin' the excess as earned profit. I bet on General Scott, you didn't."

I said, "Something is wrong here. It was mostly my five thousand that gained that profit . . ." I felt Indian Myrt pulling on my skirt and heard her saying, "You don't know how grateful we are for all you've done, Susan last night was telling me what a marvelous man you are. . . ." I'd said no such thing.

What was clear, and perhaps had been from the start, was that Bert Pettit was a canny old man, capable of all kinds of manipulations, including rigging bull-and-bear fights, and excess profits.

But there are times when you cannot win, as I was learning weekly, and this was one, was clearly what Indian Myrt's tug on my skirt was saying. Although I thought that his "profit" of $5,800 on a $200 investment was robbery, I admitted to him, trying to be both charitable and cheerful, "Yes, I did say that last night." I carefully emphasized *last night.*

I left the two of them guarding the money and walked up a block and a half to buy a satchel. There was a black doctor's bag on sale, and I thought that would be most appropriate to carry the Dix home. Returning to Adams Banking and Express, I stuffed the money into the satchel and on we went to the Long Wharf, where the *SS Oregon* was being loaded for the noon sailing.

Despite myself, I must admit I got teary-eyed as I said

farewell to Drover Bert Pettit, who would soon start his thousand-mile walk back to Taos, New Mexico, along with Cowboy Clay Carmer, Salvador Maria Baca, and Abdou Diouf. Rinaldo, Cholula, Hector, and the bitch dogs were going too, of course.

I told him to say hello to his wife, Jarramilla, and his son, Ramon Noah, and that I would, of certainty, see them someday in future travels. I kissed him on both clean-shaven cheeks and squeezed his hard hands. Indian Myrt also said her sincere farewells and we thoughtfully watched his bargeman's legs go up the dock. He was richer for having known me.

As we boarded the ship, the captain, J. P. Bucklew, in full, splendid uniform, was standing by the gangway. He smiled widely and said, "Welcome to the *Oregon.* It is always nice to have ladies as passengers. I hope I will have the pleasure of your company at dinner."

Indian Myrt said, "We would be honored," and from what I knew of riverboats, we would also be well served at the captain's table.

I got around to one side of him and asked, very quietly, "Is there a safe on this ship? This satchel is full of money."

He glanced down at the doctor's bag. "I have a safe for official specie of all kinds. Follow me."

We went along to his well-appointed cabin and office and there sat a big safe strapped to the deck and wall so it wouldn't roll around. He said, "Turn your backs, please," and I assume he twisted the combination. Then he said, "All right," and reached for the bag of Dix. Glancing over his shoulder into the big safe, I saw bars of gold bullion, pokes of nuggets and gold dust and packages of paper money. He ordered, "No looking," shut the safe, and spun the lock. I was impressed with Captain J. P. Bucklew.

We returned to the deck and mingled a little. An assortment of males returning to "the States" after their flings at
the "diggin's" were jabbering and pushing around. Not
many appeared prosperous. They seemed dazed more than
anything else. A few were carrying large doughnut-shaped
black india rubber life preservers, which gave me pause
about the seaworthiness of the *SS Oregon.* Just then,
within the babbling throng of men who were wearing everything from Mexican blankets and Peruvian ponchos to
New York topcoats, we saw Mr. Henry Gladly. He, in turn,
saw us.

"Did you know that you are the only lady passengers
aboard?" he asked, doffing his hat in greeting. We could see
no other females, at that. Luck was shining upon us, at last,
I thought. With nearly three hundred men surrounding us,
we'd be safe as Plymouth Rock.

"I do hope you'll give me the pleasure of your company
now and then," said the man who had turned the rat situation around in San Francisco. He looked mainly at Indian
Myrt, I saw. Nearing sixty, I estimate, Henry Gladly came
off as a dapper businessman type. His hair was silver-gray,
and he looked well fed. "Stout" was what people like Henry
Gladly were often called.

Mrs. Dessery smiled radiantly at him. "Sir, we'd be honored," she replied as the crowd pushed around us. I will say
one thing right off. No matter how scruffy and dissolute the
passengers looked, to the man they were courteous. Neither
would they curse, even down on their knees playing dice, if
they knew we were in earshot.

We went to our stateroom, which contained two berths,
a mirror, a washstand, and a chamber pot.

Soon, the black-hulled, high-stacked *SS Oregon* steamed
slowly past the busy wharves and warehouses and then we

turned a point of land to see another part of the city, finally putting the skyline on the stern and then entering the straits and the first uplifting swell of the Pacific Ocean. The Isthmus of Panama was 3,245 water miles to the south.

About twenty minutes later, we were again standing out on the breezy, chill deck with Mr. Gladly and he was saying, "Nearly three hundred years ago, Vasco Núñez de Balboa claimed these seas for the Spanish crown . . ."

Pardoning myself, I had to leave his lecture at that point and go throw up my breakfast.

# 9

It was explained to us by the young beardless purser that the *Oregon* was 202 feet in length and 34 in width; had a "side-lever engine" built by the Novelty Iron Works, New York, to power paddle wheels 26 feet in diameter. Five hundred tons of coal for the boilers was in a hold below-decks. If the engine stopped or the coal ran out, she had 20,000 square feet of canvas sails on two masts. I hoped, for time's sake, we would not have to use sails, and also hoped the *SS Oregon* would stop wallowing around. I was finding that the Pacific Ocean was quite different from the Missouri River in terms of motion.

At supper the next night—I had not attended the first night and only attended this night out of duty—Captain Bucklew proved to be a fine teller of sea tales, though, in reflection, I'm not sure he was wise in telling some of them. A big man, with a big voice, he had a square, red sailor's face. Said he, "On our second trip, in '50, the coal caught fire. Well, I knew I'd scare everyone if I told them, so I just buckled the hatch tight and let it burn. Smoke was coming up through cracks, but I told everyone that was natural, hah, hah, hah. Then the deck got so hot you could hardly walk on it, and I told everyone that was just the normal heat off Mexico, hah, hah, hah. Took us four days to get that fire out. I fought it between one A.M. and five A.M. every night . . ." Not much was said about that particular sea story, though Mr. Gladly did comment it was a good thing that the "fire didn't get out of hand."

The other guest, a dour man named Goldberg who had just established the Boston Notions Store in Sacramento City, and was returning to "the States" to buy new stock, remained silent.

Then Captain Bucklew told us about another time when the *Oregon* ran out of coal going north. Passengers were put to work chopping up furniture and every spare stick of wood on the ship. With no wind for the sails, Captain Bucklew put into Monterey just as the last chairs were being burnt. During the meat course, which he did not touch, he also said he'd quelled a mutiny in early '52.

After supper, I did a foolish thing, I caught up with Captain Bucklew pacing the deck, hands clasped behind his broad back. I asked, "Captain, if the ship caught on fire again, or began to sink, would you have time to get my black satchel out of the specie safe?"

He stopped to stare at me. "Diddley damn on the safe if my ship is sinking. I will be directing passengers into the lifeboats." Then he continued pacing; outraged, I think.

I suppose he was right in that priority, but it would seem he'd have another plan for saving the money.

When I returned to the side of Indian Myrt, who looked comely and pleasing this night, again wearing that black taffeta, she was in the midst of telling *our* story to Henry

Gladly. Trying to catch her eye, I wigwagged at her and cleared my throat several times. But she kept on going through the bull-and-bear fight, and the winning of the money, finally saying to him, "We have the $14,800 to save Susan's house in a black satchel in the ship's safe. . . ."

*I myself would trust no man with that information.*

Mr. Gladly asked, "Is it in dust or coins or paper?"

Why would he want to know that?

"Dix," Indian Myrt replied.

"That is fine currency," Gladly said.

I chimed in, "Yes, and there is also a live rattlesnake in that bag."

Mr. Gladly laughed heartily, but Indian Myrt frowned at that remark as if it was silly. How could she have just come right out to tell him we were transporting a small fortune?

Mr. Gladly finally realized what I'd said, separating it from jest, and came back with, "Well, the money is safe with Captain Bucklew, I'm sure, and I'll be along with you all the way to New Orleans to protect it."

Indian Myrt was suddenly starry-eyed. She crooned, "That will be wonderful, Mr. Gladly."

I didn't think so, at all. We knew nothing about this man except that he powdered his jowls after he shaved and used a lotion that I knew to be Green Tiger. The doctor had used the same lotion, but I'd never seen powder on his face.

Gladly went on. "The only dangerous parts of the trip will be the mule ride from Panama City to Gorgona, and then the bungo polers on the Chagres River. Once we get to the railhead, which is twenty miles from Aspinwall—"

I broke in. "What are bungo polers?"

"Chocos Indians who will paddle us through the jungle in their canoes."

"Why are they dangerous?"

"Well, if they know you two have money in that black bag, they'll turn the canoe over and run off into the jungle with it."

I said, "I don't plan to tell the bungo polers anything." Then I turned to look at my guardian. "Do you?" I was hoping she'd understand my message.

"Of course not," she said. It had gone right over her head.

Mr. Gladly continued, "Then there are many natural hazards. Alligators live in the Chagres River. When the bungos stop alongside the banks, look out for water snakes. They'll climb in. Also watch out for land snakes such as the bushmaster and fer-de-lance, quickest killers of all. Then you must be careful of the boa constrictors hanging from trees. Even in your sleep, you must worry. If you are a sound sleeper, jungle vampire bats drink your blood at night. In itself, that supper is harmless, but they have the potential of giving you rabies."

It seemed to me that Mr. Gladly was receiving undue pleasure from listing all the dangers. I guess some people are gleefully sinister without meaning to be. I said, "I think we'll survive."

"I hope so," he said, then added, "Of course, there are also the interesting, harmless animals such as the kinkajou and chrysothrix, found only in the Chiriqui district. . . ."

Yawning purposely, I said, "It is late, and I'm going to bed," an unmistakable hint that Indian Myrt should be coming along, too. Enough jungle talk!

Smiling at Gladly, my guardian said, "I'm not sleepy at all."

I began to wonder if the ordeal of overlanding had muddled her thinking. Was she suddenly going man-crazy?

She'd told Drover how handsome he looked after he'd shaved and bought those new clothes. Now she was making eyes at this dandified stranger.

I left them in the passenger lounge and went to the stateroom. Soon, I was in the top berth. In the chill, creaking, rolling darkness, listening to the wet pound of the paddle wheels, I thought about many things and about an hour later in she came, asking in a whisper, "Susan, are you still awake?"

"How could I sleep?" I answered, in a normal voice.

She said, "Isn't Mr. Gladly a nice man?"

"I wouldn't know," I replied. "I have been here in the darkness thinking about him, now that you've told him where the satchel is and what's in it. Any man who can trap two thousand cats may be anything but nice. Trapping five cats is almost impossible unless they want to be trapped. I've been thinking that he probably put knockout drops into milk saucers. . . ."

"What does that have to do with being nice?"

"A lot. He may be no better than Miss Puckett or Shanghai Kelly. He could get together with those bungo polers and run off into the jungle himself. He sounds like he knows what it is all about."

Indian Myrt replied crisply, "He is a fine, upstanding man and I trust him even more now that I know what he does in New Orleans. He's in investments. Trapping the cats was just a favor to his old friend, the mayor of San Francisco."

Likely story, I thought. "Investments cover many sins," I said, and promptly turned over.

A pall of silence enclosed our cabin and I finally turned over again. I couldn't see her in the darkness but said what was on my mind. "Did you really have to tell him about the black bag?"

I could hear her petticoats rustling as she took them off, answering, at the same time, "He asked me why we were traveling, where we were going."

"Couldn't you have made up a story? Did you have to tell him we were carrying a lot of money?"

"It never occurred to me to withhold the truth from such a gentleman."

I sighed and rolled back over. I well knew the reason why she'd told him. Her head had been turned by this talkative "investor" from New Orleans. He was clearly wooing her and chances were that the situation would worsen day by day. Well, Mr. Henry Gladly was in for a big surprise if he thought he was going to add to his investments at my expense. Whenever that black doctor's bag was out of the ship's safe, five of my fingers would be on the handle and the other five would be around the Presentation Colt.

The next morning, after breakfast, while my guardian and the man from New Orleans were out promenading on the deck, a whale was sighted. The *SS Oregon* tipped sharply when all the men rushed over to the left-hand side. It was exciting to see the spouting whale, but I did not appreciate the sudden tilt and said so.

Mr. Gladly, holding Indian Myrt's hand, laughed it off, saying that ships seldom tipped over from passenger movement. If we met a "green sea, look out." A "green sea" was a wave fifty to sixty feet high, he said. Between what he was saying about waves, stroking my guardian's hand, men running back and forth across the deck whenever big turtles or porpoise or whales were sighted, I was not enjoying this voyage at all. In fact, I longed to be walking beside Drover and the wonderful sheep on solid, safe, tipless U.S.A. soil.

So my mood was not at all good during this period and the next day, while Indian Myrt was washing out underwear in the basin, I found myself alone with Henry Gladly, who was out taking his "A.M. constitution" by himself. I fell in beside him and said, "I'd like to talk to you, Mr. Gladly."

"Please do so," he replied.

We went over to the rail. In the distance, off to the left, I could see faint humps of mountains, which was very reassuring. Beautiful "terra firma."

I said, "Mrs. Dessery is a well-liked widow in our small town in Iowa, with a fine reputation, and I just want to make certain it stays that way. She is an innocent and inexperienced woman." Had she been a Sweet Frenchy Moll, or a Violet Polkinghorn, there would have been no worry.

"I do not know what you mean," he said.

I doubted that very much. I said, in plain language, "I do not want advantage taken of her. I've seen you two holding hands the last two days." With that, I walked away so he could mull over the consequences.

What had also gotten to me about Henry Gladly was that he knew it all. You ask most people, "What is that?" and they'll usually answer, "I don't know." Not Henry Gladly! He'll answer, "That's a blackfish and they catch them down here for oil content." Then he'll give you the Latin scientific name and if you show the slightest interest he'll tell you where they go to breed.

Indian Myrt said, "He is the smartest man I've ever met."

I never thought I'd hear her say that.

In another two days, we were down off the long peninsula of Lower California, which is really part of Mexico, and the weather had changed. The air was balmy warm and the sea was almost as flat as the Big Muddy. It was a shame that Clay Carmer wasn't sitting in the deck chair close alongside me.

After supper, Henry Gladly suggested we all stay up to see the "beauties of the night before moonrise." When he talked like that, Indian Myrt almost swooned. He continued, "The tropic seas we have entered are surcharged with phosphoric animal culli. You'll see phenomena tonight."

So we arranged ourselves in deck chairs not too far from the bow on this black night and watched yellow-white flashes of phosphorus in the water while "Professor" Gladly said what it was all about, including such as *Acalephae* and *Infusoria*. Now and then, he'd sneak a little squeeze of Indian Myrt's hand and I could see she was squeezing back. I tried to concentrate on the unusual flashes of fire in the sea.

# 10

For those who did not travel the crowded gold rush packets, the village of Acapulco, Mexico, in a landlocked harbor, was a coaling stop eight days out of San Francisco. Steamships headed north from Panama and Nicaragua also stopped there and in the harbor, as we entered, were seven at anchor, all larger than the *SS Oregon*. In the high heat, boats were scurrying back and forth from the ships to the landing. Acapulco was of no interest to me.

Panama was seven days away, and we lost an afternoon and night at anchor in Mexico, but according to my calculations, barring "green seas" and any more stops, we'd arrive at the isthmus September 30. If the guidebook was correct, we should be at Aspinwall, which is now called Colón, located on the Caribbean Sea, sometime on October 5. That gave us less than a month to take our seats on the smooth oakwood bench in the courthouse by Cottonwood Jail. I could not wait to open the satchel before the bloodshot eyes of Judge Tuttle and see the face of G. B. Minzter collapse.

A steady ticking began in the back of my brain. Time was now flying by and I was tempted to ask Captain Bucklew if he might speed up those paddle wheels a little. Speed and time were much on my mind, I well remember.

A showdown involving those factors and my guardian and Mr. Henry Gladly was inevitable, I suppose. The day before debarking we were sitting peacefully in the deck chairs toward the stern of the ship, and he had just explained that what we called Panama was actually the new country of Colombia, founded by a man named Bolívar. Panama was the name of the old city founded by de Avila in 1519, not the isthmus. "To tell you the truth, I do not know what Panama means," he said.

Thank goodness for that, I thought.

"But we should take two days to see the city and the churches. Panama is the oldest European city on the entire continent and was thriving until pirate Henry Morgan sacked it in 1671. We can see the ancient churches, the remains of the old wall, the cannon, the mysterious alleys. Yes, two days will do it easily."

Easily, eh? Under her parasol, I saw my guardian smiling and nodding, off in some romantic dreamland.

I got up and said, "Well, if you two want to take two days to sightsee, you'll do it without me. I am heading across the jungle to catch a ship to New Orleans. I am not about to lose my house and home to look at old walls."

Mr. Gladly's patrician chin dropped, as did Indian Myrt's.

"I mean that," I said. "For days, you two have been acting like we are on some sort of pleasure cruise instead of plotting to get me home quicker."

Mr. Gladly, blinking, said, "Well, now . . ."

I said direct to him, "And I, for one, am tired of your lectures. I don't want to know anything else. I couldn't care less about *Insufores* and pirate sacking. Just tell me which ship to catch on the other side of Panama, or whatever you call it." With that, I whirled around and left them, thoroughly disgusted.

I was up by the bow, leaning over, watching the white wave curl over the black prow of the ship, knifing halfway up. It was the coolest place on the trembling *SS Oregon*.

Auntie Indian Myrt followed me up there.

"Susan, I think you're jealous," she said. I ground out a hollow laugh. "How could I be jealous of that gabby old man?"

"Why, Susan, he's been paying attention to me, something that hasn't happened very much in the last three years. It's a nice feeling, you know." I'd never seen such a look in her eyes. They were saying: Don't you understand?

I put my thumbnail under a bubble of rust on the railing and stared off toward the palm-line coast. The water was bluer than in any painting I'd ever seen. The smooth surface glittered in the sun. Why was life always so complicated?

"He told me to apologize to you. He said he just thought we'd like to know those things."

I felt awful.

"He said he will try to get you to New Orleans as quickly as he can."

I felt like jumping overboard.

# 11

I said admiringly to Henry Gladly, "I've never seen a gun like that." We were riding at anchor in the smooth-watered Bay of Panama, which is inside the island-littered, shark-infested Gulf of Panama. There was a rotting, green-jungle smell heavy in the air.

He said, "It is a French 'Apache' Fist Revolver."

It was about the size of a gambler's derringer, but the barrel was even stubbier. It threw a ball of lead less than the size of a muskenong grape but was potent enough, I suspected. I was thinking I might have misestimated Henry Gladly, but wouldn't you know he'd have a pistol no one had ever heard of. It was a firing-pin type, a wondrous weapon.

"Quite popular with French thieves," he added. New Orleans, of course, was a hotbed of the French.

Mr. Gladly was certainly not dandified this steamy early morning as Indian Myrt and myself waited patiently to enter the captain's office. He had changed to cotton trail clothes and was soon to place a big straw planter's hat over his wavy silver-gray hair. Gone was the banker's attire. Perhaps I had judged him entirely wrong.

The *SS Oregon* was anchored about two miles offshore to discharge passengers, baggage, and some cargo bound for New York and other places. Rowboats were bobbing around the accommodation ladder and dark-skinned oarsmen were yelling for business to ferry passengers ashore. Some soiled "whites" were down there, too.

One by one, or two by two, passengers reclaimed their valuables and money from Captain Bucklew's specie safe. As they exited his office, they were trying to hide what they were holding, whether it be in gold-dust pokes or carpet-bags or valises. Or satchels. They all seemed nervous. I soon discovered why.

The young beardless purser yelled, "Next," and in we went. Captain J. P. Bucklew was sitting by the safe and said, "Good morning, ladies. I hope you had a pleasant voyage."

Indian Myrt, whose stomach was lined with steel, I had discovered, said, "It couldn't have been better, Captain."

I disagreed but said nothing.

Captain Bucklew nodded his thanks for her remark and said, "I tell all my departing passengers to watch them-selves in transit across the isthmus to Aspinwall, especially those carrying specie. The miles can be very dangerous."

I said, "Mr. Gladly has already told us about the bungo polers and the bushmasters . . ."

"Diddley damn on the bungo polers and the bushmas-ters," said the captain. "It is the white scum that you have to watch out for, not the Chocos or the snakes. White human snakes from everywhere around the world have gathered in the isthmus, inhabiting Panama City, Cruces village, and Gorgona all the way to Barbacoas and Aspin-wall. Some are in those boats down there right now. When you walk out of this office with that black satchel, they'll know you're carrying money. They have spies on this ship who signal to them. I have been trying to catch those spies since '50 and have only caught one. I waited until we were

off the Gulf of Fonseca and then shot him in the head and
threw him to the sharks. . . ."

Indian Myrt and I exchanged looks. No wonder the passengers exiting from Captain Bucklew's office appeared so
nervous.

"What is your advice to us, Captain?" asked Indian
Myrt.

"It is this. My company has this shipment of gold bullion going to The Bank of New York, but I won't send it on
its way for four days, just before we sail. Twenty armed
guards will escort those wooden boxes and you could go
along, too. That is my advice."

I said, "Captain Bucklew, we can't wait four days. I have
to be back in Iowa for a court appearance November second."

"You're on your own, then," he said. "Are you going to
Cruces first?"

"No, Gorgona," I said. "That's on the River Chagres,
isn't it?"

He nodded. "That's where you'll pick up the bungos.
Watch those hotels in Gorgona. Stay away from anyone
who isn't a passenger. There's a man they call Panama Bill
who hangs around the Gorgona hotels. He'll sell you something cheap just to take a look at your purse. He's just one
of the white scum the gold rush has visited upon the isthmus. Now, ladies, kindly sign my receipt and you can be on
your way."

Suddenly, I wasn't certain I wanted to be on my way.
Spies? Panama Bill?

He opened the satchel so that we could see that the Dix
were still inside and then Indian Myrt signed the receipt
relieving Captain Bucklew of further responsibility.

"Good luck, ladies," he said, saluting us sitting down.

As we were crossing to the door Indian Myrt said, "Isn't it fortunate we have Mr. Gladly along?"

"It certainly is," I said.

Back on deck, holding the satchel, I looked around for anyone who might be signaling to the bobbing boats. I saw no one but did step close to Henry Gladly and repeated some of what Captain Bucklew had said. Mr. Gladly immediately recommended we take a boat manned by Chocos rather than the dirty-looking bearded "white scum" calling to us in the Queen's English. He went to summon a Chocos boat.

Meanwhile, I checked the Presentation Colt that was tidily holstered inside my loose-hanging blouse. I also suggested to Indian Myrt that she make sure the Navy Colt was ready. She said, "I'm of a mind to display it openly around here."

"That's a good idea," I said. "Keep it in your lap."

There was no need to pretend being ladylike until we boarded the steamer for New Orleans. That hogleg had its own silent special warning of "be careful."

Mr. Gladly returned, having engaged a boat manned by two Chocos, and sailors thereupon took our valises, plus his small steamer trunk, down the ladder. Mr. Gladly asked if I wanted him to hold the black satchel, but I declined. I do remember feeling that many eyes were fixed upon me, watching from the rail of the ship and from the bobbing boats. I felt as if I really did have a live rattler coiled among the Dix.

Gray, sinister clouds had pressed down on us that humid, windless dawn as we steamed slowly past Taboga Island to the anchorage and now heavy rain began to fall. We were soon soaked, the cloth parasols being useless, water dripping off Mr. Gladly's straw hat.

Gazing at Indian Myrt, who was trying to shield the hogleg, which was across her thighs, from rain, Mr. Gladly said, "I've never known a lady like you. Most ladies in New Orleans are occupied with their teacups. I don't say that literally."

Indian Myrt gazed back at him to say, "I've never known a man like you."

The Chocos said nothing to us or each other as the oars knocked against the boat. It was the most miserable rowboat ride I'd ever had. Shark fins were everywhere on the slick surface.

"Rainy season begins in May and lasts until December," said Mr. Gladly, water dripping off his nose and chin. "It ceases in June for a while, and this phenomenon is known as *veranito de San Juan.* Stop me if you don't want to hear anything else."

I said, "Please go on."

It would help to take our minds off the driving hot rain. I put the satchel under the seat, worried that the Dix would get wet. Now and then, as the rain let up, we could see Panama City, which sat on a rocky peninsula by the mouth of a creek. Dark hills were behind it, jungle studded with coconut palms.

"You'll be traveling a truly historic trail. Balboa was the first white man to brave this jungle, sea to sea. For a while, it was the richest trail known to man. All the gold the Castilians stole from the Incas, all the Pacific pearls, all of Bolivia's silver, maybe two hundred thousand tons, went over it, bound for Spain."

In a way, I was helping revenge the Spanish thefts. Now, my $14,800, via the "Mad-rid" gambler, would cross.

Several boats containing other *SS Oregon* passengers were in front of us, pumping toward shore, and over there several dozen mules and men were clustered. "Last time I paid twenty dollars for a saddle mule from Gorgona to Panama City, and sixteen cents a pound for my cat cages." Last time for him was spring, '51.

No sooner had we bumped the beach when the mule owners crowded around, offering services, shouting in Spanish and Choco. We ignored two "white" mule owners. In comparison to gassy Rinaldo, all of the mules here looked tubercular and weak.

Mr. Gladly bargained for four of them, one to carry baggage, and soon we started for Gorgona, by the River Chagres, about eighteen miles away. Two Choco guides led the skinny animals. The narrow road was muddy, full of deep gullies, almost impassable, and after riding for about two miles in the wet saddle I decided to walk. Hot rain kept falling and Panamanian mules, we learned, have a different gait. The wet saddles were having a corkscrew effect on us. Indian Myrt slid down from hers, as did Mr. Gladly.

After we cleared broad meadows of coarse grass, which Mr. Gladly called "savannas," thick exotic jungle and jagged high green hills arose on either side of us. There was monkey chattering and much birdsong. Parrots swooped around. Had it not been for mud up to my ankles, water seeping into my belly button and ears, I suppose I would have enjoyed it more. Even Mr. Gladly was silent most of this time as we slogged along in the tropic downpour. Occasionally, we passed soaked, glum people from "the States" headed for Panama City; behind and ahead of us were soaked, glum people headed for Home, Sweet Home.

Since leaving Captain Bucklew, I had not once let go of the Dix and it seemed to me that I only drew more attention that way. I noticed that the two Chocos looked now and then at the doctor's bag with marked curiosity. Perhaps a message had been passed from the SS *Oregon* to interested parties: *Watch for the pretty girl with the black satchel.* Was Panama Bill waiting up the road?

We reached Gorgona, which sits on a high bluff, about six-thirty. The village had one rutted, pig-squealing street, and we passed down it, looking for the best available hotel. Four came into view and we chose the Union. It would not have made any difference had we chosen any of the other three. They were all owned by the same man, six feet of tobacco-chewing red-haired Philadelphian named Howe. Behind the wooden fronts on all four hotels were canvas backs and peaked canvas roofs that leaked.

Howe showed Indian Myrt and myself to our ladies' "private room," which was separated from the next room by a piece of canvas. The next room was a "dormitory" for up to twenty-five males, sleeping on bamboo shelves.

Indian Myrt said, "Surely you can do better, Mr. Howe."

He replied sourly, "Go next door if you don't like this."

That's when we discovered he owned all four hotels. We settled on the Union. Howe had cornered all the eating places in town, as well, so we ate at the Union. Hard ham, rice, and moldy cranberries. Bananas for dessert. Since Acapulco, I'd had enough bananas to last forever. Howe's dining room, with bamboo benches and bamboo tables, had no floor. Our feet were in dirt and pigs wandered in and out. The attached saloon was the same.

After supper, batting mosquitoes, we walked around what there was of Gorgona—mostly thatched and bamboo huts for gambling; saloons to serve Jamaican rum; lean-tos of ill repute, and those "hotels." The only souvenirs of Gorgona were small stuffed alligators and we didn't buy any. Then we went down to the river to look at the bungos for tomorrow's traveling. I lugged the satchel everywhere we went, but no Yankee scoundrel approached us to sell anything; so perhaps Panama Bill was not in town.

Mr. Gladly had arranged to sleep directly next to "our wall" to protect us, and about nine o'clock, being weary, we all turned in. This many years later, I still cannot possibly describe the noise in the Union Hotel over the next three or four hours. Beside me, Indian Myrt was snoring; on the other side of the canvas wall, Henry Gladly was snoring. I was between them, sweating and suffering. Every so often, a drunken man would crawl on to the rented shelf and begin snoring. By midnight, my best guess is that there were upward of twenty-odd snorers sawing away in a space less than thirty feet wide and ten feet high. My late Daddy's description of "howlin' hell" was perfect for this vexing night.

I did fall asleep, finally, one hand grasping the black satchel and the other my Presentation Colt. A while later, maybe an hour, I awakened to the fact that someone was gently prying my fingers from the handle of the Dix bag. I was flat on my stomach, cheek to the straw mattress, my favorite way to sleep. I let the prying continue as I slowly raised the Colt to where a scoundrel's head might be, and pulled the trigger. Indian Myrt awakened with a jolt and began firing that big hogleg, riddling the canvas wall and the dormitory roof next door.

Within two seconds, all the sleepers in the dormitory were screaming and shouting. Some of the shelves collapsed, pinning occupants below. Men were running around naked in the darkness, a thoroughly frightened Mr. Gladly later said. He collided with several himself, though he had on cotton underwear. Considerable lead had gone whizzing over his head. "Pandemonium is the best way I could describe it," he said. Lanterns were lighted and things were so bad that Howe reopened the saloon and served drinks on the house for two hours.

My guardian and I did not go in there, nor did I apologize to any of those blinking, stunned men in the dormitory. Those who had slept naked had pulled their pants on. Most, except the Henry Gladly type, were still standing in their underwear, looking dazed. I simply said that "white scum thieves were operating" and let it go at that. The poor maligned bungo polers could not be blamed as they were all asleep down in their dugouts by the riverbank. Though darkness made it impossible to be certain, those were white-skinned hands laid on mine, I'm sure.

We were destined never to find out who was trying to steal the Dix that night. Maybe redheaded Howe himself. For a moment, I even entertained the sickening thought of Henry Gladly pushing his hand beneath the canvas wall. He was only two feet from me.

Howe complained about us shooting holes in the dormitory roof, but we didn't pay any attention to the complaint. That canvas was already rotten and leaking before Indian Myrt shot it up.

# 12

For the information of those who did not cross the isthmus going to or coming from California during gold rush days, the River Chagres glides swiftly by the miserable village of Gorgona and Howe's Union Hotel, pointed almost due north for the Caribbean Sea, thirty-nine twisting miles away.

Fortunately for Indian Myrt and myself, by autumn, '52,

the Panama Railroad, destined to be the first transconti-
nental railroad of the Americas, according to Mr. Gladly,
had laid tracks as far south as Barbacoas, another miserable
village of cane huts, so we only had about nineteen miles of
bungo travel through the heart of the jungle.

As we stood in the dawn downpour while our baggage
was being loaded by three lean Choco boatmen, the famous
bungo polers, Mr. Gladly said, "There are some things I
should tell you." He knew quite a lot about this trip, having
hired four bungos, three of them for the cat cages, when he
came through here on his way to San Francisco.

We waited.

I think the occurrences of the previous night had made
him a little leery of us. As the lanterns were being lit in the
dormitory, I'd noticed he'd looked at us as if we had cholera. The hot lead from my Presentation had come very
close to him, I'll admit. Now, down by the river, I noticed
that he was sizing us up again, so to speak; perhaps wondering if he had not made a mistake by volunteering to be our
escort to New Orleans. One of two things was certain to
me: He was either a man of his word or he wanted to steal
my Dix.

"The mosquitoes along the river are ferocious. Try to
protect yourselves," he said.

Well, they couldn't be much worse than those along the
Humboldt, I thought.

He said, "Vines overhang the river in some places and
quite often snakes drop off them, falling into the bungo.
Please don't panic if this happens. Please, please don't
shoot. You could hit the polers or, heaven forbid, me. The
boatmen will flip the snakes out with their poles. They go
flying out like wet noodles."

I scanned the brown boatmen. They appeared quick and

agile, as though they could easily flip snakes. They were wearing faded calico loincloths, and not an ounce of fat could be seen on them. They were all sinew.

We nodded, satisfied at that plan.

"You'll also see large alligators upon the banks. Sometimes in the water. Don't let them concern you. Unless they are crazed, they seldom attack the bungos. But I suggest you don't shoot them. Another word of caution. You will see logs now and again floating in the river as we pass. I suggest you don't pat the logs. Some may be sleeping alligators."

Why should we go down the River Chagres potshotting alligators? My Daddy had taught me to never shoot what I wouldn't eat. But I was glad that Mr. Gladly had told us not to pat the logs. It would have been just like me to reach over and do that for whatever reason.

One of the boatmen said something like "oomaligu," which wasn't remotely like Pottawattamie or Sioux, Indian Myrt soon said, and motioned for us to climb in. Another boatman tried to help me with the black satchel, but I slapped his hand and apologized later, though he didn't understand what I was apologizing for.

Hollowed out of a single log, about twenty-five feet in length and four wide, our bungo had a palm frond shelter at the stern, covering six wooden seats. So we finally got out of the rain. At that, the bungo had more class than the Union Hotel, of Gorgona. A huge basket of fresh fruit was provided for the passengers along with coconut milk. Though the bottom of the bungo was wet and mossy, I'd just as soon sleep there as in redheaded Howe's Union Hotel.

As we began the journey, propelled by the green bamboo poles, I was firmly holding the black satchel on my lap. I had reloaded the Presentation and Indian Myrt had done the same with the hogleg after the past night's usage. We were ready for further attempts at stealing the Dix.

Continuing his kind instruction, Mr. Gladly said, "These are really banana boats. This palm frond roof is to shade bananas, not people."

I looked up. Several large, black hairy spiders were crawling around in the fronds. I moved one seat forward, up beside Indian Myrt.

"If you hear howling from the jungle as we go along, do not worry," he said. "Monkeys, genus *Alouatta*, do the howling, not people."

That was fine, too.

Green darkness went to black not five feet from the banks, vines so thick in there that sunlight couldn't penetrate. Water dripped everywhere and the whole mass seemed to be a quivering, ferny, noisy ooze, sinisterly growing before our eyes.

Alligators viewed us lazily but seemed more interested in big, long-legged turkeylike birds that do not grow near the Big Muddy. Mr. Gladly expertly called them "flamingos." Monkeys howled and peered out at us from between banana leaves.

Indian Myrt, bug-eyed and in awe, said, "I cannot believe I'm going down this River Chagres in the middle of the tropic jungle. Little me, from the wide Iowa prairie." But that's what the gold rush years did to all of us.

There was considerable traffic on the Chagres. Several bungos soon passed us on the way upriver and we exchanged greetings with those happy adventurers, California-bound. One fast canvas-topped passenger-laden bungo, with five singing boatmen, came rapidly by going downriver. Playfully splashing water on us, the five Chocos shouted at us, and hah-hahed.

Soon, our own boatmen broke out in happy native song and Mr. Gladly said, a little nostalgically, "If it weren't for the mosquitoes, this reminds me somewhat of Venice, Italy."

That was another place I hoped to visit.

A little later, we heard military music ahead and around a bend came thirty-one bungos bearing soldiers of the Fourth United States Infantry, a garrison bound for San Francisco. Along with the proud Stars 'n' Stripes, their regimental flag was flying from the lead bungo, a heroic captain standing erect and eagle-eyed in the bow of that one. (Later, we learned he was U. S. Grant, destined to be a general and then President of the U.S.A.) It was a thrilling sight. The band was split between the second and third bungos. I had not heard grand military music since the Mormon volunteers marched through Kanesville on their way to the Mexican war. We all stood up to "Salute the troops," Indian Myrt almost falling overboard in the process. We were still tingling as the band music slowly faded out over the jungle. We sat down again.

Now and then, as predicted, a green snake two or three feet long would drop into the bungo from the overhanging vines and one of the polers would flip it out with sort of a hooking motion. Mr. Gladly had been correct. They did look like wriggling wet noodles as they spiraled upward and out. Twice, snakes slithered up under our seats and one of the grinning boatmen grabbed them by their tails and popped them like you'd pop a whip. Their eyes bulged when that happened.

At this point, I want to say something about the bungo polers and even Mr. Gladly admitted he'd been wrong in demeaning them. The three we had this day were fine people. They had no intention of stealing my doctor's bag and running off into the jungle with it. Mr. Gladly managed to converse a little with them and found out that some thoughtful gold rusher had given them Christian names—Moses, Jacque, and Emanuel. I said to Indian Myrt, "Let's tip those three when we arrive." She agreed.

Mr. Gladly continued to point out things of flora interest as we went along. "Those trees of honey yellow and the 'flame' trees are from the Eocene, and I would say those ten-foot maidenhair ferns are of the same. The red orchids are called 'The Seventh Deadly Sin' and the common white ones are 'Tears of the Virgin.' . . ."

We reached Barbacoas about dark after a safe journey down the River Chagres and checked into the United States Hotel, which made no pretense about wooden fronts the way redheaded Howe did up in Gorgona. The U.S. Hotel was twelve open-front thatch huts along the river with two string-hammocks in each one. The U.S. Hotel, run by a half-breed named Romero, offered no food and we were directed to a stand where roast pig was served. We decided just to eat some more fruit.

The mosquitoes were worse than ferocious, and I could hear them buzzing around under my blouse and would slap myself in the belly to kill as many as possible at one blow. There were also millions of hungry fleas.

There was nothing to do or see at Barbacoas and we went to bed about nine o'clock with Mr. Gladly next door in another thatch hut. The string hammocks were about two and a half feet off the ground and "Señor" Romero said that was to prevent snakes from jumping in.

I had spent some very bad nights on the overland trail and that awful one in Gorgona but nothing as bad as this night in Barbacoas. The mosquitoes attacked in force the minute I crawled into the hammock. I don't sleep well on my back and I had the black satchel resting on my stomach, which did not help slumber, and about three A.M., I estimate, I felt something rubbing back and forth under the hammock, at about tailbone position. I cocked the Presentation Colt and edged my face to the side of the hammock, then craned my head on over. I saw a mangy dog underneath me. He was scratching his back on mine. With the fleas as bad as they were, I couldn't blame him for that, but he did come near having his ears pierced with hot lead.

The next day we boarded the train about noon for the three-hour run to Aspinwall. Though the engine and two cars stopped every half hour to load wood for the boiler firebox, the Panama Railroad ride was heavenly. I felt as if we had returned to civilization after being in the Dark Ages.

# 13

October 14, 1852
Aboard the SS El Dorado

Cowboy Clay Carmer
c/o Post Office
Ysleta, Texas

My dear Clay:

Well, here we are aboard the SS El Dorado two days out of New Orleans, Louisiana. I will mail this from there, knowing you may not receive it for months, since I suppose you are still walking home from Sacramento City at this moment.

Well, it has been quite an experience. So far we have been as safe as Plymouth Rock, though at least one attempt was made to steal my Dix. I think many other attempts were plotted, but when our firepower was revealed the thieves decided it would be a risky venture.

Someday I will tell you about the Isthmus of Panama, especially the River Chagres, which is full of alligators. I think those River Chagres mosquitoes know how to stick their dobbers down the same hole three or four times. They are worse than the Humboldt mosquitoes and you know how bad they were.

We met a man on the ship from San Francisco to Panama named Henry Gladly and Mrs. Dessery's head has been turned ever since. The day they got aboard this ship, Mr. Gladly said something to the purser in French. Indian Myrt overheard him and that's all they've been speaking for four days. I think they talk about me behind my back. To tell you all about Henry Gladly would take pages. He is a walking book of facts or makes you think they are facts. He told me that knowledge was his hobby. Some of what he knows is useless, I think.

I am very nervous about reaching Kanesville in time for my November 2nd court date. Arriving day after tomorrow, we'll have approximately 16 days to make it. Luck will have to be with us to find a riverboat leaving for St. Louis right away, then finding another that will leave for St. Joseph and Kanesville right away.

I had hoped we could come straight from Navy Bay

off Aspinwall, to New Orleans but the route of this ship was by Habana, Cuba. We spent a day and night there and that is another place I'll tell you about some-day. The Spanish control it and have mean-eyed soldiers everywhere. There's a barracks on every street and the biggest building in Habana is the prison. We went to a cigar factory and Mrs. Dessery demanded that we buy Drover Pettit 500 cigars to further show our gratitude. So we spent $30 on *El Combates* in a flat wooden box even though he rooked me on the last morning in San Francisco.

One interesting thing about Habana is the cages of big glow worms they sell there. I bought one and read by it for three nights. Some of the women there put the cages under their muslin dresses when they go for a leisurely stroll at night. It is a startling effect.

With that, I shall say good-bye, and will write you again from good old Iowa when I am safe and sound back in my own lovely house.

Thine forever
Susan Darden Carlisle

What I didn't tell Clay Carmer about was my continual problem with seasickness. Not an hour after I'd written that letter to Clay I got my big left toe caught in an iron door when the *SS El Dorado* rolled and tossed all over the Gulf of Mexico. Most of that toe was mashed off and a tooth-pulling barber named Thomas R. Judy repaired what he could. Having my toe squashed and being seasick at the same time was almost more than I could stand. I was throwing up a lot of the time while "Dr." Tom Judy was working on my toe stump and he had the gall to call me a mollycoddle.

After we got to the smooth water of the Mississippi River I reflected upon the situation of Clay Carmer accepting a nine-toed bride. After the ordeals of the overland trail, San Francisco, and Panama, life had dealt cruelly with me almost at the end of our travels. Well, Clay would just have to accept me flawed.

Just before we docked, I thanked Mr. Gladly for all his help, and advice, and sharing of knowledge, and asked him for a favor. "I am mightily attracted to that French 'Apache' Fist Revolver of yours," I said. "I wonder if you'd trade me for the Presentation Colt?"

He said he would. He could get another "Apache" quite easily in New Orleans. I did not kiss him on the cheeks like I'd done to Drover Pettit, but shook his hand warmly. He wasn't a Dix thief after all.

Then I stood off a ways while my Auntie Indian Myrt Dessery said her good-byes to him. They jabbered in French, which I didn't think was very nice. Then when they saw me looking at them they went behind a big packing case. I finally began to limp over there just as they emerged, all smiles. I never did find out what went on behind that packing case.

Oh, well, passing fancies. Soon Henry Gladly would be but a memory alongside Drover Pettit and the late Clem Epps and Abdou Diouf and the late Charlie Quarry and Raymond H. Johnson and Hell Haggarty, and the other many men of our long journey.

# 14

We caught the *David H. Pyle* just in time in St. Louis, but it was to no avail. November 2 came and went, with helpless agony, as that steamboat took on cargo and passengers down at St. Joe. The trip on upriver seemed endless and the only thing I could do was to hope that the good Lord, in His watching-over, had found someone to dispatch G. B. Minzter to that eternal fiery hole in the ground.

Winter had settled in along the Big Muddy. The fields were brown and the leaves had fallen from the trees. There was rawness and grayness in the air as the *Pyle* pushed northward.

Indian Myrt, bundled up, standing out on the deck beside me, said, "Susan, chin up! Just because we're five days late doesn't mean you've lost." Ever since St. Joe, she'd been saying strengthening things like "Judge Tuttle might have automatically extended us" and "Lawyer Tinley, knowing we hadn't arrived, might have asked for an extension," or "Minzter might have decided he didn't want the house after all. . . ."

Among the steamboat greeters at Kanesville landing was pudgy Evan Green, down to take care of official post office business. In his other job as clerk of the court, he'd certainly know what had happened and we hurried over to him as soon as the gangplank was dropped. His first words were, "Well, you two have been gone a long time." Not a cheery hello or welcome home. His greeting matched the grayness of the day.

I said, "Mr. Green, what happened in court on November second?"

"G. B. Minzter took your property," he replied, with no bones. "Moved in that same night. Kicked the new doctor out."

I found it hard to speak.

Mrs. Dessery asked, "Was Susan's lawyer there?"

"Yes, he was. He and Judge Tuttle and Hazel Brookins worked it all out."

"Did Lawyer Tinley request an extension?" I asked.

"Yes, he did, but the judge turned it down after Hazel Brookins said neither of you had made any attempt to contact them. He further said he'd heard you both died of cholera."

Sooner or later I'd show Hazel Brookins I wasn't dead.

"Does Susan have anything left?" asked Mrs. Dessery.

"Not a thing. All the assets didn't amount to $15,450, so G. B. Minzter got not only the house and land but all furniture, pots and pans, clothing, books, equipment in the doctor's office. He's having a public auction in the barn this Saturday at ten A.M. I hear that anything he can't sell he'll turn over to Mrs. Carol Foote Thompson to get rid of at her Third Hand place."

The lump in my throat would go neither up nor down. I managed, "Did he take Gabriel away from the Blackwells?"

Evan Green nodded. "He'll be auctioned Saturday, too."

Auntie Indian Myrt took my hand firmly and said, "Let's go, Susan." The Blackwells could come down and bring back the valises.

Carrying the doctor's bag with the fruitless Dix, I limped along but wasn't sure my legs would carry me up the bluff and into town. More than that, it was the empty feeling inside me that I knew wouldn't go away for a long time. We'd tried so very hard, in so many ways, to save the finest house on the river.

"We'll get Mrs. Thompson or Mrs. Bayliss to go buy Gabriel on Saturday. You'll have him back, I promise," said Indian Myrt.

I was having trouble holding my lips together and there was a glaze of tears over my eyes. Indian Myrt kept guiding me. "We have to go to Haines and Kimball to put that money away." She tried to brighten me up. "You know that's all yours. That's a fortune for a girl your age."

On we walked and finally turned into the bank. Unlike Evan Green's unfeeling way, we were greeted warmly there. Mr. Kimball said, "You'll have to tell the whole town about it. Some experience for two ladies from Kanesville, wasn't it?"

"Yes, it was," said Mrs. Dessery.

"Mr. Kimball, I'd like to deposit this money into savings," I said, opening the water-stained black satchel.

He sniffed it and made a lame joke about it being damp. Did we tow it under the sea for a while? When we didn't laugh, he got serious again, saying, "Susan, we're all sure sorry you lost your house to G.B. I felt very bad when I had to turn over your two thousand to the court."

I said, "Just let us sign whatever we need to sign and we'll go."

"It'll only take a minute," he said.

That done, we walked out of the bank and began going up Stutsman Road, which would take me by my former house on the way to Auntie Myrt's. "Maybe we should go the long way," she said, so as to avoid the former property of Dr. Giddings Carlisle.

I said, "No, I'll be passing it for a long time to come. I'll just have to get used to the idea that someone else owns it now." Lordy, that hurt.

In about ten minutes there we were. The doctor's neat

sign was gone and G. B. Minzter's buggy was hitched near the gate, so he was "at home." I could either walk on by head high, or go up and tell him off. I had planned to walk on by, but just then, of all ill-timed luck, out of the front door and down the steps he came, followed by one of his painted women. He saw us.

"Ah-hah," he said, "you haf come back."

We looked at the chunky, square-headed, half-bald Philadelphian Dutchman. I knew Indian Myrt was eyeing the rouged floozie with disgust.

I nodded.

"Vill, I haf your hoose now."

I nodded again.

"If you vant anyting you vill have to buy it, ya. Satteeday."

Trying to keep my voice steady and eyes dry, I said, "I don't want anything from you, ever."

I was beginning to feel very ill and I think Auntie Myrt realized it. Maybe I'd throw up or faint or have something like a heart attack out there in the road. She took me by the elbow and said quietly, "Just keep going, Susan."

I did. I didn't even notice the autumn fields that I dearly loved. A pheasant whirred up and even that didn't register for a moment.

Soon we were in sight of the Blackwell's little house and Roy came running joyously up the road. "Hi, yah," he shouted, "we made sausage yesterday," as if we hadn't been gone for seven months.

I said, "Roy, come here," and I hugged that overgrown half-wit. He didn't quite know how to take that. But I just wanted to feel I was back where I belonged.

Then Mr. Blackwell came out and we all had a half-happy, half-tearful reunion there on Stutsman Road. Mr.

Blackwell said he'd poured something into Minzter's well but wouldn't tell us what it was. After that, we went into Indian Myrt's house, my new home, and fell apart.

Next day, we unpacked and I put the French "Apache" Fist Revolver away, journey over, and Indian Myrt placed the Navy Colt holster on the back of the buggy seat, to be filled whenever she traveled about. Regular life had to be resumed.

On Friday, I harnessed up old Samuel and took the buggy over to the Thompson's sod house to ask Carol Foote Thompson to buy Gabriel for me at Minzter's auction. "How high do you want me to go?" she asked.

"So long as Minzter doesn't know you're buying him for me, go as high as you need." I had plenty of money, but that wasn't what counted.

As I was getting ready to leave, the secondhand lady said, "Susan, I've already been over to the barn. He's got your clothes laid out, your old dolls and toys, things like that. He's also laid out some things that belong to your ma and pa. Do you want me to buy any o' those?"

I stood, not quite knowing what to say. The loss of the house and everything in it just kept hitting night and day. In the night I could cry, and did. In the day, I had to keep a rein. I finally said, "Well, anything that's very personal, buy for me. My Daddy's books. Not the clothing, though. You make the decision."

She nodded and tamped a load of tobacco into her pipe. "Let me tell you something. That man has your house but not a day passes that I don't spit at the gate when I go by. Most everyone else feels the same."

Saturday night Gabriel was safely back in the Dessery barn and on Sunday I rode him along the Big Muddy for almost ten miles in sunny coldness. Then I came back and wrote a long letter to Clay Carmer telling him I'd lost the house, saying that's the way life goes. I did not want to sound down, but I did have to wipe away a dumb tear from the bottom of it.

## 15

A lot of times I found myself thinking, very seriously, about doing away with G. B. Minzter. I quit riding by the house and took the long way back simply because I got riled up every time I saw the Grecian-like columns and the fluted balustrades beneath the veranda railing; the porch swing. I finally couldn't bear to look at it.

Auntie Myrt tried her best to take my mind off it, and I went to see Sweet Frenchy Moll now and then. She, too, did her best to talk about things that had nothing to do with my past life by the Big Muddy.

I went hunting a half-dozen times before the snow began to fall in earnest, taking Roy with me twice, Hans Jochem went along once. Then I began working on two quilts, one a "Joseph's Coat" pattern, and the other, "Melon Patch." That was not like the Susan Darden Carlisle I'd always known. Before going off the overland, only hot pokers on my insoles would have sent me to stitching on a dumb piece of cloth. But now I sat doing it, listening to the tick of the clock. The doctor was probably writhing up in Beulahland.

What I wanted to do was get away from Kanesville, soon to be called Council Bluffs, forever. With that in mind, I went to Isaac Lazenby's and purchased five sheets of the worst paper I could find; then went to Sweet Frenchy Moll's, almost closed for the winter, and forged a letter

from Clay Carmer addressed to me. In the scrawl, I had
Clay Carmer summoning me to Ysleta, Texas, where we'd
soon be married. That letter was to be my ticket out of
Iowa. But after looking at it for an hour or more, thinking
about it, I just couldn't bring myself to pull a forgery on
Auntie Indian Myrt. I guess I was softening up inside.

I tore the forgery up, and sank deeper into listless, de-
spairing funk.

Then came April, '53. By the third day of that month, I
had pretty much consigned greenish-eyed Cowboy Clay
Carmer to the ash heap where he belonged. He had not so
much as written me one line in six months and I had
poured out my heart to him no less than eleven times,
beginning with that letter on the *SS El Dorado.*

Evan Green said, "There is a letter here for you from
Sleta, Texas." He never quit reading the cancellations on
every piece of mail that came to Kanesville. He must have
stayed up nights to do it. I grabbed the envelope out of his
soft hand.

Outside, with shaky fingers, I leaned up against Gabriel's
rump to open it. The letter was written on the worst grade
of paper that any mill had ever made, was stained by something, and smelled of horses, but it was a letter.

*Glory all!*
*Hallelujah!*

His scrawl was as bad as my late Daddy's, but by going
slow I could read it. No salutation at all; undated:

> Well, Susan, I'm finally getting to this. How have
> you been?
> (Good Lord, he knew how I'd been. I'd told him
> every single thing.)

We got back from California all right but I never want to walk it again.

(When did he get back?)

I'm going down to Mexico in late May or so, hire me some good vaqueros, and drive a thousand head of longhorns up the Rio Grande to Sante Fe. I figure on being there in late July and will see old Drover then. D--nd if I'm going to gamble with him again.

(That was wise.)

I have received all your letters and admit I think about you now and then. I must say I don't quite know what to make of you. I told you about my sister, Lucy. She is going on 36 and I don't think she's as old as you are in most ways.

(That meant he thought I was mature.)

I'll tell you what. If you want to come up the mountain range to Sante Fe, I'll take another look at you.

(I frowned.)

Well, I have to get ready to go to Mexico and will see you bye and bye.

> With some love, yours sincerely
> Clay Carmer

I shouted so loud in front of the U.S. Post Office that Evan Green came running out and tripped, sprawling into the dirt. I felt so good that I went over to help him up and dust him off.

Then I sat down to read it again and got so mad I saw stars. What did he mean, ". . . take another look at me," and "With some love . . ." Some? How much was "some"? Then his ". . . will see you bye and bye" meant that I was automatically going up the New Mexico mountains.

I rode straight to Sweet Frenchy Moll's and asked if I could borrow some of her perfumed stationery. I then sat down and wrote to Ysleta, telling Clay Carmer that I was no longhorn he could "take a look at" and if he couldn't do better than "some love," he could stay in the mountains the rest of his life. Without me! I scalded that green-eyed Texan. I mailed it within the hour and rode home to show the Carmer letter to Indian Myrt.

"What does he mean, take a look at you, with 'some' love?" she stormed.

That's exactly what I thought she'd say.

I tried to put that cowboy out of my mind for most of May, when the false dandelions were winking at me and the tiny crepe-petaled primroses teased me from hiding places in the new grass, but I wasn't entirely successful.

Then on June 12 arrived another letter from Ysleta. This time, Clay Carmer said, "I am not much for words but I am leaning toward loving you without the some. . . ."

That was enough for me. Women were getting married all over the country with a lot less promise than that. Auntie Indian Myrt thought so, too. She said, "You can also deliver those *El Combates* to the drover."

That was true.

Then she stunned me. She said, "I'll be going away myself this summer. Mr. Gladly has reserved a room for me at the Hotel Ponchartrain in New Orleans. August first. I don't know what will happen after that. . . ."

I found out she'd been secretly corresponding with him all winter. There was no one you could trust anymore.

On the sixteenth day of June, '53, valise all packed, I climbed into Indian Myrt's buggy and off we went to town, jabbering away about the future. Gabriel was to stay with the Blackwells until I summoned him to Texas, or returned to Iowa as a spinster. I had learned not to count on *anything* anymore. Secret correspondence! My guardian had been plotting behind my back all the time.

I had already drawn money from Haines and Kimball Bank, but there was one last errand I had to perform in Kanesville. As we came abreast of the Ocean Wave Hotel & Saloon, I interrupted my guardian's talk about what attracted her to Henry Gladly to say, "Please stop a moment." She nodded and reined old Samuel to a halt. Then, being a woman of considerable coolness under fire, she fixed her eyes dead ahead, though she knew exactly what I was going to do.

I reached over behind her and lifted the well-traveled Navy Colt out of its holster and enfolded that hogleg into my new cotton shawl. Having learned many things from Mrs. Myrtle Dessery, among them that you dress up for weddings, funerals, and important affairs of any kind, I looked ravishing that early summer day when the streams were visited with moccasin flowers and yellow star grass.

I walked up to G. B. Minzter's wide doorway and looked into his crowded, noisy saloon. I saw him standing up by the bar, and let the shawl drop away from the hogleg. It fell back to my shoulders so that I could put both hands on the shiny pistol grip.

I called out to him, "G. B. Minzter," at the same time aiming the point 36 right between his eyes as he turned. Those close by the stocky Dutchman began to edge away. Some in town had said to me, "Why don't you shoot the SOB?" and I suppose they thought I was finally getting to it.

"Vat are you doink vit dat gun?" he said loudly, his eyeballs swelling.

Though I am still against profanity, I yelled at him, "You

miserable, mean Dutch son of a bitch." Cursing on G. B. Minzter's doorstep was like dropping chicken doo into a barnyard.

Then I pulled the trigger and the bullet went by his left earlobe not by an inch. It hit the new world's largest saloon mirror and you could have heard the glass tinkling all the way to Nebraska. Once again, the mirror collapsed of its own weight. Frozen there, Minzter began to whimper and at last I knew his true character.

I blew into the hogleg barrel and returned to the buggy. Indian Myrt, having heard the shot and the lovely sound of glass tinkling, was smiling broadly and on we went to the steamboat landing.

Cap'n Tom Killoran saw us coming from his glass-walled roost high on the *Prairie Queen* and gave me a little welcome toot on his whistle. Soon, I went up the gangway, happiness nipping at my heels like those 'dads from no-name creek in another time and another place.

## About the Author

THEODORE TAYLOR is the author of more than thirty books for young people and adults. *Walking up a Rainbow* is his first book for Delacorte Press. Mr. Taylor lives in Laguna Beach, California.